WHALEBONE STRICT

'*Mon Dieu,* you are gigantic!' he breathed, staring pop-eyed at Thrift's naked breasts. 'And a little wanton too. You no longer need pretend, my darling. I know it is true, and how they beat you aboard the riverboat, and how you came to climax. We French, you see, are not so reticent between man and woman as you English.'

He had taken one fat globe in each hand, kneading them as he spoke. Thrift had closed her eyes, taking a moment to enjoy the attention to her breasts, which were fully sensitive for the first time since being put in her containment bra. His mouth found a nipple, sucking hard as he squeezed the other between finger and thumb, until both were fully erect. When he pulled back again, now on his knees and still holding one breast in each hand as he began to speak once more, his voice so hoarse with excitement she could barely understand him.

'Magnificent! Your nipples are like claret corks, so big, and so stiff, and your breasts, glorious, truly glorious. On your back, you little wanton, and I shall teach you how a Frenchman makes love!'

WHALEBONE STRICT

Lady Alice McCloud

This book is a work of fiction.
In real life, make sure you practise safe, sane and
consensual sex.

First published in 2006 by
Nexus
Thames Wharf Studios
Rainville Rd
London W6 9HA

www.nexus-books.co.uk

A catalogue record for this book is available from the British
Library.

Typeset by TW Typesetting, Plymouth, Devon
Printed and bound by Clays Ltd, St Ives PLC

ISBN 0 352 34082 7
ISBN 978 0 352 34082 5

Prologue

London, the Quality Enclave, February 2006

Thrift Moncrieff's lower lip pushed out into a rueful pout as her short cotton gown was lifted to expose the plump swell of her bottom. Dr Molloy gave a click of his tongue as she came bare and paused a moment to consider her rear view.

'A fine example of British womanhood,' he remarked, and began to hum a hymn as he turned away.

He walked from the room, leaving Thrift with her face flushed with embarrassment and wondering why he'd had to bare her bottom before going out. The nurse remained, prim and immobile, yet, Thrift had no doubt, feeling thoroughly smug at having a lady in such an undignified position, and looking forward to watching the course of injections be administered.

Thrift winced, remembering how it felt to have her posterior flesh punctured by needle after needle, and how she'd disgraced herself on the previous occasion. This time, she was determined, she would take the full course with the calm reserve appropriate to a lady of the British Empire, yet when Dr Molloy finally emerged from the next room she found her pout growing more rueful still.

He was still humming to himself as he considered the notes on his clipboard, as if having her near-naked in

1

front of him was of no consequence. He was certainly in no hurry to complete her ordeal so that she could cover herself once more. Thrift waited, her bottom cheeks twitching in ever greater apprehension despite her best efforts to stay calm, and finally he gave his verdict.

'It seems that as you received the full spectrum of treatment on your last visit no further inoculation is necessary. There now, aren't you a lucky girl?'

Vast indignation welled up as Thrift realised she had been made to strip naked and lie on a couch with her bottom bare to the world for no reason whatsoever, but before she could find a suitable answer, so as to express her feelings without exceeding the boundaries of propriety, he spoke again.

'Which only leaves us with the requirement that you be waxed.'

'Waxed?' Thrift queried.

'A simple hygienic procedure,' he explained, 'and standard if you are visiting those areas in which the importance of cleanliness is not properly understood.'

'Am I going to France?'

'Your Ministry has not seen fit to make me privy to such information,' he replied, 'but merely requires you to be waxed, so if you would turn over, please?'

'Turn over?' Thrift asked in rising alarm.

'Turn over,' he repeated, as if speaking to a particularly dull child. 'If I am to wax your pudenda it will hardly do for you to be lying face down.'

'My . . . my . . .' Thrift stammered, only to find herself unable to get the word out in front of him as her face flared crimson with embarrassment. 'Oh dear . . .'

'Come along,' he urged. 'I haven't got all day, you know. Over you go, and rest your legs in these stirrups.'

Thrift made to reply, then gave in and rolled over, her eyes closed against the agony of her feelings, only to open them again in alarm as he touched her hip. He was close, but his hands were not loitering on her body, having merely brushed her skin as he raised twin stirrups into position on either side of the couch. It was very little consolation. To her mounting horror she saw that the stirrups were not merely high and wide, so as to force her to keep her thighs open, but placed so far up the bed that once her legs were in them her body would be rolled right up, spreading her quim and bottom as wide as they could possibly go, with every single private detail fully exposed. Worse still, two leather belts dangled down from each stirrup, and she knew from bitter experience that if she made a fuss she would simply be put in them and strapped into place.

She had to force herself to lift her legs, choking with embarrassment as she spread herself wide to both the doctor and the nurse. They barely bothered to glance at her, helping each other to pull on thin rubber gloves before the nurse opened a flat cardboard package labelled 'Dr Lloyd's Cold Application Hygienic Adhesives', from which Dr Molloy extracted something like a large, thick sticking plaster. Thrift closed her eyes once more as he leant in close between her open legs, wincing as he touched one thigh, and again as his hand pressed upon her well-furred pubic mound, holding on the adhesive pad.

'A moment is required for the wax to melt,' he explained as he began to smooth the pad down onto the hairy part of her skin.

Thrift bit her lip in an effort to stop herself squirming beneath the gentle pressure of his hand. She could feel the wax growing slippery as it melted to the warmth of her flesh, while the base of his thumb was pressing down on the sensitive little bud at the heart of her sex, making it close to impossible to remain detached and not disgrace herself. He began to hum again, the same cheerful hymn as before, and Thrift began to sing the words in her mind in a desperate effort to keep her thoughts from her exposure and the feelings in her sex.

'Another, if you please, nurse,' Dr Molloy remarked, 'but rather smaller.'

He had stopped massaging her quim, but she was only left in peace for a moment before another adhesive was applied, this time to one hairy lip, pressed tight and smoothed down with a single finger, all the way to the turn of her bottom. A second was applied to the other side before the doctor began to massage both into place with his thumbs. She felt the liquid sensation of the wax as it began to melt in among her hairs, tickling so badly she had to fight not to wriggle, while to add to her already unendurable shame her anus had begun to pulse and wink.

Thrift burst into tears, her whole body shaking to the sobs as she gave in to her feelings. Dr Molloy gave a disapproving tut and continued to stroke the adhesive in over Thrift's sex, now pressing the lower ends where her flesh curved down to either side of her anus. A knuckle brushed the sensitive star of flesh, provoking a small fart and Thrift's tears grew more bitter still.

'Do make some effort to control yourself, Miss Moncrieff,' Dr Molloy remarked as he pasted the final corner of the adhesive pad within a inch of Thrift's twitching anus.

Her answer was a sob. She had begun to lubricate, a trickle of fluid running from the mouth of her quim over her bottom hole and down between her well-spread cheeks, making her arousal painfully obvious. Still Dr Molloy ignored her condition, taking something from a bowl offered by the nurse and slapping it onto Thrift's quim without the slightest warning. She gasped and jerked at the sudden cold, realising too late that what he was holding was crushed ice, which he plastered liberally over her sex. Some had gone up her hole, and rather more was slithering down between her cheeks, setting her gasping and clutching at the couch, while her feet had begun to kick in the stirrups.

'Do hold still, Miss Moncrieff!' Dr Molloy urged. 'What a ridiculous fuss you make.'

'I can't help it!' Thrift wailed.

Dr Molloy gave an irritable sigh.

'The straps, nurse, if you would be so kind.'

'I will be still, Doctor,' Thrift said quickly, but she was ignored.

The nurse came close, ignoring Thrift's pleas and sobbing as she applied the straps. Thrift had begun to wriggle, despite her best efforts to keep still, and her leg had to be held in place for the second pair of straps to be applied, which left her twitching helplessly on her back as Dr Molloy continued to press the ice over and up her quim. What had gone up her had already begun to melt, trickling out between her cheeks with her natural juices and making a wet patch beneath her bottom. She could feel the wax hardening too, tugging at her pubic hair to make her skin itch and sting until she was squirming helplessly in her bonds and beating her fists on the couch, at which Dr Molloy shook his head in exasperation.

'Such a fuss over nothing,' he remarked, taking hold of one corner of the largest of the three adhesives plastered to Thrift's sex. 'Now do try to behave with a little decorum. A single treatment lasts very nearly a year, by the way, so we need not concern ourselves with a repeat prescription.'

He pulled, without warning, and hard. Thrift screamed as the thickly grown hair on her pubic mound was torn away in one agonising motion, and was left gasping for air and wide-eyed with shock. Before she could even get her breath back, much less protest, he had taken a firm pinch on both the adhesives attached to her sex lips and pulled. Again Thrift screamed, and briefly lost control of her bladder, a squirt of deep yellow urine erupting over Dr Molloy's immaculate white coat.

'Honestly, can you not control yourself at all?' he snapped, brushing at his coat as the nurse hastened to find a sponge.

Thrift didn't answer, her vision still red with pain and her breath coming in short, ragged gasps that made it impossible to speak. Her thighs were wriggling and her bottom cheeks clenched in slow, involuntary contraction. Her freshly denuded sex stung terribly, and a burning sensation was building in her hurt flesh, which had already begun to swell. Only her anus remained cool, thanks to a little mound of ice still piled between her cheeks and melting slowly to create a cold puddle around her bottom.

Both the doctor and the nurse had moved aside to clean his coat, and when Thrift could manage it she pulled her head up to inspect the state of her belly. The lower bulge was now hairless, smooth and plump – and pink, very pink. Her entire quim had grown swollen and puffy, the reddened flesh pouting obscenely from between her thighs in blatantly sexual display. It was also intolerably sensitive and badly in need of the touch of her fingers.

'A new one, if you please, nurse,' Dr Molloy was saying as he shrugged his soiled coat from his shoulders.

'Yes, Dr Molloy,' the nurse answered, as she took the coat and made for the door.

Thrift's mouth came open to protest at the breach of propriety in leaving her alone with a man, only to close again with the door. Dr Molloy glanced at Thrift's bulging, ready sex, stepped close and manipulated a lever, dropping the end part of the couch to leave Thrift's naked buttocks and open quim sticking out into the air.

'What ... what are you doing now?' she asked in rising panic.

'I think we both know what you need, my dear,' he said, his hands already at his fly.

'No, really . . .' Thrift began and broke off as a stubby penis sprang free from his fly, already erect, with the moist red helmet protruding from a meaty foreskin. 'Oh, God . . .'

'Do not take the Lord's name in vain,' Dr Molloy rebuked her as he eased his cock up her well-creamed passage.

Thrift groaned as her sex filled with cock, but made no effort to resist as her gown was twitched up to expose the full pink mounds of her breasts, nor as he began to fuck her hole. It felt too good, and her resistance was too weak, and with her legs strapped firmly into the stirrups she could do nothing to stop him anyway.

Her fucking was brief, a few dozen urgent shoves into her swollen cunt as his eyes feasted on her naked body, and then he pulled out to jerk himself off over her sore, denuded lower belly. Splash after splash of come erupted over her, to dribble down over the plump, hairless bulge of flesh, for all the world like cream on a figgy pudding.

One

'North America, breadbasket of the Empire,' Mr Warburton stated, making an expansive gesture towards the relevant continent on the immense wall map in the foyer of the Foreign and Colonial Department.

Thrift forced a polite smile in response. Her sex was still rather sore after being so suddenly and unexpectedly denuded that morning, and her hairless skin felt odd within the thick rubber of her containment pants, into which she had been put back immediately after her medical, so there had been no opportunity of relieving the feelings brought on by Dr Molloy's outrageous treatment of her body. Her ankle-length Cantlemere and Lucas corset also felt unusually stiff and tight, making her wonder if she was putting on weight.

In order to distract herself from her physical discomforts, she forced herself to listen to what Mr Warburton was saying, and to study the great marble map of the world. Those parts of the landmass subject to the British Empire were picked out in a pink shade, including Great Britain itself, Australasia and Antarctica, the Indian sub-continent, parts of Asia, all but a tiny fraction of the continent of Africa, a proportion of Europe and the entire continent of North America, at which they were looking.

8

' . . . pretty rustic, by and large,' Mr Warburton was saying, 'but apparently not without its problems, which is why Mr Fanshaw in Colonies has asked for you to be temporarily detached from South-East Asia.'

'Me, Mr Warburton?' Thrift asked in surprise.

'So it seems,' he told her. 'As you know, we have very few young ladies of quality in the department, and apparently that is what is required in this instance.'

'What will I be doing?' Thrift asked. 'I suppose I will still be with Sally Brown?'

'Naturally I'm not privy to the details of your assignment,' he responded, moving towards the magnificent staircase, 'but I think I can safely say that as you're still in training it won't be anything too onerous. As to young Brown, I fear not. We need her for a rather delicate matter that's brewing in Singapore. But pray don't concern yourself, Fanshaw will see to it that you have a suitable maid.'

'Thank you,' Thrift responded, starting up the stairs as fast as her corset would permit.

Warburton offered an arm and she took it gratefully, too glad of the support to resent the gesture and telling herself that while he might be her inferior socially, he was also her line man in the Diplomatic Service. As they ascended the stairs she was praying that Sally would have the time to make the necessary arrangements with whoever was taking her place, and especially to pass on the combination of her containment pants. Otherwise she would have to suffer the hideous embarrassment of asking to go home so that they could be unfastened and her new maid could pick up the combination.

'You seem discomfited, my dear?' Mr Warburton remarked as they reached the landing. 'You mustn't look on this as a demotion, you know, just because you'll be out in the sticks, but rather as a feather in your cap.'

'Indeed,' Thrift responded hastily. 'I do not mean to seem ungrateful, Mr Warburton.'

'That's the spirit,' he said, steering her towards the base of the next flight of stairs.

The North American office proved not only to be on the top floor of the Foreign and Colonial building, but far round on the southern face. Mr Fanshaw occupied an office considerably smaller than Mr Warburton's, looking out over the back of the Treasury. Mr Fanshaw himself was a small, fussy-looking individual with thin, sandy hair and a straggling moustache, who broke off his conversation immediately in order to greet her.

'Ah, Miss Moncrieff, pleased to meet you,' he said, rising from his chair to perform a stiff bow in her direction, then giving an equable nod to her companion. 'Warburton, very decent of you to help me out here.'

Thrift responded as best she could in the confines of her corset, dipping in a curtsey appropriate to one of her class when addressing a professional, which she judged him to be. He responded with a nervous smile and sat down again, indicating the person he had been talking to before, a woman in early middle age, tall and thin, her face marked with a severity exactly in keeping with a black bombazine dress that immediately made Thrift think of the governesses who had been responsible for her until just two years before.

'May I introduce Miss Dace?' Mr Fanshaw went on. 'Miss Moncrieff, Miss Dace. Miss Dace, Miss Moncrieff, and Mr Warburton, who you may perhaps have already met?'

'I have not,' Miss Dace replied, her voice as harsh as her features and with a curious accent Thrift found herself unable to place.

Thrift gave the smallest of curtsies, as Miss Dace was obviously an artisan of some sort, but accompanied the gesture with a smile, as it seemed likely that the woman was her maid. Mr Fanshaw quickly confirmed Thrift's guess.

'Miss Dace will be your maid and your companion while you are with us,' he explained. 'She is a native of the city of Baltimore, on the east coast, but has lived in Boston for some time and has a wide experience of the middle territories in particular and the American colonies in general, so is ideally suited to the post.'

Thrift forced another smile despite her rising irritation. Although she knew it was a lot to expect a maid as intelligent, efficient and pliable as Sally, she had at least expected a younger woman, who would do as she was told without question. Miss Dace looked as if she would question everything, and expect Thrift to do as she was told. Mr Warburton gave a carefully graded bow to Miss Dace, another to Thrift, and took his leave, closing the door behind him.

'A pleasure to have you aboard,' Mr Fanshaw went on. 'Do sit down.'

Lowering herself carefully into a chair with a creak of whalebone, Thrift took another glance at Miss Dace, but the woman's aspect had failed to improve. She sat rigid in her chair, her expression stern and attentive, suggesting unyielding rectitude and a complete lack of humour. For a moment Thrift considered protesting, only to abandon the idea. Clearly, whatever she was doing, Miss Dace had been selected by the Diplomatic Service as the most appropriate person for the task.

'As I believe you are still in training, Miss Moncrieff,' Mr Fanshaw was saying, 'and have been seconded from South-East Asia, although you are central to the assignment, you will of course be Miss Dace's subordinate, with all that implies.'

Thrift winced and felt her bottom cheeks tighten in the confines of her corset as he went on.

'Now, what can you tell me about our North American colony?'

'There are sixty-two territories in North America,' Thrift recited dutifully, 'each of which is under the control of a governor, who in turn answers to the Viceroy in Boston, currently Lord Mapledurham.

Examples include Massachusetts, the most populous state, where the Viceroy's palace is situated in the largest city, Boston; Rhode Island, the smallest of the territories and famous for the quality of its poultry; Northern Territory, which is at once the largest and most sparsely populated region of the entire Empire, excluding Antarctica; Maryland, in which the traitor Washington was executed in 1775; and California, which was purchased from Spain in 1863 and is notable for the quality of its fruit, also wine.'

She stopped, as Mr Fanshaw was clearly waiting for her to do so.

'Splendid, splendid,' he remarked. 'Your file stated that you have an exceptional memory. What do you know about the territory of Louisiana?'

'Louisiana is the most recent addition to the colony,' Thrift told him, once more reciting from what she had learnt at school, 'and was ceded to Britain at the close of the Great War in 1926. The capital city is Baton Rouge, which lies on the Mississippi, the world's third longest river after the Nile and the Amazon, also the lifeblood of the state. Principal exports are cotton, peppers and musical instruments, while . . .'

Again Mr Fanshaw's face had taken on a patient expression and again she stopped.

'Quite, quite,' he said, 'although in our case it is the socio-political situation in which we are interested.'

'I'm afraid that wasn't covered in my course,' Thrift responded, 'except in that the population is unusual in being of largely French origin.'

'Exactly,' he responded, 'which is where our problem lies. In general, the people of North America are the most loyal of His Majesty's subjects, devout, sober and generally of good character. In Louisiana, despite eighty years of membership of the British Empire, there still exists a measure of resentment – only among a troublesome minority, mark you, but it is still a matter for concern . . . although, to be frank with you, we're not a particularly busy department. In any case, disaffection with British rule exists in Louisiana.'

'Wouldn't this be a matter for the army?' Thrift queried.

'Not at all,' Mr Fanshaw told her, wagging a finger. 'Shoot one rebel and you create a dozen more, which is not the way to go about things at all. Rather, we have exploited the natural excitability of the French nation by making sure the anti-British movement remains divided, which has been pretty easy, really, up until now, and that is where you come in. There are two principal factions, the Libertistes, who want full independence, and the Gaulistes, who wish to return to French rule. Each faction despises the other rather more than it does us, which has made them easy to control, and we have done our best to maintain the situation so that neither faction comes into the ascendant. The majority of the French-descended population, the Creoles and a smaller rural group, the Cajuns, are indifferent, and likely to remain so as long as the two factions are squabbling. The British-descended population are loyal, obviously, as is the small African-descended population.'

Thrift nodded, already somewhat confused but eager to show that she was paying attention.

'The problem,' Mr Fanshaw went on, 'lies in that the Gaulistes appear likely to be about to make such absolute asses of themselves that the balance of power will swing irrevocably towards the Libertistes, which we wish to avoid. Their leader, Jean-Jacques Rougon, a hot-headed fellow even by their standards, intends to make a declaration of allegiance to France. Paris is aware of this, and somewhat embarrassed, as you may well imagine. They intend to ignore him, this being the only possible diplomatic response to such foolishness, but he is determined to press ahead, convinced, apparently, that Paris will be forced by the popular will to support him. This is highly unlikely, as most Frenchmen are barely aware that the Louisiana Territory exists.'

'How do I come into this?' Thrift asked cautiously.

'Essentially,' Mr Fanshaw replied, steepling his fingers, 'we require you to ensure than Jean-Jacques Rougon discredits himself personally before he has a chance to discredit himself more generally. His rivals within the Gauliste faction will be quick to take advantage of this, you may be sure, which should solve our little problem. To this end –'

He broke off, his already ruddy complexion taking on a yet pinker tinge, before steeling himself to continue.

'To this end, it is our intention that you should meet Mr Rougon at a social event, and er, ..., create a situation in which you can accuse him of ... of improper conduct, improper, that is, by, um ..., French moral standards, which are, um ..., as you may know, somewhat less stringent than our own. You don't actually have to do anything, of course ... naturally ... absolutely ... you merely have to be alone with the fellow long enough for your accusation to carry weight.'

'I am most relieved to hear it,' Thrift responded as calmly as she was able.

His face was now a rich puce, and he took a swallow of water from a tumbler on his desk before he was able to continue.

'Absolutely, absolutely, Miss Moncrieff, nothing of the kind. However, given the poor moral values of these people, it is plainly necessary that your accusation be, er ..., that is, your accusation must carry weight, sufficient to disgrace the fellow and make him seem ridiculous in the eyes of his supporters, and yet not actually be in breach of the law. We don't want a formal investigation, after all, do we? No, no ...'

He stopped, apparently in the grip of over-riding embarrassment, and cast an imploring look towards Miss Dace, who remained immobile, her expression, if

anything, more forbidding than before. At last Mr
Fanshaw found his voice. His words emerged brisk and
clipped, very different from his normal speech, as if he
had to physically force them out.

'It has been decided, Miss Moncrieff, that you are to
accuse Mr Rougon of ejaculating into a glass and
making you drink the yield.'

Aboard the Airship *Prince Frederick*, February 2006-01-09

Thrift stood at the window of the Quality Lounge,
watching the colossal steel finger of the Empire Tower
recede beneath her. The panorama of London widened
and fell slowly away as the *Prince Frederick* moved west,
near-silent on her four great Collins Electrical Engines.
It was a magnificent sight but also a familiar one, and
her mind was set not on the view, nor the glories of
Empire it represented, but on a remark made by the first
Frenchman she had ever met, a Monsieur d'Arrignac,
who had claimed that the giant airship mast symbolised
an erect penis. The suggestion was as absurd as it was
disgusting, and yet seemed to typify the attitude of the
French.

She wondered if Jean-Jacques Rougon would be
equally dirty in his language and habits, and if so,
whether Mr Fanshaw's plan was not unduly optimistic.
Having to make the accusation was bad enough, but she
wasn't sure if the idea was even workable. Possibly Mr
Rougon would not agree to the period of quiet, private
conversation in which she would claim he had forced his
attentions on her. Possibly he would not be fooled at all
and, realising her true intent, refuse to entertain her.
Alternatively, he might take the absence of her maid as
a genuine invitation to dalliance, in which case she
would have little option but to comply. After all, to
judge by what Mr Fanshaw had said about the Creole

habits, if she merely ran from the room screaming that he had attempted to debauch her, it would be she who ended up a laughing-stock. Then again, among such a depraved race, the act which had caused Mr Fanshaw such embarrassment that he could barely force himself to describe it might not be considered sufficiently disgraceful.

Then there was the matter of her containment pants. If she was forced to comply, then it would hardly do to pretend to seduce him, only to admit that she was in thick rubber pants specifically designed to prevent her being interfered with, which only her maid could open. That, at least, was a problem she had a chance of solving, and in doing so testing the character and resolve of Miss Dace. Since their meeting at the Ministry she had seen her companion only as they boarded the airship, and while it seemed highly unlikely that Miss Dace would prove flexible, the situation at least provided Thrift with an excuse to suggest she be allowed to discard the hated pants, without any suggestion that it was for purely frivolous reasons, let alone to allow her to touch herself.

Thrift pursed her lips, wondering how best to broach the subject. Miss Dace was either in their stateroom or in those parts of the ship in which the commonality were permitted, and could no doubt be summoned easily enough. Indeed, it might be a good test of Thrift's authority to do so, while a simple call of nature would provide an excuse for her containment pants to be unfastened and allow her to raise the topic with the minimum of embarrassment. She nodded to herself, determined. First, she would go to her stateroom and, if necessary, have Miss Dace summoned by a steward.

She turned for the door, bobbing politely to the few other quality passengers in the lounge. The *Prince Frederick* was on a long haul journey, direct from London to somewhere called New York rather than Boston, which meant the great majority of the passengers were of the professional classes, mainly merchants and no doubt involved in the shipment of foodstuffs, leather, fur and other things of which Thrift knew next to nothing. She herself was supposed to be visiting the Governors of various territories, some genuinely distant relatives, others supposedly so, which gave her an excuse to be in Baton Rouge at the appropriate time. There she would stay with yet another Governor, Sir Lionel Bartram, exactly as would be expected of her.

Miss Dace proved to be in the stateroom, apparently indifferent to the magnificent view from the window as she sat in a straight-backed chair embroidering a biblical scene. Thrift gave a stiff curtsey, embarrassed and somewhat put off by her companion's severity, both of appearance and manner. Miss Dace responded with a measured nod and continued her needlework, forcing Thrift to open the conversation.

'I wish to speak to you on a somewhat delicate matter, Miss Dace,' she said formally. 'I believe you have spoken with Sally Brown?'

'If you wish to use the convenient facility,' Miss Dace replied, sending the blushes instantly to Thrift's face, 'I intend that you shall do so at the hours of eight in the morning and nine in the evening. It is now four o'clock, or, to be precise, four fourteen.'

Thrift took a moment to fight down her embarrassment before replying. Miss Dace had returned to her needlework.

'Please do excuse me, Miss Dace,' Thrift managed, 'but given my age and our relative positions both in life and in the Service, I hardly think it appropriate that I should be . . . should be obliged to be regular. Indeed, in the circumstances I think it might be best were you to give me the combination, or, better still, that I might discard my . . . the garment in question altogether.'

Miss Dace looked up, her face unreadable, and when she spoke her voice was toneless.

'Clearly this is a matter best dealt with immediately. Come here, if you would, Miss Moncrieff.'

Thrift stepped forward, astonished that her apparently formidable companion had given in so easily. Miss Dace had set her embroidery aside, the needle tucked in beside a pattern Thrift recognised as the prophet Jeremiah coming out of the wilderness, an austere choice that seemed to exactly fit the woman's personality. Yet clearly Miss Dace was more pliable than her convictions suggested, and as Thrift began to lift her heavy skirts she was already looking forward to the freedom of going without the heavy, sticky containment pants and once more having silk next to her skin instead of rubber.

With her skirt, underskirt and all three petticoats bunched up around her middle, Thrift turned her back to her companion to allow the catches on her corset panel to be opened. Miss Dace worked with a brisk efficiency, twisting each gudgeon open before lifting the panel and fixing it up with Thrift's corset strings as the design intended. The seat of Thrift's drawers was now exposed, and that too was dealt with, her embarrassment for her exposure rising all the while, but no more so than her sense of freedom. As the panel of her drawers was in turn lifted and fastened in place her containment pants came on display, the skin-tight, form-fitting rubber making two plump black balls of her buttocks.

'Turn about once more, if you would,' Miss Dace requested and Thrift obeyed, still holding her skirts and petticoats high as she presented her companion with the combination pad that held her containment pants closed.

A few deft motions and Miss Dace had punched in the combination. It was only with difficulty that Thrift restrained a sigh of relief as the thick rubber peeled open between her thighs and behind, allowing her bottom cheeks to spill out, shamefully naked but deliciously cool from the dry air on her sweat-slick skin. She wanted to touch herself, badly, and moved towards the convenient facility, only to stumble off balance as Miss Dace pulled her sharply back. Instantly Thrift realised what was to be done to her, an all too familiar routine, as she was hauled squealing across Miss Dace's lap, but only as her wrists were twisted firmly up into the small of her back did she manage to find her voice.

'No, Miss Dace ... not that! I implore you, no ... you have no right to spank me, Miss Dace, you have no right! Please, Miss Dace, this isn't fair at all, it really isn't! Why am I being spanked? At least tell me why I am being spanked! Please! Miss Dace!'

Miss Dace didn't even bother to reply, but made short work of subduing Thrift's struggles by tying her wrists up into her corset laces. Completely helpless, with her bottom protruding fat and pink from her disarranged clothing, Thrift finally fell silent, biting her lip in consternation as she waited for her spanking. Miss Dace took her time, making herself more comfortable on the chair, rearranging Thrift into a more convenient position over her lap, and adjusting the rear of the open containment pants to expose the full globe of her victim's bottom.

Only then did she begin to spank, applying firm swats full across the meat of Thrift's bottom, always in an exact place, and to the same rhythm. It was hard, and stung badly, while being smacked on the same spot over and over made it impossible for Thrift to keep control. In moments her legs were jerking in the confinement of her corset and she had begun to wriggle her bottom in a desperate effort to spread out the smacks even a little.

It made little or no difference, and she knew it just made her look even more comic, but she couldn't help herself. Soon she was writhing over Miss Dace's lap with her bottom bucking up and down so wildly that she was showing the rear lips of her denuded quim, adding to her humiliation as the spanking continued at the same even pace. Even when she burst into tears and began to babble pleas and apologies Miss Dace took no notice, her spanking hand working Thrift's now throbbing bottom at the same relentless pace and with exactly the same force, smack after smack after smack delivered with perfect accuracy upon the wobbling, bouncing bottom cheeks.

Finally it stopped, leaving Thrift gasping with a hot behind over Miss Dace's lap, sobbing bitterly, full of self-pity and shame for her exposure and punishment. Still completely helpless with her hands tied so securely into her corset laces, she could only wait to be released. Once more, Miss Dace took her time, closing Thrift's containment pants to encase her now burning bottom in the hot, thick rubber and even buttoning up the panel of her drawers before the knot was undone.

'Stay in place,' Miss Dace ordered, the only words she'd spoken during the whole of Thrift's punishment.

Thrift obeyed, pouting furiously as she massaged her wrists and her rear clothes were arranged, so that when she was finally allowed to her feet only her skirts had to fall into place and she was once more decently dressed, though now with her bottom warm in her rubber pants and her quim full of the shameful need that invariably followed a spanking. Not knowing what to say, not even sure why she'd be punished and definitely not wanting to risk a repeat performance, she contented herself with smoothing down her skirts. Miss Dace returned to her embroidery.

Two

New York, February 2006

The giant airship *Prince Frederick* took three days to make her leisurely progress across the Atlantic Ocean. Each morning, at precisely eight o'clock, before being allowed to use the convenient facility and perform her ablutions, Thrift would have her modesty gown lifted at the back, her wrists tied together with string and her bare bottom spanked in the same firm, rhythmic fashion as the first time, with exactly twelve dozen smacks applied to the crest of her cheeks. Never once did Miss Dace vary the routine, nor did she explain herself, and, on the sole occasion Thrift managed to summon up the courage to ask why she appeared to have been put on a punishment regime so utterly inappropriate for a woman of her age and rank, she was simply hauled back over her companion's knee for another dozen blistering smacks.

On each occasion she had been put back in her containment pants the moment she had washed and Miss Dace had completed the regime of prayers she seemed to consider essential after giving a punishment. Not once had she had an opportunity to touch herself in the way that was always so necessary after a spanking, which made the punishments so much worse. Now, as she stood at the window of the Quality Lounge watching the North American coastline emerge slowly from the haze of distance, she was still very much conscious of the heat in her recently smacked buttocks, and brooding resentfully on the behaviour of Miss Dace as much as admiring the view.

Details slowly became clear: first the glitter of a system of waterways, showing bright in the winter sun between smudges of brown that then resolved themselves into rows of six-, seven- and even eight-storey buildings, set close together and back to back. There were parks among the buildings, although fewer than in London, a few great buildings, the lines of railways and, in the distance and lining the extensive docks, huge ugly warehouses of stone, red brick and corrugated iron. An airport was visible on the main landmass, with the silver needle of a jet just rising into the air, and numerous boats thronged the waterways from the tiny white specks of pleasure craft to vast commercial vessels in the livery of their companies. Several fine bridges crossed the waterways.

None of these features dominated, all either dwarfed or made to seem drab by the huge statue that rose from one of the smaller islands, towards which the *Prince Frederick* was headed. Made of greened copper, it represented a man in magnificent robes and a curling wig, one arm raised to the heavens in a gesture of command and unshakeable determination also reflected in his expression. With a flush of imperial pride, Thrift recognised Lord North, the saviour of the colony, whose personal intervention had put down the rebels over two hundred years before. She also remembered that the statue had been adapted as an airship mast, and as they drifted close she made her way to her stateroom.

Miss Dace already had their trunks packed and a boy stood ready to assist. Thrift ignored both, still piqued by her morning spanking and indifferent to the porter, but went to the window to watch the final approach, the *Prince Frederick* drifting slowly closer to Lord North's upraised finger until lines could be attached, and at last docking with a gentle shudder. Thrift left the stateroom immediately and made her way down by those elevators reserved for the Quality, emerging from the foyer at the base of the statue into cold, clear winter sunlight.

With no idea what to do, she was obliged to wait until Miss Dace came down with the luggage, meanwhile taking in the scenery and the atmosphere of the place. Her immediate impression was of cold and loneliness, and she found herself wishing she had a friend as a companion and maid instead of the taciturn Miss Dace, who seemed to take very little pleasure in anything, even spanking Thrift's bottom, a practice most of those put in charge of her had more or less openly enjoyed.

Miss Dace and the porter finally emerged and Thrift was led to a dock, from which a black-painted ferry took them across to the mainland, or possibly a larger island, where the tallest of the brown stone buildings were clustered, great solid edifices of as many as eight stories in height and several times longer than they were tall. Despite the pervading atmosphere of sobriety, there was a great deal of bustle, the roads thick with cars and vans, the pavements thronged with people, who seemed to be mixed together with no distinction for class. There were merchants in stovepipe hats and long-tailed black suits, and artisans in plainer attire, even those of the working class. The women's clothes varied from modest grandeur to shabbiness but were all black, grey or some other dull tone that made Thrift intensely self-conscious in her butter-yellow gown and rich brown furs, as did their glances, which radiated distaste, even contempt.

'Why do they look at me so?' Thrift asked as she and Miss Dace stood waiting for the porter to secure a cab.

'They think you are a streetwalker,' Miss Dace replied, her voice suggesting icy displeasure, 'which is no surprise, dressed as you are.'

'What is a streetwalker?' Thrift asked.

Miss Dace's reply was a look of withering scorn and, as her companion's meaning sank in, Thrift found the blood rushing to her face. She began to babble in outrage and humiliation, one word tumbling over the next in no sensible order, but a squat black car had pulled in to the kerb and Miss Dace had already moved away to supervise the loading of their luggage. For a long moment Thrift stood dumbstruck on the pavement, her face burning with embarrassment and shame, before she finally got hold of herself. Moving as quickly as her corset would allow, she climbed into the safety of the cab, only for the driver to turn her a knowing leer.

'The Quality Enclave,' she instructed, making her tone as haughty as she could manage.

'Tilldale's Emporium,' Miss Dace corrected as she climbed in. 'There is no Quality Enclave in New York, Miss Moncrieff, and we cannot present ourselves at any respectable hotel with you dressed like that.'

'I am dressed to the height of fashion!' Thrift responded, unable to hold back her feelings any longer.

'We in the colonies are not decadent like you Londoners,' Miss Dace replied as the cab pulled away from the kerb. 'We dress respectably.'

'I am dressed respectably,' Thrift insisted, 'more than respectably. Driver, please drive me to the best hotel this dreadful city affords, and promptly.'

'Stop the car,' Miss Dace stated.

'No, not that!' Thrift squealed, realising immediately what was about to happen. 'You cannot, Miss Dace, not in front of a man, no . . . no!'

Her last word was a scream as she was hauled bodily across her companion's lap, and she kept on screaming, and fighting, hers legs kicking furiously in her corset and her hands scratching at the thick bombazine of Miss Dace's skirts. The cab had stopped and when Thrift heard the driver's lewd chuckle she knew he was watching, which made her screams and struggles more

24

furious still. Yet her skirts had already been turned up over her head, enveloping her in rich yellow satin and mercifully blocking her view of the driver and the busy street beyond the window.

It was a small mercy. She still knew the driver was watching as her petticoats followed her skirts and her corset was exposed; maybe others too. Nor did Miss Dace make the slightest allowance for Thrift's modesty, obviously following the popular dictum that a naughty girl had no right to any such thing until she had been punished, and punishment was invariably given on the bare skin.

Thrift's bottom was stripped, not even hastily, but to the same patient routine Miss Dace invariably followed, made slower still by the victim's ever more desperate struggles. Even when Thrift's hands had been tied into her corset laces she was still fighting, her whole body writhing in furious, panic-stricken but useless remonstrance, while she wailed and begged and screamed her outrage into the worn cloth of the car seat beneath her face, ending with a long cry of utter despair as her containment pants split behind to let her plump naked bottom bulge free.

She was spanked, the usual twelve dozen firm swats applied to her cheeks, which danced and wobbled not so much because of Miss Dace's spanking but because Thrift was too far gone to have the sense to hold still, and so ended up making a far ruder and far more ridiculous display of herself than had she accepted her fate. Even when it was over she was still wriggling, her mind burning with shame and consternation for what had been done to her, her face streaked with tears and her beautifully coiffed hair a dishevelled mess, and as Miss Dace began to close the containment pants Thrift caught the driver's voice.

'How much to get a suck out of her?'

'No . . . no . . . no!' Thrift shrieked, blind panic rising once more as she imagined herself forced to take the leering common man's penis in her mouth, and to her vast relief Miss Dace's answer held nearly as much outrage as Thrift felt.

'You will mind your manners, my man, unless you wish me to report you!'

The driver's answer was a dissatisfied grunt, and Thrift's body went limp as the rubber flaps of her containment pants were pulled together and her now hot and no doubt red bottom was once more shielded from the vulgar gaze.

'Tilldale's Emporium,' Miss Dace ordered once more, her voice quite calm despite the effort of subduing Thrift and the driver's outrageous suggestion.

As the car pulled away, Miss Dace continued to dress Thrift as unhurriedly as ever. She even broke off to say a quick prayer once the corset was closed, so that Thrift was still lying prone across her lap when the car once more came to a stop.

'Do get up,' Miss Dace instructed, 'and wipe your face.'

'Of course,' Thrift answered resentfully, lifting herself to find that they were parked outside one of the very largest brownstone buildings, evidently the emporium to judge by the discreet window display.

She climbed out of the car and stood on the pavement, struggling to adjust her hair and wipe the stains of tears and mucus from her face, all the time acutely aware of the attention of passers-by, who she was sure knew exactly what had happened. Miss Dace took her time to pay the fare, and as Thrift tried to stop herself snivelling it occurred to her that her companion could perfectly well have warned her about the attitude to dress prevalent in New York, perhaps even purchased appropriate clothes before they set off.

With many of the other women who had at one time or another been responsible for Thrift's discipline it would have seemed like a deliberate excuse for a public spanking, about the most humiliating thing that could possibly be done to a girl of Quality, and something in which many governesses and companions took pleasure. Miss Dace seemed too cold and too proper for such vindictive behaviour, especially given her habit of saying a prayer each time, and yet Thrift found herself wondering as she was led into the store.

Tilldale's Emporium proved very different to the shops in London's Quality Enclave, not only being on a huge scale, but with everything imaginable under one roof instead of each tradesman or woman keeping to a single speciality. The department to which Miss Dace led her was more peculiar still, occupying the entire second floor, with thick screens to guard the modesty of the customers, but no division whatsoever so that those of different class might select garments appropriate to their rank. Fortunately Miss Dace was evidently familiar with the bizarre system, approaching a thin young woman in the brown dress that appeared to be the uniform for the Emporium, who had immediately given Thrift a look of surprise and not a little shock.

'Miss Moncrieff is from England and a lady of quality,' Miss Dace announced, at which the assistant's expression instantly changed from shock to formality. 'She will be visiting a number of Governors during her stay in the colonies and requires appropriate dress. We will require a corset of more suitable design and a selection of dresses with accessories to match.'

'Absolutely, Madame. At once, Madame,' the assistant replied, bobbing a curtsey before she moved.

'My existing corsets –,' Thrift began and shut up, realising that any protest on her part was likely to end with her bare bottom receiving the regulation one hundred and forty-four smacks in front of at least ten assistants and twice as many of her fellow customers.

Miss Dace didn't bother to comment, but stayed as she was until the assistant returned with two colleagues, one of similar age and appearance, the other an older woman with a thin edge of lace to the collar of her uniform that seemed to denote rank within the store.

'I am Mrs Clonough,' the older woman stated. 'Perhaps if the young lady would care to accompany me we might first see to the matter of her corset.'

She had addressed not Thrift but Miss Dace, who nodded politely in response and set off towards a heavily screened area to one side. Thrift followed, finding herself at last in more familiar territory, with the walls lined with the long drawers in which corsets were normally stored. Less familiar was the mobile circular screen the two younger assistants quickly erected around her and Miss Dace, who promptly began to work on the catches of Thrift's dress.

No more than mildly embarrassed by the familiar routine, Thrift allowed herself to have her dress, her underdress and her petticoats removed, leaving her in the shapely satin sheath of her Cantlemere and Lucas corset. She could just see over the top of the screen, and as Miss Dace began to unlace her she watched the two younger assistants taking corset boxes from the drawers under the supervision of the older.

As always, there was considerable relief blended with her sense of exposure and shame as the ankle-length corset came loose and she stepped free in nothing but her underwear, allowing her breasts and bottom and belly to adopt their normal feminine shapes.

'You must certainly reduce,' Miss Dace remarked with a disapproving glance at where Thrift's more than ample breasts were straining against the cotton of her chemise, 'which I shall bear in mind in the selection of your new corset.'

Again Thrift found herself biting down her instinctive protest for fear of a spanking, only for her mouth to fall open again as, to her surprise, Miss Dace began to work on the fastenings of her drawers. She could not bear the thought of the three assistants discovering that she was in containment pants.

'Miss Dace, please, need my underwear come off?' she asked.

'It is quite unsuitable,' Miss Dace responded.

'But who would see, save you and I?' Thrift demanded pathetically, despite already knowing the answer.

'Quite a few people, should it prove necessary to chastise you as I did earlier,' Miss Dace responded. 'Imagine what they will think to see you in undergarments fit only for a streetwalker.'

Thrift wasn't sure if it would be any worse that what they would think to see her bare bottom bouncing to her companion's smacks, but went into a sulky silence, sure that whatever she said would only make it worse for her. Her drawers had been unfastened and Miss Dace pulled them down, leaving Thrift in tight black rubber from the middle of her belly to her upper thighs, her disgrace obvious to anyone who saw. A moment later and her chemise had also been removed, leaving her heavy breasts on plain show and completing her embarrassment.

She was struggling not to pout and praying she would be given a gown to cover her modesty before the screen was removed, While the assistants had set out any number of corsets, they obviously weren't aware that she needed underwear too. Fortunately Miss Dace had noticed and quickly corrected the oversight, speaking to Mrs Clonough over the top of the screen.

'Miss Moncrieff will also require a half-dozen sets of suitable combinations.'

'Naturally, Madame,' Mrs Clonough replied, and signalled to one of her juniors.

Thrift watched, intensely aware of her near nudity as the girl left the screened-off area, coming back after what seemed an unreasonably long time with six identical boxes. On Miss Dace's instruction the top one was opened and the garment within taken out, a set of voluminous combinations in a coarse undyed linen. As they were held up for inspection Thrift realised that not only were they untrimmed, but the back was not a panel but a simple split among the folds of material, a design really only suitable for the lower orders.

For the third time she found herself biting down her natural outrage, instead meekly allowing herself to be put into the hideous garment, at least grateful that she had not been forced to reveal that she was in containment pants. She still felt deeply embarrassed as the screen was removed from around her, and a glance at herself in the mirror was almost enough to start the tears from her eyes. The shapeless, baggy combinations made her look like a guttersnipe, an impression relieved only by her expensive white silk stockings.

'A dozen sets of stockings as well,' Miss Dace stated, 'in brown.'

Thrift made a face, but kept it turned away from Miss Dace as Mrs Clonough extracted a corset from among the layers of tissue paper in the first box. It was a huge thing, as long as her Cantlemere and Lucas, built to cover her from neck to ankles, but there the resemblance ended. Whereas her usual corsets were of heavy satin, the new was made of some coarse tan-coloured material. Where the old followed an elegant exaggeration of her natural contours, the new appeared designed to conceal her figure as far as possible, without even a bustle to enhance the flare of her hips and buttocks. Where the old was built around a whalebone cage designed to follow the contours of her body without creating unsightly bulges, the new had at least twice as many ribs and stays, and would clearly force her flesh into a shape that seemed barely human, let alone feminine.

'This is the Vermont,' Mrs Clonough announced, holding the hideous thing up, 'a most suitable design.'

'Do you have anything a little less severe?' Thrift asked, determined to try despite the instinctive twitching of her bottom cheeks at the possible consequences.

'Please, Miss Moncrieff,' Miss Dace put in before Mrs Clonough could respond. 'As was discussed, you are a stranger to our shores and it is better that I be allowed to judge what is appropriate. Bear in mind that if you are to create a good impression it is essential that your appearance be impeccable. To this end I had something rather stricter than the Vermont in mind, Mrs Clonough: what we in Boston refer to as whalebone strict, if you are acquainted with the phrase?'

For the first time since they had met, Thrift saw Miss Dace smile, or at least that was what the brief upward flicker of one side of her mouth seemed to suggest.

'I understand you precisely,' Mrs Clonough replied. 'I have a maternal aunt from Boston.' She turned to one of the assistants. 'Miss O'Brian, the Scotian Restrictive.'

One of the younger assistants bustled away to find another box, this time from the highest drawer, which she needed a small wheeled platform to reach. A little dust had collected on the lid of the box, earning Miss O'Brian a disapproving look from her senior as it was opened, and as the corset was removed from its papers Thrift found herself wondering from what era it dated.

By comparison, the Vermont seemed light and elegant. Not only was the Scotian Restrictive a darker, duller brown in colour, but it appeared to have more in keeping with some of the peculiar medieval body armour she had seen in South-East Asia than with a female undergarment. The heavy material was not merely reinforced with ribs and stays, but woven with them, so densely as to form a cage, and in a shape that only vaguely approximated to the human body, let alone her own ample curves. Little or no provision had been made for her breasts or buttocks, while the belly piece was a rigid plate of interlocking whalebone struts

31

tightly sewn into a triple layer of material. The leg sheath tapered and would clearly leave her with even less room for movement than the Cantlemere and Lucas, while when Mrs Clonough turned the garment round the hygienic panel proved to close with not one but four locks, each with its distinct key dangling beside it.

'I really think . . . ,' Thrift began.

'The laces are sturdy, I trust?' Miss Dace interrupted.

'Absolutely,' Mrs Clonough assured her.

'I really think . . . ,' Thrift began again.

'And the neck is suitably stiff?' Miss Dace interrupted once more.

'Quite rigid,' Mrs Clonough stated with confidence.

'I really think . . . ,' Thrift began for a third time.

'Do excuse me,' Miss Dace stated, and taking Thrift's wrist, pulled her across to a chair, where despite her pleas and struggles her brand-new drawers were pulled open, her containment pants unfastened and her bare bottom spanked.

Thrift stood staring sulkily out of the window of the Imperial Hotel. It was the finest in New York, and even had suites reserved for Quality guests, one of which she and Miss Dace now occupied. As protocol dictated, she slept in the large if rather plain four-post bed, while her companion occupied a smaller room to one side. Indeed, Miss Dace has done nothing that could possibly be construed as a breach of her authority, and clearly regarded the regular spankings as not only correct but necessary.

The companion took her other duties no less seriously, standing between Thrift and the commonality exactly as she was supposed to, making certain that there was no opportunity whatsoever for impropriety or scandal, and dealing with all those they met with a cold formality that proved remarkably effective. Indeed, not even the sternest of critics could have faulted Miss Dace's behaviour, but Thrift was wishing it was otherwise.

She was bored and uncomfortable, her body squashed into the hideous Scotian Restrictive. The equally shapeless dress of dark grey wool she was wearing made her feel dowdy, while the coarse linen of her combinations tickled her nipples and made her itch all over. Now, with her bottom freshly spanked and her quim wet in her containment pants, the urge to touch herself was very near to unbearable, so much so that she was almost tempted to deliberately offend Miss Dace in some way so that she could be punished again, although she knew it would only hurt and leave her even more frustrated than before.

To make matters worse, New York had proved to be the dullest city she had ever come across, at least for a person of her class. There were very few entertainments she could possibly be seen at, and those which were acceptable all seemed to be long and impossibly tedious plays apparently designed more to reinforce the moral virtues than to entertain.

Miss Dace was praying in her room, something she never seemed to tire of, and was now doing for increasingly long periods after each occasion Thrift was spanked. She had also criticised Thrift's own brief bedtime prayers, suggesting they be twice as long and performed in the morning after punishment. Thrift had complied, kneeling beside the bed with her hands together and her eyes closed, although the state of her bottom had made it impossible to think of anything but the warm pain of punishment, the shame of her exposure and the way her body reacted to both.

She had taken what she considered a more than reasonable time, and yet Miss Dace was still busy. The companion's attitude didn't seem to be unusual by local standards. Some New Yorkers carried bibles wherever they went, and there were more churches even than in

London, aside from the enormous but severe brownstone cathedral that served as the focus of worship for New York Territory.

Miss Dace finally finished her prayers, not troubling to comment as she made for the door. Thrift followed dutifully and in silence, descending the escalator to the small breakfast room set aside for both the Quality and Professional classes, which even the most etiquette-conscious New Yorkers seemed to have difficulty in distinguishing. A breakfast was served, of tea, fruit and peculiar oatcakes in syrup that Thrift found she rather liked, and eaten in silence.

Her new corset made sitting even more uncomfortable than standing, and she was relieved when she was finally able to leave the table. Miss Dace, with no more than a somewhat heavyweight version of the short corset appropriate to her station in life, had no such difficulties but, as in all matters, never hurried and was a stickler for the proprieties.

They returned to their suite, again in silence, with Thrift wishing she had somebody she could talk to and hardly daring even to venture a comment in case Miss Dace deemed it somehow improper. The companion immediately went back to her embroidery, leaving Thrift to gaze once more across the rooftops of New York, trying not to sulk too obviously as she recalled the bright colours and exciting company of Hainan Tao and the Far East.

She bit her lip, remembering how it had felt to wear a simple sheath of beautifully embroidered silk with not so much as a stitch beneath. London had seemed stifling afterwards, and New York was worse, far worse. Possibly, she reflected, the central territories and in particular Louisiana would prove more exciting, as at the very least she would have to dress in a more fetching manner if she was to attract the attention of Jean-Jacques Rougon. Then again, Miss Dace would no doubt find some way to keep her on a tight leash and in the painfully restrictive corset.

'Why does she have to be such a pig?' she muttered.

'I beg your pardon?' a cold and all too familiar voice sounded from directly behind her ear.

Thrift spun around, to find herself staring directly into Miss Dace's face, which was set in a far from friendly expression.

'It ... it was nothing ... nothing at all,' she stammered, her bottom cheeks already squeezing together within her containment pants.

'I distinctly heard you refer to somebody as a pig,' Miss Dace stated.

'No ... I mean ... that is ... ,' Thrift babbled. 'I ... I didn't mean you, Miss Dace, not at all. I was merely daydreaming, about ... about a girl I rather disliked at Diplomatic School.'

'It makes no difference who the victim of your uncouth tongue was,' Miss Dace responded, 'to use such language is deplorable. Come here.'

'Yes, Miss Dace,' Thrift answered miserably, and allowed herself to be led to the straight-backed chair in which Miss Dace had been doing her embroidery.

As she laid herself across Miss Dace's lap, Thrift was trying to console herself with the fact that at least the coming spanking would not be in public, which made it infinitely easier to accept. Yet it was still going to hurt, and she was pouting furiously as her heavy woollen dress was turned up onto her back and her plain linen petticoats laid on top of it. Now familiar with Miss Dace's technique, she put her arms back to have her wrists tied into her corset laces, which was swiftly done.

The release of her corset panel was far from swift, each lock having to be undone separately before it could be opened to allow the rubbery black balls of her bottom cheeks to bulge out from the over-tight corset. Having her containment pants opened was even worse, as Miss Dace had considerable difficulty in getting her hands between Thrift's well-fleshed thighs in order to manipulate the pad.

As Miss Dace felt out the combination her wrist was pressed to Thrift's quim, pushing on the thick rubber pad designed to prevent masturbation. As the rubber pressed into her slit Thrift was forced to grit her teeth in order to prevent a tell-tale sigh from escaping her lips, and again as the sides of her containment pants peeled open to expose her bottom.

The corset was too tight to let it all out, which only made her bottom feel bigger still, and she could visualise her cheeks as two fat hemispheres of wobbling pink flesh sticking out for Miss Dace's attention, although with her skirts thrown up over her head she could see nothing. She could feel plenty, and bit her lip as Miss Dace's hand settled onto the fat of her bottom, trembling in anticipation of the first of what she knew would be exactly one hundred and forty-four smacks.

She squeaked in pain as the first smack landed, and again, in perfect time to the familiar rhythm of her punishment, and despite her best efforts she began to count to herself, although it only seemed to prolong the agony. Soon she was kicking her trapped legs up and down and wriggling in helpless frustration, her hands jerking where they'd been tied into her corset laces, and yet her bottom was still warm from her spanking of less than an hour before, so that before long her pain had begun to give way to the shameful warmth she could never fight against, no matter how humiliating the circumstances of her punishment.

Her cries and gasps turned to sobs, she burst into anguished tears, but still her helpless excitement grew, now seeming to rise with every smack of Miss Dace's hand, while to her undying shame she could smell the rich, feminine scent of her own quim in the air. At that her sobbing broke to a helpless blubbering, the tears cascading down her face and splashing onto the carpet, overcome by the sheer unfairness of growing excited over her own shame and pain.

Still Miss Dace spanked, eighty smacks, a hundred, leaving Thrift choking out her feelings, utterly broken, with spittle bubbling from her lips and twin strands of mucus hanging from her nose. Twenty more and something inside her snapped, as she began to try and wriggle against the rubber pad where her containment pants were open over her quim, lost to all decency and all thought of the consequences, overcome by a need that had been building within her for so long. It didn't work, for her efforts to masturbate herself were as futile as her pleas for mercy, but, inevitably, Miss Dace noticed.

'Why, you filthy little wanton!' the companion snapped, showing real emotion for the first time.

Only it wasn't anger, and the spanking grew no harder. Instead it stopped. Thrift was released, tumbling off Miss Dace's lap and onto the floor, where she rolled over. Unable to help herself with her wrists bound into her laces and her body in the tight confinement of her corset, she could only watch in astonishment as the cold, stern Miss Dace scrabbled frantically at her own skirts, hauling them high to expose the hem of a short black corset, black stocking tops held high by straining suspender straps and plain white linen drawers, into which her fingers were already burrowing.

'Miss Dace!' Thrift squealed as the thick linen drawers were hauled wide to expose a richly furred quim, blatantly wet with arousal.

'Get up here!' Miss Dace snapped back. 'No, don't ... oh God, please no ... oh God ... no, Thrift ... I can't help it ... I can't resist you, you filthy, beautiful little temptress ... get up on your knees and lick me ... I said lick me, you wanton piece of dirt!'

As she finished her voice rose to a screech and she reached down, to grab Thrift by the hair. Thrift

37

squealed in shock and pain as she was dragged close and forced up onto her knees, with her head between Miss Dace's open thighs and a moment later pressed in tight, her mouth pushed to her companion's musky, excited cunt. For a moment she tried to resist, but she couldn't pull away and her own feelings were too strong to resist. Her tongue poked out to taste Miss Dace's sex and then Thrift was licking, urgent and wanton, wishing only that she could get her fingers to her own overheated sex.

Miss Dace gave a long, contented sigh as Thrift began to lick, but kept her grip. With little choice but to obey and ever rising desire for her task, Thrift allowed her head to be manipulated. Her tongue moved over Miss Dace's sex lips and the smooth skin of her inner thighs, onto the twin tucks of the trim little buttocks and the gentle swell of the pubic mound, into the slippery, pungent slit and lastly onto the tiny bump at the top, on which Thrift began to flick her tongue as fast as she could.

The response was near instantaneous, a long, heartfelt sigh of deep bliss, thighs tightening around Thrift's head, back arched and hands locked like claws, and at last a cry of ecstasy that rose and fell twice before breaking into a shame-filled sobbing. Pulled away from between Miss Dace's thighs, Thrift rocked back on her heels. The need to touch herself was painfully strong, and for all her feelings she was immediately begging for her own release.

'Untie me, please, Miss Dace! Please! I need to do that, just as you did. Please, I beg of you, just untie my hands, please!'

Tears were streaming down her face once more, to mingle with the cream from Miss Dace's sex, while she was breathing so hard she felt her chest would surely burst, and wriggling her naked bottom against the carpet in a pathetic and futile effort to get friction to her cunt. Miss Dace looked at her, the stony expression

38

replaced with powerful emotions that flickered across her face, and suddenly she leant forward and jerked the knot binding Thrift's wrists open before running into the bedroom, streaming tears.

Too desperate to think of anything but her own pleasure, Thrift jerked her hands free of the restraint. Immense relief flooded through her and she reached back to take the hot balls of her buttocks in her hands, to squeeze and stroke them, to pull them apart in deliberate display of her anus and the pouted rear lips of her quim, to touch between, tickling the tight, rude little hole from which she did her toilet, and lower, onto the agonisingly sensitive bulges of denuded flesh and into the wet slit between.

She began to masturbate, gulping and gasping as she manipulated her aching cunt, to bring herself up towards orgasm with astonishing speed, so that she was panting for air even as it hit her, an overwhelming wave of ecstasy that left her dizzy and shaking as all the pent-up emotions of the week came out in one great gush.

Three

Not a word was said, not so much as a glance exchanged, Thrift and Miss Dace returning to their previous regime as if nothing had happened, and yet at a deeper level the relationship between them had changed completely. Thrift now knew that Miss Dace's unyielding manner was every bit as much a façade as her own attempts to come across as the ideal of young British womanhood, and that underneath lay feelings not so very different from her own. She also knew that however guilty and ashamed she felt about her inner feelings, for Miss Dace it was many times worse.

The knowledge made her spankings a great deal easier to take, at least the routine morning spankings, as she knew that whatever the pretence, it was not really done for discipline at all but for pleasure. It still hurt, and being put straight back in her containment pants was still agonisingly frustrating, but at least she knew there was a chance that Miss Dace would lose control once more. The rarer, public spankings were a different matter, no easier to endure than before, especially as she now knew that Miss Dace followed certain rules, invariably choosing situations that would be as humiliating as possible for Thrift, but avoiding those likely to lead to comment.

When they attended dinner with the Governor of New York Territory in the small market town of Albany, which for some reason was also the capital, Miss Dace behaved precisely as her role as Thrift's maid and companion dictated, and likewise at the reception given by the Bishop. Only on the following mornings was Thrift given a warning against pride, or ostensibly so, and made to go nude for her spanking, although with her hands tied behind her back as usual.

With their official engagements complete, they moved on, taking a series of short flights on the tiny local airships, and once, to Thrift's chagrin, on a jet. From New York they moved to Delaware, and from Delaware to Maryland, before turning inland across the Virginias and Ohio. In each case Thrift received only limited impressions, magnificent views from the air both of immense sweeps of cultivated land and wild, beautiful hill country and mountains, coupled with the grand hotels and the official residences of Governors and other highly placed officials. Of the people in general she saw very little and learnt less, her sole strong impression being that the deeper into the colonies she moved, the stricter and more God-fearing the population became.

In New York clothing had tended to black, shades of brown and grey, with the occasional sober blue or dull green, but in Dover the blues and greens were gone. Perhaps one person in four carried their bible wherever they went, often in a specially designed pocket that left the cross on the cover clearly visible. In Columbus few people even dared browns or greys, sombre black clothes being everywhere in evidence for both men and women, while everybody seemed to have a bible pocket.

By then Thrift was glad of her own sober clothes, as to have appeared in her preferred canary yellow or white highlighted with coloured ribbons as was fashionable in London would clearly have been considered unacceptable. Even the Governors and their immediate

41

associates dressed in the local styles and colours, and it seemed that in direct reverse of English fashion, the higher the rank the plainer the clothes.

No airship line operated from Columbus, but to Thrift's relief, after finding herself obliged to sit next to a peanut merchant on the noisy, cramped jet, they took a private compartment in a train south and west to an agricultural town with the exotic name of Cincinnati, which proved to be on a river which Miss Dace assured her ultimately flowed to Louisiana.

'Mr Fanshaw feels that we have made a sufficient number of official calls,' Miss Dace stated as they left their hotel, 'and that it would now be reasonable for you to take what is a popular pleasure excursion, travelling by river.'

'Will that not be rather uncomfortable, over so great a distance?' Thrift asked, thinking of the limited facilities provided by the pleasure boats she knew on the Thames and the Scottish lochs.

'The riverboats provide accommodation to suit even your tastes,' Miss Dace remarked, for once with a trace of humour.

'I trust I am not overly fastidious?' Thrift responded cautiously.

Miss Dace responded with the faintest of sniffs and stepped forward to their waiting car. Thrift followed, easing herself into the seat with as much grace as her corset allowed, which was a great deal more than when she was originally put in it, as despite the extreme restriction of her body it was becoming gradually familiar, if not actually comfortable.

'We are booked onto the *Sir Mark Twain*, said to be of the first class,' Miss Dace said as the car drew away, again showing surprising enthusiasm.

'I am sure she will prove satisfactory,' Thrift responded, trying to hide her doubt as she looked out at the drab streets and the prim, fastidious passers-by.

The journey was short, the car quickly pulling up beside a low white building the front of which bore discreet signs advertising the offices of what were presumably rival river companies. Miss Dace got out, moving directly to the nearest of these, beyond which rose a most fantastic structure entirely out of keeping with the understated architecture of the town. Level after level of fancifully worked wrought iron and wood rose above her, painted in glittering white and a bold, rich green and topped with a set of fluttering pennons in the same colours.

'Whatever is that building?' Thrift asked in astonishment.

'That is not a building, Miss Moncrieff,' Miss Dace replied with a sniff. 'That is the *Sir Mark Twain*, and your first taste of Creole decadence. Now do stop staring. I am surprised at you.'

'I'm sorry,' Thrift said quickly, only then realising that she had been gaping open-mouthed at the huge boat.

The green and white sign above the door announced the offices as those of the Grand Southern River Company, and as Thrift followed Miss Dace in she found herself in the company of two strikingly different men. One, seated behind a counter, was typical of the people she had so far met, his hair cropped short, his expression dour, and dressed in a severe black suit with a prominent bible pocket. The other, standing at a door that appeared to lead out to the docks, was of much the same build but with long, carefully styled hair and an opulent and rakish moustache, while he was dressed in a white linen suit of flamboyant cut, each sleeve of which was decorated with broad gold rings. Taking the first for a clerk and the second for an officer of some unfamiliar regiment but considerable rank, Thrift ignored the one and gave as full a curtsey as she could manage to the other. To her surprise he responded not with the formal and silent bow she had expected, but by tugging at the tip of his moustache and addressing her without waiting for Miss Dace to effect an introduction.

'Ah ha!' he said, stepping forward. 'You must be Lady Moncrieff, unless I'm very much mistaken? Allow me to introduce myself: Samuel Langhorne, Captain of the *Twain*. It'll be a pleasure to have you aboard, it will that.'

'Miss Moncrieff,' Thrift corrected him, the colour immediately rushing to her cheeks at his manner, and more forcefully still as he took her hand and pressed his lips gently to the back of her glove. 'A pleasure to meet you, Captain Langhorne.'

'I would think,' Miss Dace cut in from behind Thrift, 'that it would be better were we to observe the full proprieties, Captain Langhorne. I am Miss Dace, Miss Moncrieff's companion.'

'A pleasure,' the Captain responded, reaching out to take a hand that had not been offered and allowing himself a smooth chuckle as he withdrew. 'Perhaps I might have the honour of showing you to your state-room, the finest on the ship, naturally, after my own quarters – directly below them, in fact, clean across the upper hurricane deck ...'

'Hurricane deck?' Thrift queried in alarm.

'Just a name,' he said with a laugh. 'There'll be no hurricanes, not at this season, and if there are, why, you can count on me to take care of you, personally.'

He finished with a distinctly suggestive grin and Thrift found herself blushing again. As he'd spoken he had walked out onto the dockside, giving them no polite option but to follow, despite the sheaf of papers the clerk had been holding out for Miss Dace's attention. The *Sir Mark Twain* was now fully visible, almost as long as one of the big airships and rising high above them in tier after tier of decking. Three gangplanks led down to the dock, the furthest evidently for cargo and luggage to judge by the bustle around it, the next for the commonality and the closest for the better class of passengers.

For the first time since leaving New York she felt the familiar and pleasant sensation of knowing her place. Evidently she was still expected to mix with the Professional classes, but that seemed to be the case almost everywhere in America, while the stateroom sounded ideal, and as Captain Langhorne pointed it out she realised it not only had windows towards the bows and at both sides of the boat, but a fine wrought-iron balcony set out with chairs and a green and white sunshade.

'A quite magnificent vessel,' she stated, eager to please despite considerable caution.

'I like to think so,' he answered, and pointed up to the very highest level, three decks above the stateroom, where a pair of enormous gilded antlers stood out. 'Fastest time, Portsmouth to New Orleans, non-stop.'

'Portsmouth?' Thrift echoed in surprise.

'Portsmouth, Ohio,' he laughed. 'You Limeys, centre of the world, huh? Well, I suppose you are.'

He didn't trouble to explain his comment, and as Miss Dace took her arm in a somewhat pointed manner Thrift went quiet. After so long among reserved and proper people, the Captain's manner was refreshing, even a little exciting, and she knew that to be spanked in front of him would be more humiliating than anything she had endured so far. She also suspected that if Miss Dace discovered this fact it was very likely to happen, and determined to keep her feelings to herself and behave with absolute decorum.

Captain Langhorne had lit a cigar and puffed happily on it as he led the way aboard, again ignoring the officials at the gangplank. A stair led directly to the upper hurricane deck, which was plainly reserved for the Quality, with a fine open space at the stern, a well-appointed dining room and lounge, and just seven staterooms, of which theirs was much the grandest. A single room ran the width of the ship, affording magnificent views from some fifty feet above the river, while there was also a large and comfortable bedroom, a bathroom with the full range of facilities and a smaller bedroom for Miss Dace.

Thrift found herself approving, even admiring, but responded to the Captain's effusive talk and frequent compliments with polite nods, all the while wishing she didn't blush so easily or so richly. To her intense relief Miss Dace held her peace, contenting herself with ensuring that Thrift and the Captain were never alone for one moment, as any companion would do, and before long he was obliged to return to his duties. Their luggage had arrived, and Thrift went out onto the balcony as it was stowed.

Viewed from so high, and with so wide an aspect, the river and docks held all of the romantic fascination she had hoped to find in far-flung parts of the Empire. The *Sir Mark Twain* was one of four riverboats moored beside the long wooden walkways, although she was much the largest. Two others were also of good size, with three decks each, and painted in relatively drab livery that now suggested to her those territories that she had visited and presumably the majority of North America. The fourth was another southerner, much smaller but notably more exotic, with a great circular paddle wheel on either side and even a funnel, as if she belonged to the age of steam, although Thrift suspected she was powered by a Collins Engine like any other.

Beyond the docks the river spread an impressive distance to the trees on the far bank, wider than the Thames at Westminster and possessed of a calm beauty, while the view of distant, heavily wooded hills made even the drab uniformity of the town look quite pretty. Drawing in a deep breath of the fresh, sharp air she decided that she was going to enjoy her river trip, and even dared to wonder if she could reach some agreement with Miss Dace to allow her to enjoy the Captain's attention, perhaps accepting a double dose across her bottom each morning in recompense for the impropriety.

She knew she would be refused, and that to ask would certainly be disastrous, especially with the cabin boy still stowing their luggage, and she pursed her lips in vexation. Suddenly the magic of the river was gone, and she returned inside wishing that she could find some way to make Miss Dace even marginally less inflexible. Miss Dace was passing a handful of small coins to the cabin boy for some reason, and spoke immediately he had left.

'Captain Langhorne,' she stated, 'is typical of the Creole, with poor manners and little regard for God or man. He is also proud and of an age to still feel somewhat piqued at the sale of Louisiana, though not, I judge, openly antagonistic. He will make an excellent study for you so that you will know what to expect when we arrive in Baton Rouge – as, no doubt, will be other officers aboard the boat. I must, however, caution you to avoid careless intimacies, and you may be sure I will be paying close attention to your conduct, and theirs. They are a hot-blooded race, with little respect for correct behaviour or religious stricture.'

'You may of course be assured of my absolute propriety, Miss Dace,' Thrift responded, wondering if she dared go further and realising that Miss Dace's statement had given her the perfect excuse. 'As they are so bereft of personal restraint, may I suggest, should you feel I require discipline in any form, that it be confined to the privacy of our stateroom? Otherwise, might the sight not risk inflaming their blood?'

Miss Dace stiffened immediately, and took a moment before she responded.

'It is not your place to decide how you are disciplined, Miss Moncrieff, and certainly not to seek to lessen it. There is undoubtedly something in what you say, and yet no officer nor yet crewman on this boat could possibly be so lost to decency as to force himself upon you, least of all while you are across my lap. No, I shall continue, as before, to exercise my judgement as to when and where you require discipline.'

Thrift realised she had begun to pout and quickly sucked her lower lip in, only for it to quickly poke out again as Miss Dace continued.

'Furthermore, I strongly suspect that your reason for making this suggestion is not as you state, but simply an attempt to avoid your just chastisement, and therefore also a lie. You will come across my lap.'

Thrift drew a heavy sigh as she got down into spanking position.

Aboard the *Sir Mark Twain*, March 2006

The first day aboard the river boat passed without incident. Thrift had watched the *Sir Mark Twain* pull away from the docks with her bottom still hot in her containment pants and her face set in a resentful moue, then spent the remainder of her time making absolutely certain that Miss Dace could find no excuse to dish out the threatened public discipline. Feigning a slight queasiness from the gentle rocking motion of the boat, she had ensured that they ate in their stateroom and had retired early rather than join the other first-class passengers and off-duty officers in the lounge. Miss Dace had accepted the situation without comment and continued with her embroidery as Thrift lay thinking muddled thoughts in her fine bed.

Morning found them moving at good speed down a buoyed channel with cultivated fields on the bank beyond, lit bright as the sun lifted itself above the eastern horizon. Kneeling up on her bed to admire the view, Thrift wondered whether she should continue to claim to be unwell. It seemed a shame to waste her time in her cabin when she might at the very least be out on the balcony or, better still, making the acquaintance of the remaining officers and any persons of genuine quality among the passengers, to say nothing of Captain Langhorne. Set against that was the agonising prospect of being spanked in front of those same people.

A noise from the adjoining cabin alerted her to Miss Dace, and she quickly dropped back into bed, pulling the covers up to her chin. For a while she lay still, listening to the faint noises as her companion performed her morning ablutions and dressed, before rolling onto her side just as the door opened.

'Are you at all better this morning, Miss Moncrieff?' Miss Dace enquired, looking down on Thrift with what appeared to be genuine concern.

'A little, thank you, Miss Dace,' Thrift replied. 'I slept well.'

'Good,' Miss Dace responded, leaning down to place a hand on Thrift's forehead. 'Still, you do seem a little pale. No morning routine today, I think, and I shall have some weak tea and a plain oatcake sent up for your breakfast.'

Miss Dace left the room, and it took Thrift a moment to realise that she wasn't going to be given her regular morning spanking, which was normally done on the edge of her bed as soon as she got up, so that only her modesty gown needed to be lifted and her pants unfastened. She smiled at the thought as she propped herself up on her pillows, amused by how easily Miss Dace had been tricked, but managed to look suitably weak when her companion returned with the breakfast tray.

'There is no wind at all this morning,' Miss Dace stated as Thrift took a bite of her oatcake. 'I wonder if you might not have a fever?'

'I don't think so, Miss Dace,' Thrift answered. 'I get seasick very easily.'

Miss Dace didn't comment, but left the cabin, returning only when Thrift had finished her breakfast, with a heavy black bag, which she placed on the bedside table once she had removed the tray. Thrift recognised it immediately as a medical bag, exactly the same sort her previous companion had carried, which was worrying to say the least. She made to speak, but stopped, aware that too profuse a declaration of how well she felt would mean a spanking, then changed her mind.

'I am really much better now,' she insisted. 'In fact, I would like to get up.'

'We shall see about that,' Miss Dace answered firmly, digging in the bag. 'I'll take your temperature.'

Miss Dace opened a slender wooden box to reveal a selection of thermometers set in black velvet padding. One, the largest, containing red-coloured alcohol and ending in a bulb the size of a large toy marble, was all too clearly designed for insertion into a girl's anus. Inevitably it was the one Miss Dace selected, moving Thrift to immediate protest despite the risks.

'Would the oral thermometer not be more appropriate for my age and place, Miss Dace?' she asked, fighting to keep the note of pleading out of her voice.

'When you've just had a cup of hot tea?' Miss Dace responded. 'Now, roll over onto your front, and let's have no more nonsense.'

Thrift obeyed, biting her lip in consternation, and turned over onto her tummy. Her bedclothes were peeled back and her modesty gown lifted to reveal the seat of her containment pants, each exposure making the sudden churning of her stomach worse. She was forced to lift her hips to allow Miss Dace to work the combination, and as her pants peeled open to expose her bottom it was all she could do to stay still.

Miss Dace worked without fuss, apparently indifferent to Thrift's rising humiliation as she first pulled on thin rubber gloves and then chose a lubricant from her bag. Thrift's eyes were screwed up as her bottom cheeks were hauled open and the cold, sticky grease applied to her anal ring and rubbed well in, one bony finger even briefly probing her rectum.

The finger had gone in easily enough, but when it came to the bulb of the thermometer it was a different matter. It was at least twice as wide, and round, stretching Thrift's anus open as it was twisted gently in, to make her gasp and think of men's cocks being inserted into the same rude cavity. Even when her hole had closed on the shaft she could still feel it, as a gentle pressure in her rectum and between her cheeks, the glass cold and hard.

She also knew how she would look, and couldn't help thinking about it, her gown lifted and her containment pants open, her bottom bulging up, fat and pink and round, with the stem of the thermometer protruding from between her big cheeks, plainly showing that she was having her temperature taken up her bottom instead of in her mouth. To make it worse, she knew her rectum was full, and that when the thermometer was pulled out it would be dirty, a hideously embarrassing prospect.

Miss Dace began to time the regulation three minutes, but to Thrift it seemed more like three hours before her bottom cheeks were again gently parted with gloved fingers and the thermometer extracted from her anus. Even with it out she was left feeling slippery and open behind, also itchy, tempting her to touch, with inevitable consequences, though that would be impossible in front of Miss Dace.

'Quite normal,' the companion stated after a while. 'Now, I think you need the convenient facility.'

Thrift's cheeks, already warm, grew furiously hot at Miss Dace's words, and she scrambled quickly from the bed and into the bathroom, sobbing with humiliation as she let herself go, with each heavy plop from beneath her adding a fresh pang to her bruised feelings. To make it worse, Miss Dace came in to wash the thermometer, and stayed as Thrift wiped herself. Then she spoke.

'I shall leave the matter to you then, Miss Moncrieff. Do you wish to get up today?'

'I think I will, thank you, yes, Miss Dace,' Thrift replied, not wishing to risk further medical humiliations.

'A sensible choice, I think,' Miss Dace stated. 'Are you ready?'

Thinking that Miss Dace was asking if she had finished on the toilet, Thrift nodded, despite having a piece of hygienic tissue still held against her anus as she wiped the lubricant from around her ring. It came as such a shock when Miss Dace reached out to take her wrist that she could only manage a squeal of consternation before she was turned expertly across the knee, bottom up and cheeks wide, with the piece of hygienic tissue still stuck a little way in up her hole.

'I do think you might learn to wipe yourself properly, Thrift,' Miss Dace remarked, untypically using the informal address, and then she began to spank her.

Thrift took the routine punishment, sobbing and jerking across Miss Dace's lap, so full of shame she felt her head would burst, while the piece of paper between her cheeks made her bottom cheeks stick together in an odd way with almost every smack and kept her constantly reminded of its presence. Long before she'd been given her full twelve dozen smacks she was in floods of tears, and she was still crying as she stood up, and so broken down that she reached back to touch her hot bottom despite Miss Dace still being with her.

'We'll have none of that,' Miss Dace stated, gently removing Thrift's hand. 'Clearly you still need to be tied. Now, into the shower with you and we'd better see about getting you dressed.'

To Thrift's surprise, Miss Dace picked up the thermometer and left the room, giving her the opportunity to touch herself, if not enough to reach the orgasm she was once more coming to need so badly. Yet the added shame of being spanked with the piece of hygienic paper still between her cheeks had left her confused, with her feelings too raw to become erotic so quickly.

Instead she sat down on the convenient facility once more, to remove the offending piece of tissue and quickly polish her anus with another, a sensation at once so pleasurable and so rude, along with the feel of her hot bottom cheeks on the hard seat, that she very nearly risked applying a thumb to her aching quim. Fortunately she resisted, as Miss Dace was back a moment later, watching as Thrift exchanged her cotton modesty gown for the rubber one she wore to wash, peeled off her containment pants and stepped into the shower.

As always, Miss Dace cleaned and dried the containment pants while Thrift washed, only in this case the shower cubicle was directly across the cabin from the sink. With Miss Dace's back to her, Thrift found herself unable to resist the opportunity to masturbate. Twisting the shower to full in order to make it as noisy as possible, she turned her back to her companion and slid her hand up under the rubber hem of her modesty gown to her sex.

Just to be bare felt exquisite, her belly and bottom cheeks unfettered by the thick rubber of her containment pants and the harsh whalebone struts of her Scotian Restrictive. To be bare with her bottom hot from spanking was better still, and she reached back with her other hand as her control started to slip, holding her modesty gown up and rubbing the soap over her smarting flesh. It felt glorious, and she was wishing she could strip nude and go back over Miss Dace's knee, to be spanked again, long and hard, while she masturbated, then be made to lick, down on her knees with her face pressed to her companion's sex and her fingers busy with her own cunt and anus.

She was going to come, and as the soap dropped to the floor of the shower her hand slid between her cheeks. Her bottom hole was moist and slippery, allowing her finger in with ease as she remembered how the thermometer had felt going in. She began to probe the little hole, thinking of how she must have looked with the piece of hygienic tissue sticking out of her anus as she was spanked and wishing Miss Dace had made her wipe herself with her bottom stuck out to be inspected as she cleaned it.

That was the final straw. With her teeth biting into her lower lip to stop herself screaming, she applied a finger directly to her clitoris, rubbing hard as she pushed another up her cunt hole and probed her anus deeper still. The orgasm hit her immediately, with the image of her bottom thrust out for inspection as she wiped the dirty hole burning in her head as wave after wave of ecstasy flooded over her, until at last she could take no more and was forced to clutch at the shower rail to stop herself collapsing as her knees gave way.

Only then did Miss Dace speak out.

'I can see you in the mirror, Thrift, quite clearly.'

In order to prolong the agony of Thrift's punishment for masturbating she had neither been told what would happen, nor when it would happen. All she knew was that it was going to happen, and that when it did it would be a good deal worse for having accused Miss Dace of hypocrisy after she had been caught. What had happened in the hotel in New York was apparently not merely unmentionable, and to be treated as if it had never occurred, but irrelevant. Thrift, after all, was under her companion's discipline, not the other way round, and the implication that Miss Dace should therefore also be punished was very little consolation.

All the rest of that day she was on her best behaviour, despite fighting a strong urge to sulk. They took lunch at the Captain's table, although it was in fact the only table in the upper hurricane deck dining saloon, sufficiently large to accommodate the Captain himself and all eleven passengers. As always in the company of her betters, Miss Dace behaved with an almost servile restraint, her sole contributions to the conversation being to act as intermediary for the introductions and to explain that Thrift's wan complexion was due to seasickness.

Seated to the Captain's right, not only the sole English person present but of much the highest rank, Thrift found herself very much the centre of attention. Of the eleven passengers, four were senior officials of one sort of another and the remaining seven merchants. Five were from the middle Territories, and tended to blend into one another in Thrift's mind, making it hard to remember which name belonged to which face, but the other six were from the south, and notably more distinctive. She was also very aware of their conversation, hoping to pick out details that might help her when she met Jean-Jacques Rougon.

Among the six southerners, Reuben Reynolds was the owner of a cotton plantation in the territory of Arkansas, directly north of Louisiana, and while he dressed in black and carried a bible his manner was very different from what she was used to. He was fiery in temperament, seemed to have a biblical quote to cover every possible eventuality of life and was always keen to discuss them. Physically he was big, raw-boned and red-faced, clearly used to the open air and hard work despite his wealth.

His wife, Hester, at first seemed to be very much in his shadow, as she nodded at almost everything he said, but as the meal progressed it became clear that her personality was every bit as forthright as his, and that they had evidently been brought up to a common understanding of life. Like her husband, she was big-boned and apparently strong, with a harsh face that showed her fifty or so years.

Lucien Fargues was an official in the Governor's office in Louisiana, and according to Thrift's file a senior Gauliste, but his importance lay rather in his family connections than in his abilities. Tall, elegant and fastidious if somewhat effete, he was not without a certain charm and evidently of a rank Thrift could feel comfortable with, as he had ties with the ancient French aristocracy. He also seemed likely to be a useful contact, and she did her best to cultivate his good opinion, even allowing herself a little carefully gauged flirtation despite his sixty-odd years and raffish goatee beard.

Ademar Mareschal was in theory Mr Fargues' personal secretary but never appeared to do anything except smoke expensive cigars and allow his eyes to take in Thrift's figure. Clearly he fancied himself as a dandy and a rake, although his natural appearance went against these inclinations. Although tall, he was as fat and as sleek as a seal, with small, round spectacles and shiny brown hair apparently pasted to his head by some cosmetic substance. His clothes were expensive and evidently tailor-made, but the bottle-green velvet of his jacket clashed unpleasantly with his sallow complexion.

Marie-Noel and Delphyne Deix were sisters, elderly, severe by the standards of Louisiana if not the other territories, and members of one of North America's most wealthy and prestigious manufacturing families. Thrift quickly decided that as merchants they were unlikely to be of consequence, and even allowed herself the pleasure of snubbing them mildly by repeatedly providing only the briefest of answers to their numerous questions.

The meal was also interesting, a piquant soup flavoured with some herb Thrift was unable to identify, braised catfish in a rich sauce also unfamiliar to her, medallions of beef, inferior only to the very best she was used to at home, and an apple pie which was supposed to be a regional speciality but differed not at all from the ones served by the cook in her London home.

Each course was accompanied by a wine, from either New York Territory or California, and with her best efforts to be abstemious counteracted by Captain Langhorne's ready hand, Thrift found herself distinctly tipsy by the time the steward came to announce that coffee and chocolates were being served to the ladies on the promenade to the aft of the deck.

The men stayed where they were as the steward began to serve from a decanter of port, and Thrift took Miss Dace's arm as they walked out into the open air, which was pleasantly cool and fresh after the dining saloon. Adelie Young, the sole woman among the group from the middle territories and a Bostonian, asked Miss Dace a question, allowing Thrift to slip away to the rail, where she stood pretending to admire the view across the river as her mind went back to the shameful incident that morning and the possible consequences.

She knew full well that it was pointless trying not to dwell on it. However hard she tried she would soon be wondering whether it would be the cane or the strap, the whip or the quirt, all of which she had had used on her at one time or another, and all of which hurt like anything. Had Miss Dace been English she knew it would almost certainly have been the cane, the tawse from a Scot and a wooden-handled strap from a Welshwoman. Yet Miss Dace was American, and Thrift had no idea what might be the preferred implement when a girl's offence came to warrant more than the simple application of a hand to her bare bottom.

Then there was the question of the severity of the punishment, perhaps more frightening still. Thrift had never been good at accepting her due, usually squealing and in tears from what she knew many tougher girls considered trivial. If Miss Dace stayed true to form and delivered a dozen dozen, Thrift knew full well that she'd be left a grovelling, tear-streaked mess, and would undoubtedly howl so loudly that she would be heard not only by the first-class passengers but the entire crew, the commonality and probably the engineers and roustabouts down below the water level as well.

A minor question was whether she would be made to take it nude, always an added humiliation, or put through any of the shameful little extras previous companions and governesses had inflicted on her, such as being made to count the strokes or stand in the corner with her bare red bottom on show and her hands on her head. More worrying was the possibility of one or more of the other women among the first-class passengers being invited in to bear witness to the punishment, perhaps even the Captain, which would make it infinitely worse.

Lastly there was the question of her reaction. However much it hurt, however humiliating it was, her quim would grow wet and the need to touch herself urgent. In front of witnesses, the Captain especially, to be seen to grow excited as she was beaten was so hideously embarrassing she found it hard to take in at all, although even if they discovered she was in containment pants they'd know she was a wanton, which was bad enough. Without witnesses, and if Miss Dace lost control as she had before, then Thrift would no doubt end up doing exactly what she was being punished for, which was a fine irony.

Quite unconsciously, her expression had shifted to a sulky pout. She struggled to compose herself and stole a glance towards Miss Dace, who was now talking not only with Adelie Young, but also with Hester Reynolds and the Deix sisters. The expressions on the women's faces suggested a serious topic of conversation, and as Mrs Reynolds cast a glance of unmistakable disapprobation in Thrift's direction she found her stomach churning and the blood rushing to her face, hot and hotter still. Then Miss Dace started towards her.

The other women followed, and Thrift could do nothing but stand as she was, sweltering with embarrassment and shame under their gazes. Hester Reynolds had removed her bible from the pocket to one side of her gown and was holding it towards Thrift as if it were a weapon. Adelie Young's face bore the same cold disapproval as that of Miss Dace, but the Deix sisters, while full of scorn, were evidently having trouble concealing an underlying amusement.

'What a delightful evening,' Thrift managed weakly. 'Are not the lights pretty along the shore?'

'Yes, so pretty,' Miss Dace responded, 'but do you not think that in the circumstances it might be proper to show rather more contrition?'

'You have sinned,' Hester Reynolds put in, shaking her bible.

Thrift hung her head, unable to maintain any further pretence, her cheeks flaring hot and her stomach fluttering wildly as Miss Dace continued.

'These good ladies have been kind enough to advise me in the matter of your need for discipline, which is clearly great, is it not?'

'Yes,' Thrift admitted in a feeble whisper.

'I do beg your pardon?' Miss Dace queried.

'Yes,' Thrift repeated, struggling to make her voice louder around the lump in her throat. It felt as if she'd swallowed an apple.

'Yes, indeed,' Delphyne Deix put in, Adelie Young giving a single stern nod of agreement.

'You will excuse me for revealing what is usually a private matter,' Miss Dace went on, 'but I have no doubt that you are as eager as I to be cured of your habit . . .'

'Self-abuse,' Marie-Noel Deix put in, her righteous tone not quite concealing a trace of cruel amusement.

'. . . and therefore felt it best to bring your sin to a wider forum,' Miss Dace continued.

' "Keep close watch over a headstrong daughter," so saith the Lord,' Hester Reynolds quoted.

'Very wise, Miss Dace,' Adelie Young put in. 'Is this not so, Miss Moncrieff?'

Thrift found herself nodding, although no longer able to speak for her shame.

'She understands her sin, at least,' Adelie Young remarked.

'By which token her sin grows tenfold worse,' Hester Reynolds stated firmly. ' "The beasts of the fields and the birds of the air know not what they do, and man alone is sinful." '

'Her crime is the very fountain of temptation,' Delphyne Deix added, 'and must be dealt with appropriately.'

'Severely,' her sister added.

'Most severely,' Adelie Young agreed.

The women nodded in unison at the remark and Thrift hung her head lower still.

'This much we are agreed upon,' Miss Dace stated, 'and also that you will derive great benefit from receiving your discipline with the five of us present . . .'

' "She will be disgraced before the assembly," so saith the Lord,' Hester Reynolds put in.

'. . . and us alone,' Miss Dace went on, 'the presence of men being more harmful than beneficial . . .'

' "Do not let her display her beauty to any man," ' Hester Reynolds added.

'Thank you, Mrs Reynolds,' Miss Dace said firmly.

'With the five of us present and with sufficient severity to ensure that you do not repeat the offence.'

'But ... but I can't anyway!' Thrift pleaded as the tears began to trickle down her cheeks. 'I'm ... I'm in containment pants, am I not?'

'She is in containment pants?' Adelie Young queried.

'Yes,' Miss Dace confirmed, 'a pair of Haskell and Banks with combination and semi-organic action.'

'I feel that Merrill Brothers make a more efficacious product,' Adelie Young replied. 'Bulkier and more reliable.'

'A good solid chastity belt is what she needs, none of this fanciful modern nonsense,' Hester Reynolds suggested.

'She has another pair,' Miss Dace responded, 'to go with Dr Lloyd's Improved Regime, when of course she would have been catheterised. I prefer to keep her regular in order to deal with her wastes, and apply a simple morning spanking for her routine, a dozen dozen given by hand, which I thought to be sufficient.'

'Clearly it is not,' Adelie Young pointed out. 'I suggest it be doubled at least, and should you find it tiring I would be more than happy to assist.'

'Very kind of you, my dear,' Miss Dace responded.

'Perhaps when we reach Memphis we might put her on a more appropriate regime?' Marie-Noel Deix suggested.

'Dr Dupont's is most efficacious,' her sister put in.

'Is that the one in which her breasts are left bare?' Hester Reynolds queried. 'I rather think not, quite improper!'

'It serves to keep her in mind of her shame,' Marie-Noel pointed out.

'I suggest Dr Egerton's,' Adelie remarked, 'which has the same effect but without any suggestion of impropriety. Her hands are tied behind her back and her head is shaved ...'

Cowering against the rail, Thrift began to whimper.

Four

Memphis, Tennessee, March 2006

Thrift's river trip had not turned out as she had hoped. Instead of the carefree succession of days spent in pleasant and even intriguing company, her every waking hour passed in fearful apprehension of the moment when the five women would be gathered in her stateroom and she would be given whatever undoubtedly appalling punishment they had decided on. She thought about it constantly, worrying about the pain and her reaction to it, speculating morbidly over what was likely to be done to her, jumping every time Miss Dace spoke. Even the increasingly warm attentions of Captain Langhorne couldn't take her mind off it, while from the knowing look in his eye and the occasional carefully phrased double meaning in his talk she was sure he knew not only that she was a wanton but that she was spanked every morning.

After all, he and the crew were always busy about the boat, and given the changes in her routine it seemed inevitable that they would realise what was going on, maybe even hear the smacks and her squeals through the deck. There were more smacks and more squeals too, to say nothing of Adelie Young's regular visits to Thrift's stateroom. Every morning it was the same, Miss Young arriving at precisely seven-thirty, by which time

Thrift would be waiting in her bedroom, standing in the middle of the floor with her modesty gown held up to her waist and her containment pants open at the back, ready for spanking.

The two women would take turns to punish her, each taking her across her knee for precisely one hundred and forty-four smacks on her quivering cheeks while the other watched. They also talked, generally about the task in hand, commenting on the fullness of Thrift's cheeks and her need for a reducing diet and even on the appearance of her denuded sex lips, but also about other matters, the quality of apples from different territories or Bostonian politics, all the while with Thrift's bare bottom bouncing and wobbling across one or the other's lap. For some reason Thrift found such casual conversations even more humiliating than those about her.

Once she had been spanked, she would be stripped of her containment pants, still with her hands tied behind her back, put in her rubber modesty gown and taken to the shower. Miss Dace would then wash Thrift's body as Miss Young looked on, and although neither woman ever betrayed any emotion other than cold disapproval, Thrift was convinced that her companion's hands lingered longer than was strictly necessary when soaping her breasts and bottom and belly.

The shower invariably left her in a state of extreme frustration, which grew worse as she was dried and powdered, which included being rolled up on the floor to have her quim and anus done as if she was a baby. Only then would she be put back in her containment pants and her hands untied before she was dressed, which now involved Miss Dace holding her as Miss Young pulled the laces of her Scotian Restrictive as tight as they would go.

By the time she was ready she would be shivering with arousal and faint from her ordeal and the tight clothing.

Nevertheless, she would be escorted into the dining salon and have to eat her breakfast as if nothing had happened, while Captain Langhorne paid court to her and the others discussed this and that, their eyes hinting at scorn or distaste or amusement each time they rested on Thrift.

Her single, feeble attempt at protest had only resulted in yet another spanking, and now, as the *Sir Mark Twain* pulled in to the dock at the town of Memphis she stood on the balcony of her stateroom, fiddling with the front of her dress and praying that there would be no suitable doctor to put her onto a harsher regime of sexual continence.

It seemed unlikely that her prayers would be answered. Memphis was evidently an important place, almost large enough to be called a city, and the first big settlement since the Ohio River had joined the even larger Mississippi to create by far the biggest river Thrift had ever seen. Otherwise, the town was more or less typical of the middle territories, built and populated as if every building and every person was vying to be more godly than the next. Even the longshoremen and roustabouts on the docks carried ostentatiously large bibles, with characteristic gold crosses on the covers which made one of the very few splashes of colour other than the boat itself.

Possibly, Thrift considered in an attempt at optimism, the women of Tennessee were so virtuous that there was no call for doctors specialising in female continence, and yet it seemed too much to hope for. Certainly Miss Dace had expressed no such doubts as she discussed the matter with Miss Young that morning while holding a yelping, red-bottomed Thrift across her lap. Rather, she had seemed concerned at being able to make the right choice from what she assumed would be a wide selection within the limited time before the *Sir Mark Twain* moved on down river.

64

'Come, Miss Moncrieff, this is no time for day-dreaming,' said Miss Dace from behind Thrift.

'I am very sorry, Miss Dace,' Thrift answered automatically, trying not to pout as she turned around.

'There is no call to look so glum,' Miss Dace stated. 'This is for your own good, as you well know. You do wish to be cured of your nasty little habit, don't you?'

Thrift nodded, knowing that any other response would be disastrous. It was taken for granted that she wished to be virtuous, despite the fact that it was her very lack of natural virtue that made her suitable for the Diplomatic Service. It also made her unsuitable for just about any other role in life, including marriage, as no young man of quality would ever take a known wanton for his wife. Not that being cured would make any difference, as a girl cured of being a wanton was considered little better than a wanton anyway, but this was not a line of logic she was tempted to place before Miss Dace.

'Come along then,' Miss Dace urged, leaving Thrift no choice but to take her arm and allow herself to be escorted from the stateroom.

Miss Young was waiting in the lounge, and immediately took Thrift's other arm, so that they descended the gangplank as if a pair of wardresses were leading a delinquent to prison. Thrift was unable to find the strength even to keep her chin up, and let herself be led meekly through the offices of the Grand Southern River Company and out onto the streets beyond.

'Now, the matter of a suitable doctor,' Miss Dace remarked.

'Perhaps if we were to visit a hospital or sanatorium?' Miss Young suggested. 'They might be expected to know.'

'An excellent idea, my dear Miss Young,' Miss Dace answered and turned to one of the porters from the *Sir Mark Twain* who was nearby unloading the trunks of a passenger from the lower hurricane deck. 'Boy, are you familiar with Memphis?'

'I am, Miss,' the porter answered, bowing.

'Are you able to direct me to the nearest medical facility?'

'There's the sanatorium in Beale Street,' he replied, 'two blocks left and turn into town, but –'

'That will do nicely, I am sure,' said Miss Dace, cutting him off before he could continue. 'Here is a sixpence for your troubles.'

She passed him the coin and Thrift was led away, along the dockside and in among tall houses of a brick so dark as to be almost black. The sanatorium was immediately evident, a forbidding-looking edifice set somewhat back from the rest behind iron railings. It proved necessary to ring a bell in order to attract attention. Thrift waited with all the patience she could muster, looking glumly at the legend above the door proclaiming the sanatorium as run by the Sisters of Divine Mercy.

Presently the door opened and a woman emerged, not in the severe black dress and white apron Thrift had been expecting, but in full religious robes, while she held in one hand a thick leather strap. Thrift winced, remembering how just such straps had felt across her bottom during her time at Weathercote House of Shame and wondering if there was some mistake and the place was a similar establishment. It certainly looked the part, but in any event Miss Dace spent only a moment in conversation before withdrawing with a polite bow.

'Dr Corraghan is the local specialist in these matters, apparently,' she told Miss Young, 'and by good fortune he does much of his work here and has his consulting room at the rear of the premises.'

Thrift's heart sank at her words, but she let herself be led down a side alley to a black door set in a high wall with only two windows as openings, both high above the ground, little more than slits and set with bars. Miss Dace rang the bell and presently a small hatch in the door came open to reveal a none too friendly face. After another brief conversation they were admitted, and Thrift found herself in a tiny hall between two doors, the second of which could not be opened until the first had been locked shut, then at the base of a stone staircase, which they ascended.

Dr Corraghan's office proved to be little more inviting, a windowless box on the third floor, almost entirely bare and smelling of rubbing alcohol, ether and something rather more unpleasant Thrift was unable to place. He himself was a huge, loose-limbed man with a great red beard, dressed in the usual severe black suit with his bible laid on the desk in front of him. The servant who had let them in spoke briefly with the doctor before he turned to Thrift and her companions.

'She is in need of further restraint, I understand?'

'We feel it appropriate,' Miss Dace confirmed.

'I see,' he replied, 'and who is her home doctor?'

'Dr Molloy,' Thrift supplied, 'of London, the Quality Enclave.'

For a moment Dr Corraghan looked surprised, then reached for the telephone on his desk. It took a moment for the call to be connected and another for Dr Molloy to answer, and Thrift found it impossible to follow the muttered conversation. The doctor's behaviour seemed remarkably brusque, even in the circumstances, but Thrift said nothing and both Miss Dace and Miss Young seemed resigned to patient acceptance. At length Dr Corraghan put the phone down and turned to them.

'Dr Molloy informs me that she has been on Dr Lloyd's Improved Regime and another of his own, neither of which have proved effective. She is still in her containment pants?'

'Naturally, Doctor,' Miss Dace responded.

'She is beaten regularly?'

'Certainly, Doctor.'

'And yet still she persists,' he said with a shake of his head. 'Extraordinary.'

'Quite so, Doctor.'

'Such extreme recidivism is rare, admittedly,' he went on, 'although I am nevertheless somewhat surprised that you should come to me. However, extreme measures are sometimes the best.'

He rose to his feet, frowning, then spoke again.

'Naturally, given her station in life, you will not wish her condition to be unduly obvious?'

'We had felt that some evidence of her sin might be appropriate,' Miss Young replied, 'if only in an attempt to shame her out of it.'

'No, no,' he said, 'matters have gone far beyond that point. Quite evidently her mental condition has deteriorated to a point at which she no longer has any self-control to exert, not matter how frequently she is punished, nor how plain the vile nature of her behaviour is made to her.'

Thrift opened her mouth in outrage, but promptly shut it, sure that anything she could possibly say would only make it worse. He had opened a drawer and was leafing through a thick black directory of some sort as he went on.

'A purely physical regime is what is needed. Continue to beat her as before, although perhaps rather harder, as there may still be hope of building a link between her self-abuse and punishment. That is to be done bare, naturally . . .'

He trailed off, placing one long, bony finger on a page of the directory as he began to scribble on a pad. Presently he tore off the piece of paper he had written on and extended it to Miss Dace, who took it, gave a single glance at the unintelligible scrawl of his writing and bobbed a curtsey to him.

'Thank you, Doctor Corraghan, and is this guaranteed to be efficacious?'

'Absolutely,' he assured her. 'You will need to go to Smith and Smith in King George IV Street, a supplier I use myself, just two blocks east of here and immediately to the right.'

They left the building, Thrift with immense relief despite not knowing what was coming to her. She had expected to be stripped, examined, perhaps even taken advantage of, then put into some ghastly device similar to the one she had worn for Dr Lloyd's Improved Regime, which had caused her endless torment but only succeeded in making her involuntary arousal worse.

At the very least she seemed to have escaped the indignity of exposure in front of a strange man, and as they reached the shop Dr Corraghan had suggested she found herself hoping that whatever device he had prescribed would be at least no worse than those she'd had before. Smith and Smith occupied a double front, with heavy black curtains drawn across the interior of the windows and a simple stencilled name announcing their trade.

Again it was necessary to ring in order to gain admittance, and within was a screened-off anteroom with a single sour-faced clerk seated behind a counter. Miss Dace passed the prescription across and it was handed back through a slot in the screen. Presently they were admitted into an inner room, the centre of which was occupied by a medical couch, beside which a squat, massively built woman was waiting. She took one look at Thrift and nodded, then spoke.

'Undress her, if you would.'

Thrift's heart sank, but as Miss Dace and Miss Young began to work on her clothes she was telling herself that at least there were no males present to witness her shame, only for two dark-skinned men who appeared to be technicians to enter just as her combinations were being opened across her breasts, in full view. She put her hands up to cover herself, but nobody took

69

the slightest notice, the two men starting to prepare some worrying-looking machinery while the squat woman arranged a paper sheet on the couch.

'She has evacuated?' the squat woman asked.

'About an hour and a half ago,' Miss Dace answered.

The squat woman nodded as Miss Dace punched the combination into Thrift's containment pants. They peeled open and were quickly pulled down and off by Miss Young. Stark naked and shivering badly, Thrift climbed onto the couch. The squat woman immediately took her legs, hauling each one up and strapping it into a stirrup to leave Thrift spread to the air. Her wrists were pulled up above her head and fixed into further straps, making her completely helpless, her heavy chest rising and falling to the motion of her breathing, her stiff nipples and already puffy quim betraying the sexual reaction she could do absolutely nothing about.

The squat woman raised her eyebrows slightly as she came to stand between Thrift's open thighs, but she said nothing. Instead she reached out to lift a cloth from a trolley on the far side of the couch, revealing a selection of implements, including several large syringes. One of these she took up, inspecting the contents as Thrift's eyes and mouth grew gradually wider with alarm, carefully pointing it upwards and depressing the plunger until a little plume of the murky green liquid within shot up, then abruptly plunging the needle into the swollen, denuded mound of Thrift's sex.

Thrift gave a squeal of shock and pain, followed by an involuntary whimper as the plunger was pushed home and she felt her pubic area swell to the liquid. Even before the needle had been withdrawn from her flesh she could no longer feel it, and the whole of her sex was quickly numb. A squirt of urine erupted from her pee-hole as her muscles went fully slack, but she was unable to feel the warmth or the wet as it dribbled down over her anus, only when it began to soak into the paper

70

sheet beneath her bottom, which was as sensitive as ever. She was now sobbing with shame, sure her bottom hole was also open and that she was about to disgrace herself in the most humiliating way possible, by defecating in front of them all, but to her vast relief nothing happened. The squat woman put the syringe down and cast a critical glance at Thrift's open sex, then spoke to Miss Dace.

'She is married, I see. Am I to presume her husband no longer requires access?'

'Married?' Miss Dace echoed. 'No, not at all.'

'She has had intercourse,' the squat woman pointed out, indicating the mouth of Thrift's vagina.

'The matter is complex,' Miss Dace replied, 'but suffice to say that she is an incorrigible wanton.'

'These people should be better cared for,' the squat woman remarked, shaking her head. 'It is a disgrace. So then, a double plug, if you would, Mr Abercrombie.'

Thrift, now with her entire genital and anal area completely numb, had begun to wonder if they thought her rationality was impaired, but held back from comment, sure that it would merely prove to be the interpretation they put on her wantonness, and too overcome with emotion to argue. She was naked, her sex spread for inspection, her quim numb yet oddly hard, her anus no doubt slack and gaping, while they seemed likely to be about to plug her body in order to keep her natural fluids in.

Sure enough, the two technicians had finished manipulating their machine and now opened it with a gentle hiss. Thrift saw that it was some sort of press, or possibly a biotechnic vat, as they were removing a large black object, rubbery in texture and still wet on the surface. Two large plugs protruded, both substantially thicker than any cock she had had inserted into either of the holes they were obviously destined for.

With a last, sullen sob she closed her eyes, but she felt nothing beyond a curious sensation of increased weight and the occasional touch to her inner thighs. Yet she knew in her mind that two men, complete strangers, were inserting hygienic plugs into her anus and vagina, and they could see every private detail of her body, every line and bulge of her open bottom hole, ever moist pink fold of her quim, and were undoubtedly thinking how it would feel to ram their erect cocks deep into her body and fill her with hot thick semen . . .

Thrift deliberately cut off the train of thought, but even as the technicians patted the hideous thing now encasing her sex into place she had to make a conscious effort to hide a wry smile. Her sex was completely numb, and yet her mind had reacted as it always did, dwelling on her exposure and the possibilities it offered, despite her clear knowledge that it was wrong. She could also feel the pressure of the plugs inside her body, swelling both vaginal cavity and rectum, as she was numb only around the mouth of each hole.

'The initial dose will last some twenty-four hours,' the squat woman was explaining to Miss Dace, 'but there are sensors in the pad to detect the swelling of her pudenda as she becomes aroused, which will automatically trigger another injection from a reservoir in the belly panel, which holds enough for a week, typically. All you need to do is refill her reservoir with the preparation, stock of which I will provide, while it is available in all good pharmacies. Just ask for Smith and Smith's Patent Neurological Corrective. Her urine collects in this sack, and I trust she is already regular?'

'Absolutely,' Miss Dace assured her.

'Then you should have no difficulty.'

As she spoke, the squat woman had folded the heavy black substance up around Thrift's thighs. It took hold, clinging to her as if trying to envelope her for ingestion in a way that made her flesh crawl, although she knew that it was simply a half-living fabric and entirely harmless. Even the catheter proved to be self-inserting, tiny papillae extending to spread Thrift's pee-hole wide and a tube crawling in up the passage before her quim was encased. More of the substance had surrounded her thighs and belly, also pushing in under her buttocks to encase her from waist to mid-thigh in a slick black integument that might very well have been a second skin.

'A biodynamic?' Miss Dace enquired.

'Rather an advanced one,' the squat woman explained with pride, 'very nearly fully alive, self-activated and self-repairing. The integument is considerably tougher than the best rubber, and supported on a skeleton of steel wire. It feeds from her wastes, although not in sufficient quantity to eliminate the need for evacuation. That is something we're working on.'

'I see,' Miss Dace responded, 'and how does one open and close it?'

'Now that is rather clever,' the squat woman explained, now with open enthusiasm. 'It can be trained to recognise and respond to vocal commands from a specific person, yourself in this case, and in a wide variety of ways. For your needs I suggest that just three commands will be adequate, one for evacuation, which will cause it to withdraw the plugs and open between her legs, one for her punishment routine, which will expose her buttocks, and one for complete removal should that at any time prove necessary. Naturally you must return here if any adjustments need to be made. The system was only licensed on the first of this year, but we have great confidence in our product.'

Thrift grimaced, less than convinced and thinking of a dozen awful ways in which things might go wrong, but Miss Dace appeared satisfied and responded with a complacent nod.

'No further regime is required,' the squat woman continued, 'as those areas which lead to excitement and immoral thought are entirely without feeling.'

'I do not wish to seem indelicate,' Miss Young put in, 'but what of her breasts and buttocks?'

'Naturally she needs to retain feeling in her buttocks if she is to be chastised effectively,' the squat woman explained, 'but we can supply an adapted version of the system for her breasts if you wish. In fact, we have the pair on special offer this month, if you are interested?'

'I think so, yes,' Miss Dace replied, ignoring Thrift's despairing groan. 'Why not?'

'An excellent decision if I may say so,' the squat woman responded, giving a brief, obsequious curtsey. 'Mr Abercrombie, another former, if you would.'

The taller of the two technicians withdrew as the squat woman once more selected a syringe, held it up to eject any air that might have become trapped, took a large pinch of Thrift's breast flesh and plunged the needle home. Thrift's instinctive squeal was ignored and the process repeated with her other breast, after which she was left to lie as she was, with the numbness creeping rapidly over her chest as her containment bra was prepared and the squat woman went about programming Miss Dace's vocal commands into the pants.

She was soon ready, with the three commands 'convenience', 'chastisement' and 'disrobal' selected for her hygienic needs, spanking routine and complete exposure respectively, along with counter commands to make the pants seal themselves afterwards. By then the containment bra was complete and she was obliged to sit up and place her hands on her head as it was held across her numb breasts. As with the pants, it clung to every contour of her skin, encasing her breasts in what looked like wet black rubber, but concealing nothing of their shape and size, save where a triangular bulge rose in the lower part of her cleavage to hold the reservoir of serum and the system for injecting her.

'There,' the squat woman stated with satisfaction as she looked down at Thrift's fully encased breasts, 'that should be an end to her difficulties, and quite possibly mark a turning point in her condition.'

'Thank you, you have been most kind,' Miss Dace replied.

The technicians had begun to tidy away their apparatus, and Thrift swung her legs from the bed. As she moved, so did the bra and pants, making her shudder, and little waves of pressure moved across the skin of her buttocks and back. It felt odd, as if she were in the grip of some voracious animal, while being unable to feel her quim and breasts made it odder still.

With no choice but to put a brave face on it, she scrambled off the couch and began to climb into her combinations, grateful to be covered not only because of her nudity but because of the shame of being in full containment for the first time. Miss Dace had picked up the Scotian Restrictive from where it hung rigid from a stand, and Thrift extended her arms to allow herself to be put into it. For once the all-enveloping whalebone was a relief, as it hid the last evidence of her shame, and she even pressed the sides together to make it easier for her companion to adjust the lacing.

'I must say,' the squat woman remarked, 'she is remarkably rational for one in her condition. You would hardly know it.'

'She is quite rational,' Miss Dace replied, 'merely wanton.'

'But you came from Dr Corraghan, did you not?'

'Why, certainly. We were recommended to him.'

'Is she not a patient at the sanatorium?'

'No, no, not at all.'

The squat woman accepted the information with a lift of her eyebrows and Miss Dace continued to work on the laces and clips of the corset, both unaware of the rising horror on Thrift's face as she realised the full truth. Quite plainly, the sanatorium was not a medical facility in the normal sense, but a home for those unfortunate souls who had lost their minds, which explained why it was run by nuns and had a resident doctor. Outrage and indignation filled her, but she said nothing because, with her body already in full containment and both Miss Dace and Miss Young so full of approval for the system, she knew they would merely say that it was appropriate for her, and only add to her humiliation.

Once she was again fully dressed and Miss Dace had dealt with the matter of payment they left Smith and Smith, this time walking slowly back towards the docks and admiring the discreet displays of goods in the shop windows. Miss Dace was far more voluble with Miss Young than she had ever been with Thrift, and even allowed herself the occasional smile, while the topic of Thrift's containment and spankings came up more than once.

Again Thrift wondered if it might not be possible to make Miss Dace accept the reality of their relationship, or her own nature, only to dismiss the thought immediately. Evidently Miss Dace had buried her needs too deeply beneath the layers of religious devotion and propriety to even understand what she was doing. Once more thinking back to China and the deeply hypocritical but more self-aware Nurse Bode, Thrift hid a sigh. At the time it had seemed unbearable, but this was worse.

Nurse Bode had spanked and humiliated Thrift at every opportunity, but she had been completely shameless about wanting her quim licked afterwards, and had also understood that once spanked and licking, Thrift needed to masturbate. Never had she imagined wishing she was once more in Nurse Bode's charge, but as she walked the streets of Memphis with her half-alive bra and pants squirming on her flesh and her breasts and quim numb, she was beginning to do so.

At last they returned to the boat, where Thrift was once more forced to behave as a polite young lady of the British Empire should, despite every single person there being aware of her shame. Hardest of all to deal with was the Captain, who clearly found Thrift attractive, despite, or more probably because, she was wanton, so that his attention not only filled her with embarrassment but put lewd thoughts into her mind, which the Smith and Smith containment system did nothing to relieve.

That night, as she lay in bed trying to ignore the squirming of her pants and bra to every movement of her body, she found it impossible not to dwell on what might have been had Miss Dace been less upright in her manner, or perhaps corruptible. There would have been the secret arrangement of a rendezvous, the excitement as she waited for the Captain to visit her in her stateroom, the thrill of his compliments and caresses, the joy of having her body explored and exploring his in turn, and at last the pleasure of his cock, in her mouth, between her breasts, in her vagina, perhaps from behind so that she could enjoy the glorious blend of shame and arousal that came from raising her bare bottom for a man to penetrate, and would allow her to rub at the little bump between her sex lips until she reached her climax.

She rolled over, her mouth twitching into a wry smile. Full containment might stop her abusing herself physically, but it was not going to make her any less of a wanton. Unfortunately it did mean that thinking erotic thoughts was merely tormenting herself, so she began to count sheep jumping over a stile, which soon gave way to childhood memories of the Scottish countryside, and sleep.

Thrift lay on a beach, naked, in bright sunshine. Above her the sky was a perfect blue, with the vivid green of the southern Chinese jungle cloaking a slope behind her. To be nude felt exquisite, unutterably wonderful, with the memory of the rubbery caress of her containment set still harsh in her mind. She could feel her breasts too, and her hands went to them, her eyes closing in bliss just to feel the roundness and weight of the heavy globes and the sensitivity of her skin. Her quim was equally receptive, not numb at all, and deliciously accessible.

She spread her thighs, deliberately showing herself off as she caressed her breasts, lost in the sheer ecstasy of being nude and able to touch as she pleased, too lost to see the strange black creature that had crawled from the sea until a flat, rubbery tentacle touched her thigh. A gasp of shock escaped her lips as she jerked upright, and a scream as she saw what had caught her, a great black octopus, its body oddly flat, its thick, muscular tentacles already wrapped around her spread thighs to deny her any possibility of escape.

Again she screamed, writhing in the monster's grip as more tentacles began to envelope her body, encasing her thighs and bottom and hips, her belly and her breasts. Its flesh was squirming against hers, squeezing and stroking in a manner horribly reminiscent of the caresses of a lover. She tore at its body, her fingers clawing at the rubbery flesh, but it only squeezed the harder, and as she felt twin bulbous extrusions press to her cunt and anus she knew it was going to fuck and bugger her, and there was nothing she could do to stop it.

A long wail of despair broke from her lips as she was penetrated, her vagina filling with thick, rubbery penis, her anus giving way without resistance, both holes simply spreading to the pressure until she was bulging with the creature's flesh, more of which was pressed directly into the slit of her cunt, and which had begun to pulsate. It was squeezing her nipples too, and had set up a gentle, wavelike rhythm on her buttocks and breasts, bringing her up to a helpless ecstasy for all her terror.

Then it happened, a single, massive jolt of pleasure, so strong it set her entire body jerking in the creature's grip, utterly helpless as she gasped and shook in orgasm and the thick cocks worked in her cunt and bottom hole. Again it hit her, and again, until she was sure she would die of ecstasy and began to fight with a new and demented fury, tearing at the beast's flesh, kicking at it, biting at it, which for some bizarre reason made her face tickle, until she realised that she was not on a beach at all, and there was no creature. Instead she lay in her bed on the *Sir Mark Twain*, her containment set squirming to the movements of her body as she wriggled in her nightmare, her sheets tangled around her and her teeth clenched in her goosedown pillow, which had burst.

She lay back in the darkness, gasping. Her body was prickly with sweat and trembling with reaction, her mind still full of dark fears despite knowing that she was safe. It had been a terrible nightmare, and yet another emotion had begun to push up through her fear, a deep longing, for being nude, for being able to feel her breasts and sex, which were as numb as before, and yet there was also a savage satisfaction, because although it might have been in the grip of an imaginary octopus, her orgasm had been real.

Five

The *Sir Mark Twain* had set off at first light, and Thrift awoke to the gentle motion of the boat on the placid waters of the Mississippi. It took her a moment to remember why her hair was full of feathers, which brought a shock of fear and longing, only for the longing to fade to simple fear at the thought of Miss Dace's likely reaction. She shook her head as she sat up, resentful of the coming spanking but not so much for the pain and indignity as for the hypocritical pleasure of the two women who would be administering it.

The clock by her bed showed that it was a quarter past seven, and she quickly wiped the sleep from her eyes. Miss Dace would be in at any moment, but there was at least a chance of hiding the damaged pillow. Climbing quickly from the bed, she gathered up as many feathers as she could and stuffed them under the mattress, only to freeze at the gentle click of the door from directly behind her.

'Whatever are you doing?' Miss Dace enquired.

'I . . . I had a nightmare,' Thrift explained. 'It's my containment set, the flesh . . . the integument or whatever it is, it squirms. I bit through my pillow.'

'What a very peculiar girl you are, but never mind, we will deal with the matter in due course. Stand in the middle of the room.'

'Yes, Miss Dace,' Thrift responded, stepping to the exact centre of the green and white rug that decorated the floor.

She had lifted her modesty gown to her waist automatically, but Miss Dace gave a thoughtful nod, then spoke.

'Lift your gown higher. As you are in a containment bra, you should show it to help keep you in mind of your sin.'

Thrift obeyed with a fresh touch of chagrin as she raised her modesty gown to the level of her neck, exposing the jet black orbs of her encased breasts.

'That is better,' Miss Dace confirmed. 'Now – chastisement.'

She had said the word slowly and clearly. Immediately Thrift's containment pants split open at the back, peeling away from her bottom to leave both plump cheeks completely exposed and ready for spanking. For some reason her bra had also opened, allowing her breasts to spill out, heavy and naked and fat in the morning light. Miss Dace raised an eyebrow in surprise.

'How peculiar,' she remarked.

For a moment Thrift thought Miss Dace was actually going to laugh, and her lower lip pushed out into an involuntary pout as the thought of how absurd she must look.

'No matter,' Miss Dace continued, 'I dare say you may be spanked like that as otherwise. Stay as you are.'

Miss Dace walked from the room, leaving Thrift standing exposed on the rug and feeling very sorry for herself indeed. She could see the clock, and watching the minutes tick by with agonising slowness, all the while acutely aware of her exposed bottom and breasts and thinking of the smack of the women's hands on her flesh. Her cheeks had begun to twitch, and she wondered if her quim was growing wet despite the lack of feeling, although with the plugs still in her vagina and anus there was at least the small mercy that her excitement would be hidden from view.

At last Miss Young's gentle knock sounded on the stateroom door. Thrift's heart jumped and she bit her lip as she listened to the two women's quiet, genteel conversation, which continued as they entered the bedroom. There was no mistaking the amusement in Miss Young's face as she saw Thrift's exposed breasts, but nothing was said.

'Would you care to go first today, Miss Young?' Miss Dace offered politely, indicating the straight-backed chair across which Thrift was usually given her spankings.

'That's very kind, thank you,' Miss Young responded, taking the seat. 'Come across my knee, Miss Moncrieff.'

Thrift obeyed, making sure to keep her modesty gown lifted as she draped herself across Miss Young's knee, so that her breasts were dangling once she was in proper spanking position. They still felt heavy, despite being numb, while her bottom seemed bigger and more prominent than ever because of the lack of feeling in her quim.

Miss Young took a moment to adjust Thrift's modesty gown, making absolutely sure that both breasts were on full show, accepted the piece of cord they used from Miss Dace and tied Thrift's wrists securely behind her back, then began to spank. Like Miss Dace, Miss Young tended to aim for the very fattest part of Thrift's cheeks, perhaps a style typical of Boston, but unlike Miss Dace she varied her strokes a little, making sure that the full spread of Thrift's cheeks was slapped up to a rosy glow by the time she had completed her dozen dozen.

By then Thrift was panting and prickly with sweat, also crying softly for the humiliation of her punishment and the lack of feeling in her sex, which was no relief, but merely frustrating, while it made the pain even harder to endure. Her bottom was swollen and hot, and she could feel the pressure of the plug in her rectum, although nothing of her straining anal ring. As she stood to wait for Miss Dace to take over, the need to touch her smacked cheeks was overwhelming, setting her fingers fidgeting behind her back.

As soon was Miss Dace sat down Thrift was pulled back over and the spanking began again, as hard and rhythmic as ever, to set her kicking and wriggling immediately, her dangling breasts bouncing up and down. She found herself counting, smack after stinging smack, until a sudden wetness between the rubber of her open containment pants and one thigh made her realise that she was lubricating, and copiously.

A sense of triumph welled up through her misery. They had failed to rob her of her pleasure, both mentally and physically. She could still grow ready for penetration and she could still reach orgasm, as wanton as ever despite the severity of the Smith and Smith regime, or perhaps simply because the idiots had failed to realise it wasn't designed for girls in full control of their senses.

She came close to laughing as she was finally let up, despite the tears and mucus streaking her face, and once she'd been sent into the corner with her modesty gown held up to show off her red bottom, while Miss Dace and Miss Young enjoyed a cup of tea, she allowed her mouth to curve up into a secret smile. They had more than failed; they had pushed her so far that she no longer even felt guilty for her wantonness.

A day passed, and the following night, with Thrift once more beginning to worry about her major punishment. The right bank was now the territory of Arkansas, with vast, flat cotton fields stretching away into the distance and only the occasional clump of trees or white-painted house to break the monotony. Mr and Mrs Reynolds were due to disembark where the river flowed past their own great plantation and Thrift was very sure that Hester Reynolds was not going to want to miss out on the beating.

Sure enough, as they sat at breakfast, Thrift's bottom still hot in her containment pants, Mrs Reynolds was seen to speak a quiet word in Miss Dace's ear. The response was a reserved nod, and Thrift immediately felt her stomach tighten. Suddenly the oatcakes in syrup, which had tasted so delicious a moment before, seemed to turn to ashes in her mouth, while her stomach began to churn frantically.

Imagining that she was going to be sick, she hastily excused herself and fled for her stateroom, followed by the surprised looks and disapproving comments of her fellow passengers. On the balcony she stood for a moment, looking out over the river, her heart fluttering and her hands tight on the rail. Fifty feet below her, oily brown water moved sluggishly past the hull of the *Sir Mark Twain*, and for one brief moment she considered leaping in and striking out for the shore, only to dismiss the idea. It was too far, and she knew her heavy clothes would drag her down.

Instead she braced her body, telling herself that she was a lady of the British Empire, that what she had coming to her was an entirely reasonable punishment for the filthy and sinful crime of self-abuse, and that she should accept it with good grace. Unfortunately the idea was less than convincing and did little or nothing to quieten her sulky resentment, let alone her fear.

At length she turned from the rail and walked into the stateroom, just as the door opened to admit Miss Dace, then Miss Young, Mrs Reynolds and the Deix sisters. Thrift went still, save to hang her head and fold her hands in her lap in shame and submission. Miss Dace spoke.

'The time has come for your punishment, Miss Moncrieff. You are to be given one hundred and forty-four strokes of the paddle, naked.'

Thrift's mouth fell open, but she was unable to speak, or even to look up. Miss Young and Mrs Reynolds had come forward, and began to unfasten Thrift's dress as Miss Dace went into her own bedroom. Numb and unresisting, Thrift allowed her dress to be opened and pulled off over her head. Her under dress followed, and as the dark material was lifted from in front of her face she saw that Miss Dace had come back into the main room, and was holding in her hand the paddle with which Thrift was to be beaten.

It was huge, a great flat thing perhaps a foot long and half as much across, made with a wood that was either naturally dark or stained dark from the sweat of its victims, and a good inch thick. The handle was bound with string and two faded letters showed on the back, in Greek script, omega and pi.

'What a fine paddle!' Miss Young remarked immediately, showing more enthusiasm even than when Thrift had been put in her pants and bra.

'From my sorority house at Boston Diplomatic College,' Miss Dace remarked, making no effort to conceal her pride. 'I was president.'

'I imagine it has been put to good use many a time,' Miss Young responded. 'Come, let's have her clothes off.'

Hester Reynolds gave a haughty sniff at Miss Young's indecent enthusiasm, but her disapproval didn't stop her from making quick work of Thrift's corset laces, while the elderly sisters were making no effort at all to conceal their enjoyment at the sight of Thrift being undressed and the prospect of her beating. As the Scotian Restrictive came loose Thrift started to shiver, making her containment set squirm against her flesh.

'You are to be fully nude,' Miss Dace remarked as Thrift's combinations were peeled open and down. 'Disrobal.'

Thrift's containment set immediately split wide, the bra to fall down around her waist, the pants to drop to her thighs and into her half-removed combinations. She gasped at the sudden exposure of her most intimate parts, her shivering growing stronger still as Marie-Noel Deix raised a lorgnette to better admire the full curves of Thrift's naked body.

With her shoes and stockings gone and the rest pulled down around her ankles she was left to step out of her clothes, stripped nude as had been promised, and feeling completely vulnerable in the ring of five fully dressed women.

'Twenty-nine strokes each, near enough, I make it,' Delphyne Deix stated happily. 'My, it is quite a while since we beat a girl, is it not, Marie-Noel? And she is delightfully full. I do like a good, fat bottom when it comes to giving a paddling.'

'Is it not somewhat unseemly to take such open pleasure?' Hester Reynolds remarked. ' "A silent wife is a gift from the Lord," so saith the Lord.'

'You are over-fond of Ecclesiasticus, my dear,' Delphyne Deix responded. 'We're all going to enjoy thrashing the little trollop, so we may as well admit to it. Would anyone care for a chocolate?'

She extended a small gold box, affording Thrift a brief respite as the five women made their selections.

'You may have one afterwards, my dear,' Delphyne Deix addressed her, 'once you've been properly spanked.'

The elderly lady put so much satisfaction in the final word that Thrift found herself blushing as she remembered how it had felt when each session across a woman's lap was likely to end with grovelling thanks provided by her tongue.

'What position shall we have her in, Miss Dace?' Marie-Noel Deix asked with every bit as much enthusiasm as her sister.

Miss Dace was still savouring her chocolate and took a moment to reply.

'Kneeling on the sofa would be most convenient, I think. Come along, Miss Moncrieff, place your knees to either side of this. You are not to tread about in that silly way you do, and you are to keep your back well in.'

As she spoke she positioned a small cushion at the centre of the sofa. Thrift stepped forward, her whole body shaking as she climbed onto the sofa. The position left all five women with an excellent view not just of her bottom but also of her dangling breasts and, as she pulled her back in as instructed, of her pouting, denuded cunt and the wrinkled star of her anus, both, she suspected, still a little open from the plugs so recently withdrawn.

It was a hideously embarrassing position, everything on show and all five women watching, three in mock disgust, two with open delight. Marie-Noel Deix even leant closer to make a brief inspection of Thrift's anus and quim through her lorgnette.

'Is she naturally bald?' the old lady queried. 'Or do you shave her, Miss Dace?'

'She has been hygienically waxed,' Miss Dace replied, picking up the paddle once more and offering it. 'Perhaps you would care to be first, Miss Deix, as you are senior among us?'

'Oh, yes, please, what fun!' Marie-Noel responded, drawing another sniff of disapproval from Hester Reynolds and a sob from Thrift. 'Don't worry, my dear, we all get bent over like this when we're young, and your turn to do the paddling will come soon enough.'

'Miss Deix, please!' Miss Young remarked.

'You Easterners, so very prim,' Marie-Noel chuckled, and brought the paddle down across Thrift's bottom.

The meaty smack of wood on flesh rang out, echoed by Thrift's cry of pain, and the punishment had begun. Every blow of the paddle across her buttocks made her cry out and jump too, making it impossible to keep still, so that after just three smacks she was treading up and down and bending her back, exactly as she'd been told not to. Miss Dace told her sharply to get back into position and the paddling stopped, but only long enough for Thrift to get over her shock and once more stick her bottom out with her cheeks spread and her cunt on blatant view. Yet as soon as Marie-Noel began again, Thrift began kicking and wriggling and stamping and squealing. Again Miss Dace stopped the punishment.

'I think she would be better in restraint,' Miss Young suggested. 'I shall fetch her cord.'

'That won't stop her kicking,' Hester Reynolds pointed out. 'Better we just hold the brat down, Arkansas fashion. We should put something in her mouth to stop her caterwauling. There are men on the texas deck, and it won't do to have her inflame their blood.'

'There is something in that, I confess,' Miss Dace admitted. 'Very well.'

'Use her drawers for a gag and tie them off behind her head with the strings,' Delphyne Deix suggested. 'That's how we quiet the maids at home.'

'She was wearing combinations,' Miss Dace pointed out, 'but a stocking will do, and the other to hold it in place. Open your mouth, Miss Moncrieff.'

Thrift obeyed, sulky, yet also grateful that Captain Langhorne wouldn't hear squeals as she was beaten. Just seven strokes and her bottom was already burning, so that she knew she would lose control completely, long before they had finished with her. As she opened her mouth one balled-up stocking was thrust well in, then the other used to tie it in place, leaving her mute, and then helpless as one woman took each of her limbs, spreading her out across the back of the sofa with her well-parted bottom the highest part of her body.

'How many had I given her?' Marie-Noel Deix asked vaguely.

'It is your responsibility to keep count,' her sister pointed out. 'Now you'll just have to start again.'

'I do apologise, ladies,' Marie-Noel said, and once more began to beat Thrift.

If it had been bad before, now it was unendurable, and yet there was nothing she could do about it. Gagged and held down, she could only squirm in their grip and gasp out her emotions into the soggy ball of silk blocking her lips as smack after smack of the horrible paddle landed across her bottom. Soon she was blubbering, with tears spraying from her eyes and snot spattering the rug beneath her with every impact. She had lost count of how many strokes she had received long before it stopped to leave her shivering and wet with sweat.

'Delphyne, dear?' Marie-Noel remarked, and a moment later the grip on one wrist had changed and the beating had begun again.

It was harder if anything, and Delphyne made no pretence of not enjoying it, deliberately pausing between smacks and alternating between Thrift's buttocks to make both the pain and her already raw emotions harder still to cope with. Worse, still, there was none of the compensating warmth in her quim, which had always made hard beatings easier to take before.

Now there was only the blaze of her bottom, the heavy slap of the paddle on her flesh and the shame of being nude in front of them. In a desperate effort to lessen the pain she forced herself to think dirty thoughts, of how the same situation might have been in China, where such a beating might have been followed by being made to kiss and lick as many as a dozen beautiful girls, ending in a pile of wriggling limbs and eager tongues on the floor.

To her amazement it worked, and when the paddle was passed to Miss Young the pain quickly gave way to sexual heat, despite her numb cunt and the Boston woman's harder and painfully accurate strokes. Ten were delivered, and twenty, by which time Thrift had begun to whimper and sob as much with passion as pain, and her thoughts had turned to how it might be if the five women lost control of themselves and used her.

She remembered how it had felt to be held close between Miss Dace's thighs, pulled in by her hair and made to lick with her bottom hot behind her and her wrists strapped tight behind her back. She thought of how the same treatment would feel from the stern, elegant lady now applying the sorority paddle so effectively across her meaty cheeks. She imaged the intensity of lying prone as the two sisters took turns to drop curtsies on her face, fully clothed and showing nothing, yet with their drawers open beneath their dresses to smother Thrift's face in bare, musky bottom so that the tiny, dirty holes between their cheeks could be licked clean.

'Disgusting!' The voice of Hester Reynolds suddenly cut through Thrift's fantasy, and the spanking stopped.

'Well, I never!' Miss Young added. 'I thought they'd put a stop to that.'

'Evidently not,' Miss Dace said coldly, and Thrift realised that she had begun to juice and that they could all see.

'She is really quite incorrigible!' Marie-Noel Deix declared, with as much surprise as the others, but also amusement.

'Whatever is to be done with her?' Miss Young queried.

'Beat her harder, that's what,' Mrs Reynolds suggested.

'I shall,' Miss Dace agreed, 'if you have finished your turn, Miss Young?'

Thrift was unable to see, but had begun to twitch in fear again as her left ankle was released and then once more taken in a firm grip. Her body had closed up a little as she was beaten, and they now spread her out more fully, splaying her buttocks to leave her anus pointing almost straight up in the air. She chewed on her gag as she waited for the beating to begin again.

She heard the swish of air, the pain exploded across her bottom at the same instant as the smack of wood on meat rang out, and a muffled scream burst from her lips. Her legs began to kick immediately, in terror of the next stroke, but the women merely held onto her more tightly and it came anyway, harder even than before. In desperation Thrift tried to think dirty thoughts, of every filthy act she'd ever been subjected to, for punishment or for pleasure.

It made little difference, but it made some, and she forced herself to focus even as her body writhed in the women's grip and the paddle slammed down on her bottom again and again. Miss Dace was beating her and she knew Miss Dace would be growing excited. Miss Dace was beating her, and she had to want her quim licked, perhaps late that night, if Thrift crawled in and begged for it on her knees, or waited until the evil bitch was masturbating over her wicked behaviour and then offered her face as a seat.

At the thought of being made to insert her tongue into Miss Dace's anus Thrift's entire body went tight, a sensation on the edge of orgasm for all her numb breasts and cunt. Again the paddle smacked down across her bottom and again she jerked, only for it to stop, Miss Dace slightly breathless as she stood back. Thrift's right leg was released. Mrs Reynolds took up the paddle, and spoke as she positioned herself behind Thrift.

'Now you'll see how a wanton should be beaten, Arkansas style. "A wilful woman is a shameless bitch," Ecclesiasticus: 26,25, so saith the Lord!'

With the last word she brought the paddle down across Thrift's bottom with all the force of her brawny arm. As the responding smack rang out around the stateroom Thrift was knocked forward across the chair, her entire body gave one frantic jerk in reaction and her limbs almost pulled from the women's hands. Another smack hit, and a third, setting Thrift screaming through her gag, at which the big woman laughed, her reserve completely gone, and replaced by a savage joy in the beating that struck Thrift as near demented even through her pain.

Yet the image of Miss Dace dropping a curtsey on her face was still there, and she held on it, now imagining the humiliation of having it done in front of the other women. Her body jerked again, but not to the paddle, which smacked home an instant later. Again Thrift pictured Miss Dace's trim bottom being lowered into her face, the cheeks wide to show off a tight, wrinkled anus, which she was going to have to kiss, to lick, to push her tongue up until both ring and hole were quite clean, and all as the other four women looked on in amusement and pious satisfaction.

Again the paddle smacked in, and this time Thrift lost control completely, her body suddenly tight, her back arched and her bottom thrust high and wide, her denuded cunt spread open, in a helpless, shuddering orgasm. Something wet touched her leg and she knew she'd started to spray, making her jerk around, pulling free of the sisters' grip as they cried out in shock and disgust, just in time to see a fountain of milky white fluid erupt from her pee-hole, full across Mrs Reynolds' dress.

As she stood on the balcony of her stateroom, Thrift's bottom felt as if it had been reduced to one huge bruise, and yet she was finding it very hard indeed not to smile. The steward had arrived to announce that a launch had come alongside to pick up the two Arkansas planters, just minutes after she had come all over the wife's dress. Mrs Reynolds had still been too full of shock and outrage to do more than demand smelling salts and shout for her maid, who was travelling on the lower hurricane deck and in fact busy packing.

By the time Thrift had been hustled into her bedroom to be dressed by Miss Dace, and the mess cleaned up by the Deix's sisters' unfortunate maid, the Reynoldses' launch had already left. For two hours Thrift had been kept locked in her room with her hands tied behind her back, but come the dinner hour they had been forced to release her. Even now, as she watched the lights on the Mississippi Territory shore drift slowly by, Miss Dace and Miss Young were conferring urgently together in the stateroom. Thrift was back in her containment set and very likely to get another punishment, and yet she found herself feeling oddly detached.

There was also the fact that they would soon be in Louisiana, and Miss Dace would be obliged to put rather less of her energy into tormenting Thrift and more of it into their assignment. At the very least that meant a pretty dress, and possibly even being allowed to wear her old corset, as the file from Mr Fanshaw stated quite clearly that Thrift was to make herself attractive for Jean-Jacques Rougon, and under no circumstances whatsoever could the combination of her Scotian Restrictive and drab colonial dresses be considered attractive.

She thought longingly of the collection of ball gowns in her luggage; a beautiful scarlet silk creation that went perfectly with her tumbling brown hair and which had a neckline so daring that her throat was left entirely bare; another of similar cut but in rich blue satin, with a fuller skirt and a huge bow at the back to enhance the shape of her bustle; and a third in heavy black velvet, cunningly cut to make the very best of her waist. All three were beautiful, and while it would be hard to choose between them, to be in any one would be bliss, better still with her beautifully made Lucas and Cantlemere underneath.

With a gentle sigh she turned back from the rail and stared into the stateroom. Miss Dace and Miss Young sat as before, their faces set in serious, concerned expressions as they talked, no doubt discussing Thrift's abominable behaviour and how best to deal with it. No doubt they were also secretly enjoying themselves immensely, just as they had done when they beat her, at least until she had ejaculated all over Mrs Reynolds.

Again Thrift's mouth curved up into a smile, only to open in an O of surprise as she caught a movement above her and looked up. A head appeared to be protruding from the side of the texas deck directly above her, although she had to lean backwards to discover that it belonged to Captain Langhorne. She responded with a polite smile more or less by instinct, although it felt rather foolish when she was leaning back over the rail and looking up into the night sky. In response he put a finger to his lips, causing an immediate shiver of anticipation in Thrift.

Evidently he was up to something, and it could only involve her. She gave a brief nod, signalling her acquiescence in that first flush of excitement without worrying about the need for modest conduct. After all, she told herself, if she was such a wanton and a trollop and a slut and all the other things more proper women called her, then she might as well behave like one. She would be beaten anyway.

With no idea what he planned, she could only continue to lean on the rail, staring out across the dark waters of the Mississippi and, supposedly, thinking on her sinful behaviour and the consequences of it, which was what Miss Dace had told her to do. No more than a minute had passed before she saw Miss Dace turn her head to a knock at the stateroom door. A steward appeared, bowed politely and said something Thrift was unable to hear. Miss Dace gave a polite inclination of her head in response and rose to her feet, as did Miss Young.

Thrift watched in astonishment as both women left the room, Miss Dace locking the door behind her. Evidently they had been invited somewhere and, despite the gross breach of etiquette in a companion leaving her lady, Miss Dace had accepted. Unfortunately it seemed to leave Thrift locked in the stateroom on her own, which was very little improvement, or so she thought until once again her attention was attracted by a noise from above her head.

Again she looked up, this time to find not a head but a pair of feet, just emerging from the central window of the texas deck. A leg followed, a length of knotted rope, another leg, and finally the whole of Captain Langhorne, who had swiftly let himself down and swung in to join Thrift on the balcony. He returned a grin to her polite curtsey and took a long draw on the cigar he held clamped between his teeth.

'What an unexpected pleasure, Captain Langhorne,' she said, 'but quite improprietous, as you know. Miss Dace . . .'

'Is being entertained to cocktails by my First Officer,' he explained. 'You weren't invited, on account of having been punished.'

He chuckled and Thrift found herself blushing hot but he went on, apparently oblivious to her embarrassment, or enjoying it.

'They whacked you good, huh? Noisy enough, that's for sure, and don't worry, everyone knows, so when Billy sends the steward down with a hint that you should be left to feel sorry for yourself, why, they took the bait.'

He chuckled again, evidently well pleased with himself, and Thrift found herself smiling through her blushes.

'You are most resourceful, Captain Langhorne.'

'I like to think so,' he told her, 'and hell, I wasn't going to get to the end of this trip without getting better acquainted with you, was I?'

'That is very kind of you,' Thrift responded, wondering how long she had and how much small talk he would make before embracing her, which was obviously his intention.

Unfortunately he seemed in no great hurry, puffing on his cigar and talking about his time on the river. Thrift answered politely, wondering if he was shy, which seemed unlikely; teasing her, in which case he was certainly succeeding; or simply felt that a girl of her class and background, even a wanton, would take a little while to seduce, which seemed most likely. As he gradually shifted his conversation towards complimenting her on her looks she decided that he was indeed attempting to soften her up until he felt she was ready for a more direct advance, at which point she raised a finger to her lips, cutting him off in mid-sentence.

'You must excuse me, Captain Langhorne,' she said, forcing the words out through her blushes but determined to go on, 'but as you have clearly divined I am given frequent physical discipline for my wanton nature. Moreover, I have spent some little time in Hainan Tao, but recently ceded to the British Empire, where the native customs might surprise or shock even a gentleman of French ancestry like yourself. Therefore I feel we may safely dispense with the formalities.'

As she finished she let her hand move forward, to do what she had wanted almost since their first meeting in Cincinnati, and pressed her fingers gently to his bulging crotch. His cock felt bulky and soft within his trousers, sending an immediate shiver through her despite the numbness of her genitals and breasts.

'Well, I'll be damned!' he said, but made no effort to stop her.

'As you may have determined,' Thrift said softly, 'I am in restraint, so must ask that you allow me to indulge myself as best I am able.'

'You just go right ahead, my girl,' he assured her.

Thrift leant forward and kissed him, trying to ignore the taste of cigar as their mouths opened together, and all the while with her hand gently kneading his cock and balls through his trousers. He had immediately began to swell, a sensation she wanted in her mouth, and she wasted no time, sinking slowly to her knees with a creak of protesting whalebone.

Three quick motions and she had unbuttoned his fly, two more and she had pulled his cock and balls from his underwear, to lie warm and heavy and desirable in her hand. Just to hold him felt exquisite, after so long and so much deprivation, making her want to fill herself with the smell and feel and taste of him. For a moment she tried to hold off, savouring the moment, but her excitement was rising too fast and she had quickly popped him in. Her eyes closed in bliss for the sheer joy of having his cock in her mouth, of feeling it start to swell to the motions of her tongue and lips.

She looked up, to find him staring down at her in mingled lust and astonishment as his cock grew in her mouth. He was thick and quite long, adding to Thrift's delight as he became stiff enough for her to move her head up and down on his shaft, deliberately fucking her own mouth, then taking him in hand and licking at the swollen head as she masturbated him. She put her other hand to his balls, gently kneading the heavy sack as she sucked and licked and nibbled at his erection, lost in bliss to have a man's cock to pay court to, and wishing only that she could feel her poor quim and get a hand into the slippery groove between her lips to stimulate herself as she enjoyed him.

'Sweet Jesus!' he remarked, and his hand closed gently in her hair.

Thrift began to suck more eagerly, worried that Miss Dace might return unexpectedly because she was in full view of the stateroom window. If she was caught, she knew full well what would happen. The Captain, a man, would be reprimanded and then excused, for he had done nothing but follow his natural lusts. Thrift, a woman, would suffer the full consequences of her unpardonable sins, giving in to her wanton nature and, worse, taking a penis in her mouth.

His breathing was growing deeper and she knew he would soon spend his seed in her mouth, which filled her with need as well as disappointment that her experience would be so quickly ended. Her sucking grew more urgent still, and as it did so she came to realise that her quim and breasts were no longer fully numb. She could feel the urgency between her thighs and the hot point of desire between her lips, and her nipples too, hard and sensitive within the thick black integument.

She began to wriggle her bottom, praying that she could get enough friction to her sex to make herself come, and sucking on Captain Langhorne's cock with demented urgency as she masturbated him into her mouth. He gave a deep groan and salty, sticky seed erupted into her mouth, making her eyes pop – and pop wider still as the needles of her containment set jabbed deep into her breasts and cunt mound to pump her with the numbing serum, a sudden shock of pain that took her to the very brink of orgasm, and over it as she felt the swell of fluid in her tender flesh, so that she was still jerking and squirming her way through her climax as she went slowly numb.

Six

Baton Rouge, Louisiana, March 2006

Thrift stood in her favourite place on the balcony of her stateroom as she watched the *Sir Mark Twain* approach Baton Rouge. Ever since reaching the point at which the western bank of the now vast Mississippi passed into Louisiana, the atmosphere of the river had changed. Everything seemed gayer, from the houses set back among the cotton plantations to the other craft using the river. Some even sported the colours of France, or another flag, showing three golden lily flowers on a white field, which she knew to be the symbol of the Libertistes. Every building seemed to have its flag, some even with bunting as well, including a gigantic Union Flag fluttering from the top of an airship mast, visible beyond the next bend in the great river.

For a while the *Sir Mark Twain* had been moving almost directly away from the mast, but now she swung back into a long straight, with the houses of what Thrift knew to be Baton Rouge at the far end. In size, the town seemed to be on a par with Memphis, but the atmosphere could hardly have been more different. Where Memphis was drab, Baton Rouge was bright. Where Memphis was staid, Baton Rouge was alive. Where Memphis was quiet, Baton Rouge was full of music, which seemed to involve a great many cymbals and horns.

'Is there a festival in progress, do you suppose?' Thrift enquired as Miss Dace came to stand beside her.

Miss Dace gave a sniff of distaste before she answered.

'Quite possibly, although, as you know, the behaviour in these parts is notoriously lax. Their conduct towards young women is especially reprehensible, so please attend to my remarks. You may expect men, even men of the lowest sort, to compliment you and even address you directly without an introduction, so familiar are they.'

'Dressed as I am?' Thrift asked in surprise. 'And surely only those of appropriate rank would think to introduce themselves?'

'To the contrary,' Miss Dace assured her. 'The lower their rank, the more vulgar their behaviour. In any event, you must ignore all such attention. As you walk, look neither to your left nor to your right. Keep your chin up and your hands folded in front of you. On no account meet anybody's eye, wink or flutter your eyelids.'

'I am versed in the fundamentals of etiquette,' Thrift stated.

Miss Dace gave another sniff, this time doubtful, and continued.

'Be that as it may, your corset and containment system protects you from the most vile of intrusions, and I shall be keeping you under close attention. Is that clear?'

'Abundantly,' Thrift responded, drawing a warning look from Miss Dace, who then went on.

'Miss Young, regrettably, is continuing south to New Orleans, a naval base where she has some business or other, so I will be obliged to give you your full routine each morning, which is a nuisance. Furthermore, as Messers Smith and Smith have failed to live up to their promise, it would, in any place less ungodly, be better

100

for you if your hands were to be tied in front of you, both to remind you of your shame and allow others to see. As it is, your wantonness, rather than inciting righteous disgust, will only serve to encourage improper conduct. In order to cope with both these matters, I intend to use my hairbrush on you from now on rather than my hand.'

'If giving me discipline is so irksome a task, you really need not concern yourself,' Thrift replied, and immediately wished she hadn't.

Miss Dace drew a heavy sigh, reached out to take a firm pinch of Thrift's ear, and led her squealing back into their stateroom. There Thrift was made to lie across Miss Dace's knees and suffer the elaborate and undignified process of having her bottom exposed before the usual one hundred and forty-four smacks were applied.

'Next time,' Miss Dace stated as she applied the final swat to Thrift's now reddened and quivering bottom, 'it will be the hairbrush. Don't pout; it is most unbecoming and also suggests that you have failed to learn your lesson.'

'I'm very sorry, Miss Dace,' Thrift answered, 'and I have learnt my lesson.'

'I doubt that very much,' Miss Dace answered. 'Never have I known such a brat, to say nothing of your incorrigible wantonness. End chastisement.'

At Miss Dace's final words Thrift's containment pants pulled closed over her bottom, a sensation that still made her stomach lurch. The companion then began to fasten Thrift's clothes, and by the time she had finished the *Sir Mark Twain* was approaching the heart of Baton Rouge. A steward arrived to deal with their luggage, and with Miss Dace now busy, Thrift went back out onto the balcony to watch them come in.

Close to, Baton Rouge was even brighter and gayer than from a distance. Both the dozen or so big riverboats and the buildings were painted brilliant white with highlights in a myriad different colours. Flags, pennons and bunting were everywhere, in all three styles, while a constant swell of happy noise rose from the bustling dockside, mixed in with music, some of it from a five-piece band that was playing to welcome the *Sir Mark Twain* to her home port.

Thrift watched in fascination, her sole regret her drab, shapeless black dress, which she could see would make a sorry comparison with the way the Creole women dressed. Fortunately there were quite a few women from the middle territories about, their disdain evident as they moved through the butterfly crowds, and most of them with one hand on their bible.

As with the riverboats and buildings, pure white was the dominant colour for both men's and ladies' clothing, although there was always a splash of colour: linen suits were relieved by cravats and pocket handkerchieves of flamboyantly coloured silk, dresses set off by sashes, wide ribbons, bows and silk roses. The ladies' style struck Thrift as particularly fetching, with corsets apparently designed to flatter the figure and yet leave the legs free, a trifle indecent perhaps, for one of her rank, but undoubtedly pretty and infinitely better than the way her body was crammed into her Scotian Restrictive.

The faintest of bumps signalled that the *Sir Mark Twain* was against the dock, and Thrift made her way back inside. Miss Dace was waiting for her and took her arm to escort her from the vessel, Thrift managing a wistful smile as she curtsied to Captain Langhorne. He returned an open wink, and as they reached solid ground Miss Dace made a quiet remark.

'Do not encourage dalliance, Miss Moncrieff. That will be another dozen dozen.'

'No, please, not here, Miss Dace,' Thrift begged.

Miss Dace had already slowed, glancing around for a suitable place to sit for Thrift's spanking. There was nothing close by, but a little way along the docks a great pile of cotton bales stood ready for loading aboard the boat. Some had been taken out for inspection, providing ideal seating, and Miss Dace began to pull Thrift in their direction, lecturing as they went, only to stop for no apparent reason, smooth down her dress in a somewhat self-conscious manner and start back the way they had come.

Thrift's heart was hammering in her chest, and she was unsure what was happening. Certainly it was not that giving punishments in public was considered inappropriate, for nearby a young girl had been upended and her chubby pink bottom laid bare among a froth of petticoats as she squealed and kicked her way through a spanking, which both men and women were watching with amusement. When it was done the girl got up and to Thrift's astonishment took a moment to inspect her smacked cheeks, with her skirts lifted high as she craned back over her shoulder, her face full of consternation but apparently indifferent to the fact that she was displaying her bare bottom to a large audience.

Thrift recalled the words of Monsieur d'Arrignac from her time at the Diplomatic School: 'In France, when a girl must be spanked, her bottom is bared, but this is not to humble her, merely for convenience.' She felt a shock at the thought of being so casually exposed, and was gratefully reflecting that she was not in the same sorry situation herself, when Miss Dace stopped and curtsied to a splendidly dressed woman of middle years who was standing near where the gangplank came down from the *Sir Mark Twain*.

'Ah, Susannah, there you are,' the lady said as she turned, then, addressing Thrift, 'and you must be Miss Thrift Moncrieff? Pleased to meet you. I'm Felicity Adams, our man in Baton Rouge, so to speak.'

Thrift curtsied, somewhat taken aback by the lady's abrupt, almost masculine manner, which was not only bizarre but greatly at odds with her beautiful white silk dress, made striking by clusters of black silk roses. Perhaps more surprising still was Miss Dace's response, a deep curtsey and then silence, and no remark at all at the use of her first name, which implied that the two of them knew each other very well indeed.

Miss Adams continued to talk as they started in among the buildings of Baton Rouge, enquiring after their journey and asking Thrift how she found the colonies, but never once mentioning why she had been brought to Baton Rouge until they were in the car, a gleaming Healy Norfolk evidently newly imported. The driver was a large black man in a white linen suit, and to Thrift's surprise he grinned in a most familiar manner as he held the door for them.

'Miss Thrift Moncrieff, Mr Tobias Kobo. Toby, Miss Thrift Moncrieff.'

Thrift curtsied, deeper than she might otherwise have done, although the very casual manner of Miss Adams's introduction made it hard to be sure of Mr Kobo's position, save that he was evidently no mere servant. After a moment while Thrift was assisted into the car, Miss Adams spoke again, as casual and effusive as before.

'Mr Fanshaw will have filled you in on the background, and the situation is much as it was at the beginning of the year. Rougon is still trying to negotiate with the Frogs, who won't budge, and has set the date for his grand announcement for some festival they have, Bastille Day. That's not until July, so we're in no hurry. Still, no sense in dallying, so I suggest you attend a couple of bun fights to get to know the fellow and make your move when the time seems right. Mark you, if we want old Rougon to give you the glad eye we'll have to dress you properly. Whatever did you put her in that get-up for, Susannah? She looks like she's going seal hunting, and it must be damnably hot.'

'I felt my choice appropriate for the middle territories,' Miss Dace answered, but for once the cold certainty of her voice was gone.

'My costume is a trifle warm, I confess,' Thrift added, 'and clearly inappropriate for a ball.'

Miss Dace managed a furious glare, which Thrift ignored. Miss Adams was evidently quite senior, while the sudden change in Miss Dace's behaviour on the docks suggested strongly that for whatever reason a public spanking had been inappropriate. What happened later was a different matter, but then, Thrift was already going to get the hairbrush, so might as well make the best of the situation.

'Utterly inappropriate,' Miss Adams was saying. 'Turn the temperature control a notch to the cool, would you, Toby? I take it you have some decent gowns, Miss Moncrieff?'

'I have three evening gowns, thank you, Miss Adams,' Thrift responded, blushing a little to be discussing clothes in front of a man.

'Splendid,' Miss Adams answered, 'but I think we'd better go shopping this afternoon in any case. We can't have you walking around Baton Rouge as if you've just been to a Pittsburgh funeral, can we? You too, Susannah.'

'I am quite well as I am, thank you,' Miss Dace answered with what to Thrift seemed extraordinary timidity.

'Nonsense,' Miss Adams replied. 'You're supposed to be escorting Miss Moncrieff on a tour of the colonies, not introducing her to your Boston set, so you'll jolly well dress the part. That's an order.'

'Yes, Miss Adams,' Miss Dace answered, and Thrift found herself struggling to hide a smile.

'That's more like it,' Miss Adams went on, 'and besides, I'm sure Miss Moncrieff would like to see Baton Rouge, and not have everybody staring at her. We'll go to Claralinda's, I think. They're not exactly Bond Street, but they know what they're doing. Where was I? Ah, yes. We'll do the round of bun fights, just as you'd be expected to do anyway, and I'll lay a guinea to a goldfish that old goat Rougon makes a pass at you before long. When he does, scream the place down. After that, just leave it to me and everything should go smoothly. Toby here will be keeping an eye on you just in case the Gaulistes catch on, and then you're off on the next airship for home.'

'You make it sound so simple,' Thrift responded.

'Oh it is,' Miss Adams assured her. 'Plain sailing.'

Thrift found it impossible not to smile as she admired the corset she had selected for herself. Claralinda's had proved even better than she expected, a large emporium catering specifically for ladies of wealth, although, as seemed to be the case almost throughout the territories, the Professional classes were allowed to mix with the Quality. Likewise, the corset was not, strictly speaking, appropriate to her rank, being much too short, but it was too beautiful to resist, a confection of pink satin and delicate cotton lace, designed not for day wear but to go under a ball gown.

'Do you think this might be permitted?' she asked Miss Adams, who had accompanied her after telling Miss Dace off to unpack and sort out the suite of rooms she and Thrift would be occupying at the Governor's residence.

'Permitted?' Miss Adams asked with a touch of surprise. 'Ah, yes, a trifle short for a lady of Quality, isn't it? Never you mind that, we're a long way from London and you'll find some of the Creole girls are a sight more daring. Yes, try it on.'

'Would you be so kind as to assist me, Miss Adams?' Thrift asked, preferring Miss Adams to the two shop assistants who were hovering respectfully but would doubtless be utterly horrified to discover that Thrift was in containment, Creole or not. Miss Adams at least already knew.

'Yes, of course,' Miss Adams offered, 'and I think Felicity will do while we're off duty, if you don't mind me calling you Thrift?'

Thrift hesitated, unsure of Miss Adams' rank and therefore of correct etiquette, but was quickly reassured.

'I am cousin to Lord Ludlow, by the way.'

'In which case I would be delighted,' Thrift responded immediately, warming to Miss Adams even more, 'and may I say what a pleasure it is to meet a fellow lady in the colonies.'

Private cubicles had been provided, not as discreet as those in London or Edinburgh, but completely enclosed. Thrift still felt embarrassed as Miss Adams began to help her with her dress, especially when her underdress and petticoats had been removed to reveal the bulky, heavily ribbed Scotian Restrictive.

'Good heavens!' Miss Adams exclaimed. 'Susannah has been taking you seal hunting, hasn't she?'

'It is a Scotian Restrictive,' Thrift answered, allowing herself a little smile, 'from Tilldale's Emporium in New York, and frankly I doubt I could pursue a tortoise, much less a seal.'

Miss Adams laughed and shook her head, continuing to talk as she began to work on Thrift's corset laces.

'Susannah's been enjoying herself then, I don't doubt. I suppose she's put you on a routine?'

'Yes,' Thrift admitted, her need to talk easily out-weighing her embarrassment about the subject. 'I am spanked every morning and when she deems it necessary.'

'That sounds like our Susannah,' Miss Adams chuckled. 'Always strict with the girls.'

Miss Adams was clearly amused by Thrift's plight, but there was also a measure of sympathy in her voice.

'I do think she's rather unfair,' Thrift said. She hesitated, and suddenly began to pour out her woes. 'It's horrid to spank me for nothing, every morning, and it is really quite unnecessary to tie my hands into my corset laces. I wouldn't mind if it was just a couple of dozen smacks, but she gives me a dozen dozen, very hard, and . . . and always on the same spot, and on the boat she got another woman from Boston to help, and they used to take it in turns with me, and . . . and now the other woman's gone she says she's going to use the hairbrush! I know I'm a wanton, Miss Adams . . . Felicity, and I accept that I deserve discipline, but I don't think she's very fair at all.'

'She was a beast at college too,' Miss Adams agreed, 'especially when she was sorority President.'

'You were at college with Miss Dace?' Thrift queried.

'Yes,' Miss Adams confirmed. 'Boston Diplomatic has the only ladies college in the territories. Good grief, this thing is like plate armour!'

'I thought the same myself,' Thrift agreed and sighed as her laces finally came loose.

Miss Adams began to work on the gudgeons holding Thrift's corset panel closed, and for a moment they were silent. Only when the panel came loose and the corset began to open did Miss Adams continue, her voice warmer and more friendly than ever.

'There we are, old thing, a guinea to a goldfish that feels better. Step out of it then.'

Thrift complied, emerging from the corset to allow her flesh to return to a more natural shape. Miss Adams stood back, admiring Thrift's figure and nodding before she spoke again.

'If old Rougon doesn't make a pass at you I'll eat my bonnet. No, my entire collection of bonnets.'

Thrift found herself blushing, and hoping Miss Adams wasn't going to comment on the slices of black integument visible where the containment bra showed.

Sure enough, she ignored it, despite it being obvious and knowing Thrift would be in containment. Eager for the sympathy, made bold by Miss Adams' effusive manner and desperate for somebody to share her feelings, Thrift spoke out again after a moment.

'When you were at college, did she use that horrible paddle on you?' 'Did she use it on me?' Miss Adams laughed. 'Good heavens, no! I was two years her senior, and I used to use mine on her. Snivelling Susannah, we used to call her, or just plain Snivels, because she always used to have a snotty nose after a beating.'

'You used to spank Miss Dace?' Thrift asked in something close to awe.

'Oh yes, many a time,' Miss Adams answered casually as she picked up the beautiful pink satin corset. 'We used to line them up in the dormitory, kneeling in just their drawers, and we'd play a little game. Tears at Bedtime, we used to call it. Each one got a question, in turn, and if she got it wrong she'd go bare bottie. Two wrong and it was time for a spanking, three wrong and she got the paddle. We'd tie their hands into the laces of their drawers too, which is no doubt where Susannah picked up that little habit. Happy days!'

'She gave me the paddle,' Thrift said bitterly as she slipped into the corset. 'A hundred and forty-four strokes, in front of all the ladies from the first class deck, and she let them use it on me too.'

'Did she, by God!'

'Yes. My poor skin is still bruised.'

'She was in her rights, I dare say, but I think that's a bit thick, turning you over to outsiders.'

'It's really unfair, and she spanked me in front of several men!'

'Oh dearie me!'

Again there was both amusement and sympathy in Miss Adams' voice, also a hint of rather familiar interest.

'Perhaps you'd like me to warm her buns for her?' Miss Adams offered.

'Oh, I couldn't possibly!' Thrift responded, genuinely shocked despite an underlying desire to see Miss Dace spanked and spanked soundly. 'She has only done her duty, although she is rather strict. Perhaps, though, if you could speak to her about putting me on a more appropriate routine?'

'I'll take care of you,' Miss Adams assured her, 'now just hold on tight.'

Thrift was now in her corset, and took hold of a pair of bars on the wall designed for the purpose as Miss Adams began to pull the laces tight. It felt curious not having her bottom and legs encased, and distinctly sexual, while the front was so low that instead of creating the usual undivided bosom her breasts were pushed up and out into full and, given their size, slightly unnecessary prominence, a sight at once embarrassing and exciting.

'That'll make old Rougon stare,' Miss Adams chuckled. 'Yes, we'll have a couple of these, the pink, and perhaps the yellow? Let's get you some decent underwear too, and look, I'll speak plainly here, and hope you'll excuse me, but old Rougon's quite likely to want those boobies of yours out, and it'll do no harm to let him, so we'd better have you out of whatever peculiar containment device Susannah's put you in, don't you think? The top part anyway.'

Despite the immediate rush of blood to her face, Thrift found herself nodding heartfelt agreement.

The apartment reserved for Thrift proved to be very fine indeed. The Governor's residence was built on what passed for a hill in the Louisiana flatlands, and she had been installed as guest of honour, directly above the Governor's own rooms. The windows looked out across a long ornamental lake towards the Mississippi, with the town spreading out on both sides.

110

Sir Lionel Bartram proved to be a bluff, genial man who had been to school with Thrift's uncle and extended a warm welcome, while Miss Dace was obliged to maintain her role as a servant. With the Governor living directly below, and under direct orders from Felicity Adams, Thrift's spanking routine had been suspended. She had also been allowed the choice of her own clothes, and so as she stood admiring the view in a pretty white and pink Louisiana-style gown purchased at Claralinda's with her Cantlemere and Lucas beneath, she was feeling distinctly smug.

'I shall wear my scarlet silk this evening, Miss Dace,' she stated. 'One cannot underestimate the importance of making a good first impression.'

'No doubt,' Miss Dace answered.

'With suitable accessories, if you could be so kind as to lay them out,' Thrift continued.

'At once, Miss Moncrieff,' Miss Dace answered.

Thrift turned, puzzled at Miss Dace's tone, which, while as level as ever, had simultaneously managed to carry oddly contrasting hints of servility and mockery. After being together so long and also meeting Miss Adelie Young, Thrift had come to realise that Bostonians were not as cold and emotionless as she had at first thought. It was more a matter of extreme reserve, with the full range of human emotion expressed, but with great subtlety. In this case it was more than a little disturbing.

Cautiously, she went into her dressing room, in which Miss Dace was sorting out what would be needed for the reception that evening, at which Sir Lionel Bartram was to greet the Governor of Jamaica and Thrift would be able to meet Jean-Jacques Rougon.

'Do you think my ruby choker would be too ostentatious?' she asked, needing something to say.

'Here, only married women wear jewellery in the evening,' Miss Dace responded. 'Silk flowers worn in your hair would be more appropriate, although

111

appropriate is hardly the word. I purchased some this morning, to match all three of your gowns.'

'How thoughtful, Miss Dace,' Thrift responded. 'Oh, they are beautiful!'

As Thrift spoke, Miss Dace had laid out a hair ornament of tumbling silk blooms in the same brilliant scarlet as the gown. Thrift picked them up to admire them, and as she did so noticed something else on the dressing table between her gloves and her fan. It was a highly polished length of wood, or more accurately, two woods, one dark and hard, the other pale and, to judge by the three notches cut into it, correspondingly soft. One end was rounded, the other pierced by a delicate silver chain.

'What is this?' she asked, picking it up.

'Have you never seen a tally stick before?' Miss Dace responded.

'No, never,' Thrift admitted.

'They are used in circumstances where, for whatever reason, discipline cannot be given directly after the offence,' Miss Dace explained. 'Instead of a spanking, a notch is cut in the stick, which the girl wears around her neck so that all may see, and at the appropriate time she is given her just deserts. That is your tally stick.'

Thrift had already realised, and begun to pout.

'In the circumstances you may wear it under your gown,' Miss Dace offered.

'Miss Adams has ordered that I am not to be spanked,' Thrift pointed out.

'Miss Adams has ordered that your spankings be suspended,' Miss Dace corrected her, 'which is why you need a tally stick.'

'Very well, if you insist,' Thrift said, struggling to keep the frustration out of her voice, 'but why are there three notches already on it?'

'One is for your lewd behaviour in front of Captain Langhorne,' Miss Dace replied, 'the second for your morning routine and the third for seeking to evade fair chastisement by speaking to Miss Adams when all such questions should be left to my responsibility.'

'Oh,' Thrift responded, although quickly playing over her options in her head. They were not good. In Baton Rouge she might be able to evade punishment, but as soon as they were on the airship she would be entirely at Miss Dace's mercy.

'You did not expect to avoid punishment, did you?' Miss Dace asked.

'No, not at all, Miss Dace,' Thrift answered quickly, knowing full well that to admit she had would mean yet another spanking.

'Then that will be two notches,' Miss Dace replied, 'one for seeking to evade just punishment, and one for lying.'

Thrift made a face, unable to find an answer without risking further trouble. Miss Dace took a tiny, pearl-handled penknife from her bag and very carefully cut two more notches into the tally stick. Thrift noted with apprehension that the notches were cut deliberately small so as to leave plenty of room.

'Are you ready to bathe?' Miss Dace enquired as she put down the tally stick. 'The reception starts in nearly four hours and to rush spoils a girl's equanimity.'

'Quite ready, thank you, Miss Dace,' Thrift answered, avoiding the temptation to point out that being threatened with spanking also spoiled her equanimity.

She began to prepare, first undressing to her containment set and pulling on her rubber modesty gown before Miss Dace removed both bra and pants, then washing in a huge enamelled bath, which was a delight after so many days of showering on the boat. Once she was scrubbed to a healthy pink glow, her hair was given a final rinse and she got out, to be dried and powdered under the watchful eye of Miss Dace, including the invariably humiliating experience of having her legs rolled up for her quim and anus to be done, during

113

which her hands were tied to prevent any risk of self-abuse.

Once dry, she was put back in her containment pants and her cotton modesty gown for her hair to be dried and brushed out into a cascade of shiny auburn curls. She was grudgingly allowed to pull on a chemise and a pair of panel-back drawers, newly purchased from Claralinda's, before removing her modesty gown and adding her stockings. Her new corset was put on, accentuating her bottom and pushing out her breasts to Miss Dace's open disapproval and her own delight.

Her three petticoats were added, the inner of heavy flannel, for cleanliness, the middle of cotton with a heavy lace trim, for modesty, and the outer of taffeta, which would rustle as she walked. Her underdress went on top, then her gown, before she was sat down to have her hair arranged and finally allowed to put on her gloves and a pair of scarlet silk slippers. By then over three hours had passed, and as she went to the full-length mirror Thrift had to admit that whatever faults Miss Dace might have as a companion, she was an efficient maid.

Thrift's reflection put a delighted smile on her face. Not since setting off for the colonies had she felt so pleased with her own appearance, which left her confident of being at least as fetching as the Creole girls, while she had the added advantages of her rank and novelty. Lifting the edges of her gown, she allowed herself a single, elegant twirl to show off the way the built-in bustle exaggerated the swell of her hips and bottom, only to stop halfway around. To her consternation she saw that Miss Dace was cutting a sixth notch in the tally stick.

'I do not mean to dispute your authority, Miss Dace,' she asked, 'but in what way have I misbehaved?'

'To dress as you are is more than sufficient to earn you a spanking,' Miss Dace answered. 'You look positively indecent, to say nothing of your unseemly pride in your appearance.'

'I am supposed to be pretty,' Thrift objected. 'Both Mr Fanshaw and Miss Adams have made this clear. How else am I supposed to attract Mr Rougon?'

'To be pretty and demure is one thing,' Miss Dace responded, 'to look like a trollop and be proud of the fact quite another.'

She cut a second notch.

'Two?' Thrift asked.

'One for indecency, one for pride,' Miss Dace answered. 'Now, put this on, and if you will excuse me, I must get ready myself.'

Thrift was pouting furiously as she accepted the tally stick and put it around her neck, taking great care to ensure that it was tucked well in and out of sight. With a few minutes to pass before Miss Dace was ready, she went into the main room of the apartment, feeling more than a little sulky as she once more stared out across Baton Rouge, now twinkling with lights as dusk gave way to night. The way things were going, her bottom would be warm all the way from Baton Rouge to London, and it was quite obvious that Miss Dace was merely trying to make the best of her opportunity to spank Thrift, which she so clearly enjoyed. Briefly, and with a little flutter of her stomach, she wondered if Miss Dace might not lose control again. It seemed unlikely, which was a shame, as her trip would undoubtedly have been far more exciting had her companion been able to accept her own feelings and make Thrift her lover.

Thrift was barely conscious of the footman as she lifted a glass of champagne from his tray. All around her men and women in immaculate evening dress were talking together or dancing, filling the great ballroom almost to capacity. The men were invariably charming and generally handsome, the women as pretty as nursery dolls in their brightly coloured gowns. She had received all the attention she had anticipated, even from the Governor of Jamaica himself, Sir Talavera Groves, a gigantic man with skin the colour of mahogany, but even such high flattery was beginning to pale.

From the conversation of the guests and the way those who were Creole tended to fall quickly silent if she passed close to them, she had come to realise that the situation was a great deal more tense than either Mr Fanshaw or Miss Adams had made out. The gay atmosphere of the ball was no more than superficial, while the conversations were very serious indeed and focused almost entirely on the question of secession. The majority opposed it, and yet both the Gaulistes and the Libertistes clearly meant business, so much so that she found herself grateful for the discreet presence of Mr Kobo in the background.

Most alarming of all had been her introduction to Pierre Mareschal, father to Ademar Mareschal, the second most influential man in the Gauliste movement and the one who was expected to take over and maintain the political balance once she had disgraced Jean-Jacques Rougon. He was tall, dark-haired and hot-eyed, and had insisted in speaking French and addressing her as Mademoiselle, to which fortunately her education at the Diplomatic School had enabled her to respond. He had also spoken freely and fiercely of the time when Louisiana would once again be a French territory, which Thrift had found both impolite and frightening.

Jean-Jacques Rougon himself had been only marginally less alarming. His photograph had belied both his height and his impressive bearing, while his steel-grey hair and pale, bright eyes leant him such authority that she found it hard to imagine herself facing up to him at all, much less accusing him of something he hadn't done. He had also been charming and was clearly taken with her, so much so that she had little doubt that Mr Fanshaw's scheme was practical, knowledge she took in with mixed feelings.

Now, with the reception well under way, she had done all that Miss Adams had expected of her first encounter with Mr Rougon and was free to enjoy herself, at least as much as the presence of Miss Dace at her elbow allowed. Her dance card was full, and she made an effort to put her misgivings aside as her next partner approached and greeted Miss Dace with a stiff bow. He was a member of the Jamaican delegation, exceptionally tall and darker of skin even than the Governor, a combination that made Thrift's heart flutter.

'I believe I have the honour of a dance with Miss Moncrieff?' he addressed Miss Dace.

'You are correct, Mr Monroe, sir,' Miss Dace replied after a brief glance at the card she held, her voice as formal as the plain black chin-high evening gown she had selected.

Thrift curtsied and offered her arm, mindful of the feel of the tally stick between her breasts and so determined to follow correct etiquette exactly and not to allow so much as a hint of impropriety. Mr Monroe took her arm and she allowed herself to be escorted to the floor, with Miss Dace walking on her other side, alert for any over-familiar behaviour or an attempt to arrange an assignation.

Moving out onto the highly polished circle of the dance floor, Thrift allowed Mr Monroe to guide her through the intricate steps of a lawn glide, all the while thrilling to the size and power of his hands on her shoulder and waist. Soon she was lost in the pleasure of the dance, only to be brought abruptly down to earth as the gradual swelling of her quim triggered the needle in her containment pants, puncturing her flesh and filling her with serum as her eyes popped in surprise and discomfort. She also missed her step, so that he was forced to catch her up to prevent her falling.

'Are you quite well, Miss Moncrieff?' he asked.

'A trifle faint, I confess,' Thrift answered with some difficulty as the numbing sensation crept over her quim.

'It is rather close,' he responded. 'I shall fetch you a glass of champagne.'

He had already steered her to the edge of the floor, with his arm not supporting hers, but around her waist. Miss Dace was waiting with her face set in open disapproval, but waited until Mr Monroe had gone in search of a footman before she spoke, and then in a whisper.

'I suppose you have some excuse for that little display? Really, it must be the oldest trick of all, to pretend to stumble so that your partner can take a more intimate hold. Do you think me a complete fool?'

'Not at all,' Thrift answered, 'and it was not a trick. My . . . my horrible pants triggered, if you must know!'

'You grew aroused while dancing?' Miss Dace queried. 'Extraordinary!'

'How could I help it?' Thrift asked.

'Give me your tally stick,' Miss Dace demanded, ignoring Thrift's question.

'Here?' Thrift countered. 'People will see!'

'So much the better,' Miss Dace began, and despite herself Thrift's hand had gone to her neck.

She pulled the tally stick out, shaking with humiliation and praying Mr Monroe would take his time finding the champagne. Unfortunately he didn't, returning almost immediately, so that he was standing with the glasses in his hands as the notch was cut. Worse still, it was quite obvious from the expression of surprise that quickly gave way to both amusement and lust that he knew exactly what the tally stick was and what the notches meant.

He was too polite to make a remark, but Thrift was still blushing furiously as she put the tally stick away and took her champagne. The dance was still in progress, leaving her with no option but to make polite conversation and wonder how much the handsome and attractive Mr Monroe would enjoy seeing her given a bare-bottom spanking. Only when the strains of the lawn glide at last began to fade and partners were exchanged did he finally retire, leave Thrift feeling hot under the collar and badly in need of fresh air.

Unfortunately she was marked to dance again, and had no option but to allow her new partner to escort her out onto the floor and follow his rather clumsy lead as best she could. The dance was a formation waltz, and as she went into the elaborate pattern she had soon lost sight of Miss Dace, making her wish Mr Monroe had made a later choice, as not only was her current partner less appealing, but the numbness between her thighs was a constant irritation.

A break followed, to her relief, and as she made her way back to the edge of the floor she found Miss Dace in conversation with Felicity Adams, now in a ball gown of rich blue velvet with diamonds at her neck and in her hair. Thrift smiled and curtsied. Miss Adams responded in kind, swallowed the remains of her champagne and fielded another glass from a passing footman before speaking, her voice rich with both amusement and drink.

'Susannah tells me you're wearing a tally stick, Thrift, my dear?'

'Yes,' Thrift admitted.

'I thought it best,' Miss Dace put in, quickly defending herself, 'as while I naturally respect your decision, Miss Adams, I must be allowed to retain my authority.'

'Oh absolutely, no question at all,' Miss Adams agreed. 'You are entirely within your rights, but it was rather poor form to do it in front of quite so many people, don't you think? Indeed, if it was not for the fact that at least a dozen Creole partisans might wonder at

119

my behaviour and make certain assumptions, I think I'd put you across my knee and spank that little round bottom of yours bright pink, here and now. How would you like that, eh, Snivels?'

Miss Adams gave a cheerful wink and turned on her heel, leaving Miss Dace, for once, showing emotion that was far from subtle, her cheeks a rich red colour and her wide mouth open in humiliation. Thrift found herself trying desperately not to laugh, and failing, her hand going to her mouth to hide a giggle despite herself, at which Miss Dace turned to face her and spoke.

'You may be sacrosanct in Baton Rouge, you snotty, stuck-up little brat, but believe me, once I get you on that airship you won't be able to sit down until you've been back in London a month!'

'That's not fair!' Thrift protested, her voice rising to a petulant whine only to be abruptly cut off as she realised somebody was approaching, Jean-Jacques Rougon himself.

He bowed, and a second time in response to Thrift and Miss Dace's answering curtsies, then spoke.

'A little contretemps, ladies? Inevitable, I fear, the way you English arrange these matters. Now in France, you see, and indeed in Louisiana for our own entertainments, we have a much better system. The young ladies are free to hold their own dance cards and to make their own arrangements, although always under the watchful eye of Mama, of course.'

'A system which, I dare say, suits the French very well,' Miss Dace responded.

'You imply that we are decadent?' Mr Rougon laughed. 'No, no, I take no offence, for I think you will find that if we measure the degree of what you English call "moral rectitude" among different cultures down the ages, you will find that modern French culture more closely approximates the average than does English.'

120

'Undoubtedly,' Miss Dace responded. 'As civilisation advances, so must, or so should, moral rectitude advance, and I am sure even you would agree, sir, that the British Empire represents the peak of civilisation.'

'Not at all,' Mr Rougon responded. 'Far from it, indeed. Even after the ruination of my country in the Great War our culture outshines any other as the beauty of Miss Moncrieff outshines that of any woman in this room.'

'Nevertheless,' Thrift put in, blushing for the compliment and eager to join in the conversation, 'you must surely admit that Miss Dace's statement has merit. As humanity has evolved, so has our morality, ever since the time when we were mere apes.'

'Are you comparing me with an ape, Miss Moncrieff?' Mr Rougon retorted, throwing Thrift into immediate blushing confusion and speaking again as she was still attempting to stammer an apology. 'I speak in jest, naturally, Miss Moncrieff, and only because you blush so prettily and I wished to see it. It was cruel of me.'

Miss Dace evidently wanted to say something, her face set in stern disapproval, but she held back, allowing him to continue.

'Another custom we French enjoy, and which you would no doubt consider morally dubious, is that should a Mama be keen to make a suitable match for her daughter, or indeed, find herself in a state of pecuniary embarrassment, then she may be inclined to turn a blind eye for a while, permitting a brief *tête à tête*, or perhaps something rather more.'

He raised an eyebrow as he finished, and again Miss Dace opened her mouth to speak but closed it again, her moral instincts clearly fighting against her sense of duty. Mr Rougon gave a low chuckle and went on.

'For instance, purely as a hypothetical example, you understand, let us say that I hoped to arrange an assignation with Miss Moncrieff. Then you, Miss Dace, in return of course for a suitable consideration, might allow or even facilitate the matter. Is that so very outrageous?'

'Absolutely,' Miss Dace responded, no longer able to contain herself.

'Yet, Miss Moncrieff herself says nothing,' he observed, turning his penetrating gaze on Thrift, 'while certain remarks made by my cousin Delphyne, whom I believe you have met, lead me to suspect that if such a situation were to arise, my attention might not be entirely unwelcome.'

Thrift hung her head, blushing, and before the outraged Miss Dace could reply he spoke again, changing the subject completely.

'What does a lady's companion earn, Miss Dace?'

'I receive adequate remuneration, thank you, Mr Rougon,' Miss Dace replied, her voice more frosty than ever.

'Ah, yes,' he said, 'I had forgotten that you English consider money to be vulgar. Still, I will warrant that it is no great sum, not so much, for instance that an extra five pounds might not come in useful.'

Thrift kept her head hung, her heart now hammering in her chest as she allowed them to negotiate. Miss Dace didn't answer, and had begun to sip her champagne – too abrupt a change in attitude, Thrift thought, but Jean-Jacques Rougon merely chuckled then spoke again.

'For the companion to a lady of Miss Moncrieff's rank expenses are no doubt rather greater, but I suspect ten pounds would be worthwhile. No? Twenty perhaps? Thirty even?'

At last Miss Dace found her voice.

'Such a thing is unthinkable, for any sum, Mr Rougon,' she stated, 'and I trust that as a gentleman you would not seek to take advantage if, for example, I were to be obliged to conduct Miss Moncrieff to her rooms during the next break and became indisposed for a short period.'

'You have my word on it,' he assured her, smiled and bowed to each of them.

Thrift tried not to make a face, realising that she had effectively been sold, and a moment later the music had struck up again. Her next partner had been hovering nearby and quickly moved close, going through the brief ritual of recommending himself to Miss Dace before taking Thrift onto the dance floor.

She was only half aware of him as they danced, her mind running through what she had to do over and over again. It was simple, in theory, just a matter of acquiescing to his demands until enough time had passed, then screaming for Miss Dace and making her accusation amid a flood of tears. In practice it seemed a very different matter, and she knew it would require every ounce of courage she had.

The dance came to an end, the next began, and Thrift found herself counting down with much the same feelings of apprehension as on the many times she had watched a clock while waiting outside a door for the hour at which she was to face punishment. As then, time seemed to have slowed down but still to be moving with inexorable force. As the third dance began she began to tremble violently, to the delight of her partner, Ademar Mareschal, who mistook her fear for arousal and attempted to make a proposition.

Nor did he give in easily, still wheedling earnest protestations of desire into her ear as they made their way from the floor. Thrift simply ignored him and he was forced to give way to her next partner. Struggling to compose herself, she accepted his arm and stepped out once more, holding herself rigid until they were done in what seemed moments. The fifth dance seemed swifter still. The time had come.

Thrift was having difficulty walking as Miss Dace took her arm and led her towards the staircase, but forced herself to smile and bob at acquaintances. Miss

Dace never spoke, as stiff and perhaps as nervous as Thrift, and when they reached the landing of their floor she paused to squeeze Thrift's arm and smile, the first gesture of proper affection she had shown. Thrift returned both and slipped quickly into the apartment, composing herself in a chair as if resting.

No more than a moment had passed before she caught a hurried conversation outside the door, which then opened. Thrift looked up, forcing a coy smile as Jean-Jacques Rougon stepped into the room. Miss Dace followed, but quickly slipped through the door into her own bedroom. Thrift stood and curtsied, hoping that he would take the lead. Sure enough, no sooner had Miss Dace's door closed than he had stepped boldly forward, clasping her in his arms and trying to press his mouth against hers.

'Please,' she managed, pushing him back in an effort to feign reluctance, 'take a little time with me, at the least.'

'Time?' he answered, his voice thick with passion. 'I cannot take my time, Miss Moncrieff . . . Thrift. I am no coldblood like you English. I burn for you, Thrift, and I mean to have you.'

'Sire, please,' Thrift responded, but she allowed his hands to stray to the fastenings of her dress, 'you are too hasty.'

His answer was to press his mouth to hers again. Thrift resisted for a moment, then gave in, at first allowing her lips to open, then her tongue to meet his. He kissed with bruising passion, and all the while his fingers were fumbling with her gown, and making slow work of it as men invariably did. For all her feelings it was easy to melt into his kisses, and she put her arms around him, surrendering herself even as a small, clear part of her mind waited for the crucial moment.

At last he had the back of her dress open and broke away from her mouth as he peeled her gown off her shoulders. His lips found her neck, kissing with rising passion, and lower, across her chest and the upper slopes of her breasts, his mouth hot on her skin. Her sighs were real, and her gasp as he suddenly placed both hands under her corset cups and gave a sudden, upward thrust, bouncing both her breasts out to lie plump and round among the silk and lace of her dishevelled clothes.

'*Mon Dieu,* you are gigantic!' he breathed, staring pop-eyed at Thrift's naked breasts. 'And a little wanton too. You no longer need pretend, my darling. I know it is true, and how they beat you aboard the riverboat, and how you came to climax. We French, you see, are not so reticent between man and woman as you English.'

He had taken one fat globe in each hand, kneading them as he spoke. Thrift closed her eyes, taking a moment to enjoy the attention to her breasts, which were fully sensitive for the first time since being put in her containment bra. His mouth found a nipple, sucking hard as he squeezed the other between finger and thumb, until both were fully erect. Then he pulled back again, now on his knees and still holding one breast in each hand as he began to speak once more, his voice so hoarse with excitement she could barely understand him.

'Magnificent! Your nipples are like claret corks, so big, and so stiff, and your breasts, glorious, truly glorious. On your back, you little wanton, and I shall teach you how a Frenchman makes love!'

He'd began to push her down onto the rug, fumbling her dress up around her waist and still kissing at her breasts. She realised that it was the perfect time for her to scream, but the words wouldn't come. Before she could do anything more she was on her back with her legs held up as he fumbled for the buttons that held her drawers closed. She steeled herself, only for him to lose patience and tear the panel open, then stop, eyes wide, as he exposed not the soft bulge of her naked quim but the shiny black integument of her containment pants.

'What is this?' he demanded. 'Some new fashion to preserve your brittle English modesty? How do they come off?'

'They . . . they don't,' Thrift managed in an agony of embarrassment. 'That is, they do, but only Miss Dace can open them.'

'I suppose the bitch needs another thirty pounds to do it?' he demanded. 'Well, she'll be disappointed. I'll fuck your tits and mouth and have done with it!'

Again Thrift made to scream as she was caught by the hair and pulled up into a sitting position, but he'd already managed to extract his cock from his trousers and all that came out was a bubbling noise as her mouth was filled with erect penis. He began to fuck her head, gasping and grunting as she batted at him in pathetic remonstrance. His hands were both twisted into her hair, painfully hard as he jammed his cock deeper and deeper down her protesting throat, all the while calling her a wanton and a harlot, a trollop and a slut, insults that broke off in a choking, gurgling sound as with a final convulsion he ejaculated the full volume of his semen deep into Thrift's gullet.

He pulled out immediately, flopping back to leave her gasping for air and blowing come bubbles from both nostrils, her anger at the way he had treated her making it easy to gather her breath for a scream to end all screams. It never came. Her furious expression turned to shock as she realised that Jean-Jacques Rougon definitely should not still be in convulsions so long after coming, nor suddenly so still.

Monsieur d'Arrignac, she recalled, had referred to orgasm as *la petite mort*, the little death. Jean-Jacques Rougon, it seemed, had gone one step further.

Seven

Thrift remained as she was long after Jean-Jacques Rougon had given a final twitch and expired. Only when Miss Dace at last opened her bedroom door did Thrift react at all, turning to her companion in open-mouthed horror.

'What happened?' Miss Dace demanded. 'Is he dead?'

'Yes,' Thrift managed.

'For goodness sake put your breasts away then!' Miss Dace snapped.

Thrift reacted to the order from sheer habit of obedience, making herself decent as quickly as she could while Miss Dace came to kneel beside the body, which she quickly confirmed as dead.

'What shall we do?' Thrift asked as Miss Dace returned the dead man's penis to his trousers with a look of fastidious distaste.

'I will fetch Felicity. She'll be the best person to decide,' Miss Dace responded, even her sense of propriety forgotten in the moment.

Thrift nodded and climbed to her feet as Miss Dace hurried from the room. The dead man's face was set in an expression of mingled ecstasy, horror and pain, an intensely unpleasant sight. She looked around for something to cover him, decided to fetch a sheet from her bedroom. It took her just a moment to pull it free and she came back, to find herself face to face with Ademar Mareschal, a hastily assembled bunch of flowers he had evidently intended to present to her hanging limp in one hand, his mouth as round as his spectacles as he stared at the dead face of Jean-Jacques Rougon. An instant later the flowers lay scattered on the carpet and he had fled, screaming a single word over and over again.

'Assassin!'

Blind panic hit Thrift. She needed to be as far away from the body, and as quickly, as possible. Dropping the sheet to the floor, she ran from the room, along the corridor and away from the main stair, from which screams of accusation could still be heard. Other voices were answering the screams before she'd reached the end; there were shouted questions, then cries of rage. The instant she reached the servants' stair she darted down it, immensely thankful for her short corset as she took the steps two and three at a time.

The stairs led down to a great open room bustling with people, servants of every sort doing all manner of tasks, but Thrift had eyes only for a door left open to let in the cool night air. Curious glances were turned her way as she pit-patted her way across the floor, nothing more, and she ran outside to find herself behind the residence. The reek of decay caught her nose, and she saw that vast refuse bins stood beside her. For a moment she considered hiding behind them, even in one, before dismissing the idea as she at last began to get a grip on herself. She needed to get clear, to the Diplomatic Service building, where she would be safe.

Moving quickly to the gate of the service yard, she peered out along the front of the residence. A long line of cars was parked beside the lake, with knots of drivers standing among them in conversation, and, to her immense relief, Mr Kobo, just getting into a sleek white

128

Bentley. Again she ran, knowing she was in full view of the open residency doors as she scampered over the gravel, all the while waving frantically. He hadn't seen her, his back to her as he opened the door, even as he swung himself into the driver's seat, but she had made it, scrambling into the back and already babbling instructions.

'Quick, take me to –'

She stopped as she realised that there was somebody already in the car with her, staring in astonishment: not Felicity Adams, nor any of her fellow staff, but Sir Talavera Groves, the Governor of Jamaica.

'Miss Moncrieff, I believe?' he asked.

'Yes, I . . . um . . . that is to say . . . , I . . . ,' Thrift managed, about to admit what she'd done, deciding against it, about to admit she was in the Diplomatic Service and remembering she wasn't supposed to, and finally turning to the only other reason she could think of for her behaviour. 'Might I speak to you, Sir Talavera, on a matter of some delicacy?'

She lowered her eyes, trying to look coy and hoping that her ragged breathing would be mistaken for passion. He took a moment to respond, clearly astonished that a young woman of her rank should behave in such a manner, but quickly collected himself.

'I would be honoured, Miss Moncrieff, but your companion?'

He left the question open, allowing Thrift a chance to withdraw gracefully.

'My . . . my companion, Miss Dace, is of a malleable disposition,' Thrift answered, a statement so clearly a lie that his eyebrows rose once more.

'But your reputation?' he asked, still cautious.

'I feel certain, sir, that as a British gentleman you will ensure that my reputation remains unscathed.'

'And as a British lady I feel equally sure you will extend me the same courtesy,' he replied. 'James, the boat, if you would.'

It was only then that Thrift realised the man she had mistaken for Tobias Kobo was in fact James Monroe. Still too flustered to do anything other than act on the instant, she glanced back towards the residence as the great car pulled smoothly out from its space. The front doors were wide, showing the brilliantly lit interior and a few figures, but the only people outside were the footmen at either side of the steps. The lights were still on in her apartment, but with the curtains drawn it was impossible to see if anybody was there.

She closed her eyes, trying to block out the picture of Jean-Jacques Rougon's dead face and force herself to behave as she would be expected to. All Sir Talavera Groves knew was that she had rushed out to him to make an assignation, abandoning her companion and risking her supposedly precious reputation. It was extraordinary behaviour for a woman of her rank. She would be disgraced anyway, and probably sent to the doctors, where she would almost certainly be diagnosed as a wanton and put in containment.

Thrift had been sent to the doctors long before and was already in containment, which was going to prove a problem if Sir Talavera Groves expected to seduce an eager but essentially innocent virgin. She had no choice but to admit that she was disgraced, which would at least go a long way to explaining her behaviour, while for the sake of his own reputation she could definitely count on his complicity. The car was now moving out through the residency gates and there was no turning back. Collecting her wits, she forced herself to speak.

'You must think me very forward, Sir Talavera?'

'Frankly, I've never seen the like,' he admitted, 'but now you're here, would you care for a drink?'

'Yes, please,' Thrift answered with genuine feeling.

He leant forward to open a small refrigerator, from which he took a bottle of champagne, another of brandy, and two tall, slim glasses.

'Say what you like about the French,' he said as he began to work on the champagne cork, 'but they make the best wines, brandies too. This is Ay champagne, one of the finest, and a cognac that's been in barrel longer than you've been about, like as not.'

Thrift managed what she hoped was an encouraging smile as she watched him mix the cocktails, then accepted her glass, draining most of it at a gulp.

'My, but you are a thirsty girl,' he said. 'Still, I suspect you need it. I know I do.'

Quickly swallowing what remained in her glass, Thrift passed it back to be refilled. Already somewhat drunk, her head was spinning from the potent cocktail, while her body was beginning to go limp as her panic and fear drained away. She sipped at her second glass, making her eyes big for him over the rim but still unsure what to say. He didn't seem to mind, talking casually in an effort to put her at ease, in a soft, strong voice Thrift knew she would have found appealing in less fraught circumstances.

The car quickly reached the waterfront, where the Governor's private yacht was moored beyond the berths reserved for the commercial riverboat lines. James Monroe was given his instructions, which he carried out swiftly and without comment, clearing the way for Thrift to be taken aboard without arousing suspicion. She was immediately guided to the Governor's private quarters, where another glass of the powerful champagne cocktail was put into her hand and she was left for a moment before the Governor himself came in.

'We are now quite alone,' he assured her, 'and those few who know you are here can be trusted. I believe there was a matter you wished to discuss with me?'

He was smiling as he spoke, leaving no doubt at all as to his meaning, the more so as he had sat down on the immense bed and now patted the space beside him. Thrift came to him, far from aroused but badly needing

131

to be held and prepared to assuage his lust if that was what it took. His arms came around her immediately, immensely powerful, so that it was easy to melt into his embrace, although she had to make herself respond to his kisses.

She was on the edge of exhaustion as his hands explored her body, teasing and cajoling her out of her clothes, a little clumsy, but evidently with practice. Soon Thrift's gown had been undone and turned down around her shoulders, allowing her breasts to be pushed up from her corset. The motion also exposed her tally stick, and from the brief flicker of amusement that crossed his face it was evident he knew what it was. Then he began to enjoy her breasts, taking his time over them, stroking and squeezing the heavy globes, licking her skin and suckling at her nipples until at last her body began to respond for all the turmoil in her mind.

He had taken out his cock as he fed on Thrift's nipples, and now guided her hand to it, thick and heavy and quickly stiffening as she began to tug. His hand closed in her hair, to guide her gently but firmly down towards his growing erection, as if unsure if she would be willing, or have the experience, to take him in her mouth. She gave no resistance, feeding him into her mouth and sucking. It felt oddly soothing to have the big penis swelling in her mouth, distracting her, while he continued to fondle her breasts as she sucked.

Only when he began to bunch up her skirt did she pull back, leaving his now rock-solid penis standing up from his open fly as a proud, rich brown pole of meat, wet with her saliva. He took a moment to adjust himself, pulling a heavy, dark scrotum out and asking gently if she would suck his balls.

'Gladly,' Thrift admitted, 'but I have a confession to make. I am in containment pants, which makes it impossible for you to enjoy me fully, and for me to take my full enjoyment of you.'

'So you suffer from wantonness?' he asked. 'I had guessed you might. May I still touch?'

Thrift hesitated, then nodded her acquiescence. As she once more went down, this time to open her mouth around the bulk of his scrotum, he began to haul up her skirts once more, piling everything onto her waist until her drawers were exposed. She had begun to masturbate him as she sucked on his balls, fighting down her first flush of embarrassment as he undid the panel of her drawers and lifted it up to expose the twin black bulges of her buttocks.

He said nothing, squeezing the full, rubbery balls of her encased bottom cheeks and as she opened her thighs stroking the bulge of her quim, where the integument was pulled tight over the shape of her sex lips. She moved her attention back to his cock, masturbating him into her mouth and squeezing gently on his scrotum as she sucked and kissed at his helmet. He spoke again, his voice now hoarse.

'Do you enjoy it when your companion punishes you? I know many girls who do.'

Thrift nodded on her mouthful of cock, much too far gone to deny her guilty secret. He gave a low chuckle and began to slap her bottom, stinging her and making the integument squirm against her flesh. She pushed her hips out for more, a gesture only half false as her pleasure rose, and an instant later he was ejaculating gout after gout of thick white come into her mouth, then over her face and breasts as she pulled back. His hand left her bottom and he gave a long and contented sigh as he lay back on the bed, with Thrift still squeezing the last of his come from his erection.

'That was a delight,' he said after a moment to catch his breath. 'I am only sorry it could not be more fulfilling for you.'

'I will take my fulfilment when the opportunity arises,' Thrift told him, 'and I shall think of our time together.'

'Which, I fear, has been all too brief,' he replied. 'Should you not return to the Residence?'

Thrift hesitated, taking a drink of her cocktail as she struggled for an excuse. Simply pretending to faint could only postpone her problems, while to ask to be taken to the Diplomatic Service building would raise all sorts of difficult questions. Meanwhile on the yacht she was safe, both from the territorial authorities and the vengeful Gaulistes. She decided to stay, and hope that his sense of honour and the prospect of more sex would outweigh his undoubted objections.

'I would really rather stay a while,' she said, turning so that he could see the full expanse of her bare chest and the tally stick between her breasts.

She had begun to toy with the tally stick, deliberately self-conscious, and he nodded in understanding.

'I find myself in a difficult situation,' she went on. 'I could not contain my desire for you, and I do not regret what I have done for a moment. When I return to the residence Miss Dace will undoubtedly discipline me, not as she usually does, which I admit can be pleasurable, but most severely, and all the more so if I refuse to tell her whom I have been with, a secret I am honour bound to keep.'

'Absolutely,' he agreed with conviction.

'Therefore,' she continued, 'for both our sakes I think it best if I remain with you here for a while.'

'I understand that you are scared,' he replied, 'and believe me, there is nothing I would like better than to entertain you here for a while, but you will have to face the music eventually, and the longer you are away the more concerned your companion will become, which will inevitably mean she increases the severity of your punishment. Not only that, but I leave for Arkansas first thing in the morning.'

'Take me with you!' Thrift said immediately. 'I . . . I will visit the Governor in Arkansas, make up some story or other, in which you can support me, have my companion dismissed for ineptitude –'

'Isn't that a little unfair?' he broke in. 'She is only doing her duty.'

'That is true,' Thrift admitted, thinking desperately, 'but I am still reluctant to go back, and I would like to enjoy you once more, at the least.'

'As would I,' he assured her, 'but it is really for the best, and your smarting will soon go, leaving you with only this pleasant memory.'

'Miss Dace can keep me smarting for a very long time indeed,' Thrift replied with feeling. 'You saw my tally stick? Each notch represents one hundred and forty-four smacks, with a hairbrush, or with a horrid paddle she has.'

'That is severe,' he admitted, with genuine sympathy despite giving his cock a squeeze. 'Ah, yes, do use my handkerchief.'

Thrift had been trying to wipe the sperm from her face and breasts with her own minute lace handkerchief, and gladly accepted his much large silk one as a substitute. He watched as she cleaned her breasts, clearing enjoying the view despite having just come, making Thrift wonder if she might not be able to persuade him to take her to bed and at least delay the inevitable until morning, or perhaps later still.

'You're right,' she said, hastily reversing her argument. 'She can only beat me so often and so hard, and I am already on a routine so strict she would hardly dare increase it. I will probably be put in hand restraints, and perhaps made to wear my tally stick above my clothes, but I do not care. I want to spend the night with you, and in the morning Miss Dace can do her worst.'

'You flatter me,' he responded.

The Mississippi, March 2006

As Thrift emerged from sleep her immediate memories seemed to be a series of vivid dreams, but she came awake with a shock as full awareness returned. Jean-Jacques Rougon was really dead, she was really on the Governor of Jamaica's private yacht, and she had really pleasured him until she finally passed out from sheer exhaustion in an effort to ensure he overslept.

He had, his great body lying beside her in the bed, clad in the mauve pyjamas she had teased him about until he took her across his knee for the playful, erotic spanking which had initiated their third bout of sex. There had been two more after that, lasting deep into the night, until his final orgasm had produced no more than a dribble of clear fluid and she had no longer been able to keep her eyes open.

With no instructions to the contrary, whoever was captaining the vessel had left first thing in the morning, as intended, and the big yacht was now in motion, perhaps some miles up river from Baton Rouge, as they seemed to be moving at a good speed. Thrift lay back on the pillows, trying to think out her next move rather than dwell on what had happened.

Nobody knew where she was, so it was evidently important to communicate with Felicity Adams as soon as possible. That could be done as soon as she could get to a telephone, although she didn't like the thought of what Felicity was likely to say to her. She frowned, wondering just how bad it would be. Her record was hardly immaculate after she had made such a fool of herself on Hainan Tao, and at the very least she would be hauled back to London, even dismissed from the service, and at the not so tender mercy of Miss Dace all the way.

That assumed she was cleared of any involvement with the death of Jean-Jacques Rougon, and running away when Ademar Mareschal caught her was bound to cast suspicion on her. At the very least the Gaulistes would suspect a conspiracy of some sort, and were therefore not likely to accept any information given out by the British authorities. Clearly she needed to stay well away from Louisiana. The most sensible thing to do was therefore to disembark in Arkansas and stay with whoever represented the Diplomatic Service until she could be picked up.

She nodded, but was still feeling distinctly sorry for herself as she propped herself up on the pillows. For the moment there was nothing to be done, as the longer Sir Talavera Groves slept, the further up river they would be. Being naked but for her containment pants felt odd, and she took a moment to find her chemise among the discarded clothing beside the bed, pull it on and fasten the laces across her chest. Doing so brought another problem to mind, her pants, because while her anus was safely plugged she had eaten rather a lot of the delicious food served at the reception and her tummy was starting to grow uncomfortable.

Now frowning, she wondered if it might not be possible to imitate Miss Dace's voice, allowing her to remove her pants. By their own admission the Smith and Smith system was new, and not really designed for an active, mentally alert girl anyway. She decided to try before her belly grew any more uncomfortable, and carefully slipped her legs out of bed.

The second door she tried proved to lead to Sir Talavera Groves' convenient facility. It was somewhat Spartan and masculine, but at that moment a bush would have done well enough. She closed the door, took a moment to compose herself, then spoke in what she hoped was a good imitation of Miss Dace's flat Bostonian tone, but softly, for fear of waking the Governor.

'Disrobe.'

Nothing happened, not so much as a tremor in the thick black integument.

'Disrobe,' she repeated, a little louder, but still nothing happened.

She paused, suddenly no longer sure if the command had been 'disrobe' at all. The others had been used more often, and at least she was certain of them.

'Convenience,' she said, again attempting to imitate Miss Dace's accent.

Nothing happened, and she had to bite down her frustration before trying once more.

'Convenience.'

Her pants remained obstinately closed and she had to catch herself before she said a rude word.

'Convenience,' she repeated, as loudly as she dared, but still nothing happened.

'Convenience, convenience, convenience!' she snapped, but her pants held firm.

'Convenience,' she said once more. 'Oh, for heaven's sake. Convenience. Convenience. Disrobe . . . if that's it. Convenience. Disrobe. Chastisement. Convenience. Disrobe. Chastisement!'

Her containment pants split behind and a sigh of the deepest relief broke from her lips as she felt cool air on the skin of her bottom, only to be cut off as she reached back. It was the last command that had worked, leaving her bottom on show, ready for spanking, but with the plug still firmly embedded in her rectum that was worse than useless. She was also sure her pants needed to be closed again before another command could be given, at least to judge by the way Miss Dace had done it.

'End chastisement,' she said.

Nothing happened.

'End chastisement,' she repeated, but still nothing happened.

Thrift stamped her foot in annoyance, which only made her bottom wobble.

'End chastisement!' she ordered, not even bothering to imitate Miss Dace.

This time something happened, Sir Talavera Groves' voice sounding from the bedroom with a distinctly diffident query as to whether she needed the assistance of a female crew member. Thrift was far too embarrassed to reply, and wished she'd had the sense to bring her drawers with her. Yet there was nothing she could do save come out of the convenient facility. Sir Talavera tried not to grin at the sight of her with her bare bottom cheeks sticking out at the rear of her containment pants.

'I can't get them off,' she admitted, blushing. 'I can't even get them open properly.'

'How very awkward,' he said, one corner of his mouth twitching up slightly as he tried to hide his amusement.

'It's not funny,' Thrift insisted, her cheeks going gradually redder because of his amusement and the growing discomfort in her belly, 'and hardly a suitable topic of conversation between a gentleman and a lady, however well acquainted they may be.'

'I do apologise,' he said. 'Perhaps we could cut them off?'

'Not easily,' said Thrift. 'It's very tough, and there is steel wire inside as well.'

'Maybe we could peel it a little more open then?' he suggested.

'There's ... there's a plug up my bottom,' Thrift admitted, blushing more furiously than ever.

'Remarkable,' he said. 'I realise that female containment against the vices is a serious matter, but I had no idea they went to such extremes.'

'They do,' Thrift assured him, and winced as her belly contracted on the load in her bowel.

She ran for the convenient facility, determined to try his suggestion. Squatting low over the bowl, she dug her fingers in around the tuck of her cheeks where her pants had opened for access to her bottom, and pulled. Her pants rolled back, a sensation that made her stomach crawl, but she could feel the thick plug pulling slowly from her anus, which was no longer completely numb. She pulled harder, grimacing and red-faced with effort because of the absurd posture she had been forced to adopt, squatting over the bowl with her bottom stuck out ready to go.

The plug came out a little way, stretching her anus so wide she was gasping in reaction, and wider still as it emerged slowly from her bottom, immediately followed by the full contents of her bowels, falling into the water beneath her with a series of heavy plops in time with her gasps and sobs as she evacuated herself. At last it was all out and she let go, only to have her eyes pop and her mouth come open in shock as the big plug squeezed itself back in up her anus.

She was fully sensitive, and realised with a little concentration she might be able to make herself come, something she needed badly. Immediately she was telling herself not to be so trivial, and yet she knew it would relax her, and after so much ultimately unsatisfying sex during the night her wantonness had come to the fore. Having the plugs inside her felt rude, and what she'd done oddly exciting, especially the way her pants had squirmed against her quim as she struggled to extract the plug from her anus, just like the great black octopus in her dream.

Knowing she had to be quick enough to get her orgasm in the brief time between the reaction of the needle and growing numb, she closed her eyes and lifted herself a little, once more slipping her hands beneath her bottom to spread the sides of her containment pants. The integument began to squirm even as the plug started to pull from her anus, a sensation at once disgusting, frightening and immensely desirable. She pulled a little harder, until the plug had emerged far enough to stretch her anus as wide as it would go, then relax to let it suck back in as her pants squirmed against her cunt.

She repeated the motion, and again, slowly and gently buggering herself as she thought of how it might have been if instead of the plug it had been the Governor's thick brown penis, jammed deep up inside her rectum with her bottom spread for his enjoyment. A little whimper escaped her mouth as she imagined him buggering her and she began to tug faster, making the plug squelch in her anus to add a new and filthier dimension to her fantasy.

He would do what the bullies at the Diplomatic School had done to her, holding her head down the lavatory and rubbing her off, then pulling the chain just as she came, disgracing her utterly before she was made to kiss their bottom holes and lick their cunts. The Governor would put her head down the toilet, but he'd bugger her, and flush it as he filled her rectum with hot, sticky sperm.

She was coming, wriggling her bottom into her spread containment pants and biting her lip to stop herself screaming as wave after wave of ecstasy tore through her to the filthy fantasy. Only at the very peak of her climax did the needle trigger, jabbing into her flesh to bring her up one last time, and she could feel the mound of her quim filling with fluid even as she sat down exhausted on the seat.

Her relief was so great it almost made up for her embarrassment, and only then, with her cunt growing gradually numb, did she realise that without Miss Dace to supervise her there was nothing to stop her draining the remaining serum from her pants, although she would presumably still get punctured every time she grew excited. The valve was tricky, designed to defeat any but the most determined attempt, but she managed to do it, and drained the reservoir.

Feeling that she had at least won a small victory, although not looking forward to Miss Dace's reaction, she set about her ablutions. She took her time, washing her bottom thoroughly even before peeling off her chemise to step into the shower. When she was finally clean and dry, Sir Talavera Groves was propped up in bed, wearing a black silk dressing gown and sipping at a cup of coffee. As Thrift emerged he indicated the breakfast tray beside the bed.

'Do help yourself,' he offered. 'You do realise, I trust, that we have left Baton Rouge?'

'I know we are under way,' she told him, 'but I have no wish to inconvenience you. Perhaps if you could put me ashore in Arkansas?'

'Alone? A lady of your rank? And what of your companion?'

'I will telephone her, if I may, and please do not be concerned for me. Even a lady, with my condition, need not be as scrupulous as she might otherwise.'

'Not with that contraption on, no,' he responded, 'but I cannot simply leave you alone at some remote landing in the middle of nowhere. I don't suppose you even carry money?'

'No,' Thrift admitted.

'Do you know anybody in Arkansas?'

'A Mr and Mrs Reuben Reynolds, who own a cotton estate not too far north of the Louisiana border.'

'They sound respectable.'

'A most respectable couple.'

'We will arrange to have you met, which leaves only the question of how you are supposed to have got to Arkansas at all?'

'You have my word of honour that your name will not be mentioned,' Thrift assured him.

'Very white of you, if I may say so,' he responded.

'Very red, by the time Miss Dace has finished with me,' Thrift joked, and managed a wry smile.

Eight

Arkansas, March 2006

The landing was little more than a jetty, with a cluster of houses behind it, including a shop outside which stood a telephone box, the familiar red shape strangely incongruous among the cotton fields and woody marshes of Arkansas. Thrift glanced around, trying to remember if she had ever been anywhere so bucolic and deciding she hadn't. The sign announcing the shop to be 'Seth's Stores' was even hand-painted, while Seth himself had gone so far as to remove his black coat and was dozing in a chair on the porch with his hat pulled down over his face.

She had called Felicity Young from the yacht, but had only managed to speak to a flustered young man who had told her to wait at the Reynoldses until she received further instructions. The Reynoldses at least had been enthusiastic, immediately agreeing to collect her, although there was no sign of them. James Monroe, who had rowed her to the landing against all the rules of propriety, glanced at his watch, oddly nervous compared with his suave manner at the reception.

'I don't think they'll be here for a while yet,' he remarked. 'Would you care for anything from the shop? A sarsaparilla perhaps?'

'Thank you, no,' Thrift replied.

He smiled, began to speak, thought better of it and turned to stare out across the Mississippi to where the yacht had anchored well out in the stream. Thrift followed his gaze, admiring the sleek lines of the vessel, which was larger and more luxurious than all but the very grandest of those she had been on before.

'I imagine that in our Caribbean colonies it is most useful to have such a magnificent vessel,' she said, more for the sake of conversation than anything.

'She comes with the post of Governor,' he responded. 'He is a most fortunate man, Sir Talavera.'

'No doubt he has worked hard to achieve his current eminence,' Thrift responded, 'and perhaps, in due time, you too might aspire to the post.'

'If I do,' he replied, laughing but with his voice tinged with passion, 'I doubt I will have beautiful girls of the Quality climbing into my car of an evening. Can you imagine how that felt for me, Miss Moncrieff? And when we danced I allowed myself to think you might have some affection for me.'

'You danced beautifully,' Thrift reassured him, 'and . . . and matters are not, perhaps, quite as they seem.'

'No?' he answered. 'They seem very plain to me. You flirted with me, and all the while –'

'Perhaps if you had sought to make an assignation?' Thrift broke in, determined not to let him delve too deeply into events at the reception.

'Would you have accepted?' he asked in open astonishment.

'If it was practical,' she admitted.

To her surprise his face contorted as if in physical pain and he clenched his hands in emotion before replying.

'And you tell me this now, when it is too late? I could scream!'

'The opportunity did not present itself before now,' Thrift pointed out, then broke off in a squeak of surprise as he came forward and took her in his arms.

'Would you?' he demanded. 'Now? There is still time.'

'Would I . . . I . . . ,' Thrift responded as he tried to kiss her. 'We can be seen from the yacht, Mr Monroe, and the shopkeeper is watching us!'

'You would then?' he asked. 'In among the cotton-woods?'

'Oh, for heaven's sake!' Thrift exclaimed. 'Really, Mr Monroe, you are most importunate. I cannot do what you ask for . . . for private reasons, but I will show you I am not so unkind as you seem to imagine.'

His response was a grin, all his anguish and nervousness gone on the instant as she took his hand and led him quickly in among the trees. The biggest of the cottonwoods was so thick around the trunk that it hid them completely from sight as without delay she peeled down his fly and took out his cock and balls. He sighed in pleasure, leaning back against the tree and looking down as she flopped him into her mouth, sucking with very real pleasure as she caressed the heavy, dark sack of his balls.

With his impressively large cock growing in her mouth it was impossible not to respond, and she let her hand stray to her own body as she sucked, caressing her bottom through her skirts and holding her breasts in turn, until in her rising excitement she was wishing she was out of her containment pants and could take him inside her. What she got was a stab of the needle, which activated as her cunt began to swell, although there was no serum left to pump into her body and spoil her pleasure.

She could feel the plugs in her vagina and anus too, tempting her to slip a hand between her legs and try to bring herself to ecstasy. Quickly she adjusted herself, burrowing her hand up underneath her skirts to find the smooth surface of the integument where it covered her quim, tracing every bulge and crevice of her flesh. She began to massage herself, now masturbating him into her mouth with her eyes lightly shut, revelling in the pleasure of sucking on a large, hard penis as she toyed with herself.

His breath was growing hoarse and she rubbed harder, determined to get there first so that she could have her moment of ecstasy with her mouth full of penis. It was going to work too, her clitoris sensitive beneath the integument, her pleasure rising as she thought of how naughty she was being, how utterly improper, sucking a man's cock more or less in public and masturbating as she did it.

That was enough. She felt her thighs and buttocks start to tighten and she was there, squirting fluid into her containment pants as she came in a long, tight orgasm, all the while jerking furiously at his erection in the hope of making him come in her mouth while she was still high.

He came, but not in her mouth. At the last moment he snatched his cock free, to jerk it over her face. Still in ecstasy, Thrift opened her mouth wide to take his sperm, only for the first eruption to jet high across her face, falling into her hair and leaving a long, sticky streak running down over one eye and one cheek. A second gout splashed out over her nose, a third across her chin and the other cheek, before he had popped himself back in her mouth to have her suck him clean.

She took it all, revelling in having her face soiled and in swallowing his seed even after she had started to come down from her orgasm. He even wiped his cock in her face, smearing his come over her skin and leaving her sticky and foul with it as she finally rocked back on her heels.

'Might I trouble you for a pocket handkerchief?' she enquired, giggling.

As she stood up she thought she caught a glimpse of movement near the track, and quickly took the offered handkerchief to wipe her face, thinking that the

Reynoldses had arrived. They hadn't, but as they walked back a black Austin Baron appeared around the corner of the track.

Thrift found herself smiling at her own naughty behaviour as she recognised the plump, dignified features of Hester Reynolds peering from the window of the car. She was in the back, with a female driver who held the door for her. Thrift curtsied politely.

'May I introduce Mr James Monroe, a Jamaican gentleman. Mrs Reynolds, Mr Monroe. Mr Monroe, Mrs Reynolds.'

Mrs Reynolds gave the briefest and stiffest of curtsies to Mr Monroe as he bowed.

'You must excuse my appearance, Mrs Reynolds,' Thrift continued, already deeply embarrassed. 'I was attending a reception in Baton Rouge and have been unable to change.'

Instead of the expected disdainful sniff, or the possibility of Thrift being taken straight across the knee, Mrs Reynolds answered with at least limited sympathy.

'How unfortunate, and yet such events must be common in the life of a wanton, I would suppose?'

'Hardly that, Mrs Reynolds,' Thrift replied, blushing furiously for the presence of James Monroe despite what they had just done. 'It was simply that events became . . . somewhat confused.'

'I do not wish to know,' Mrs Reynolds replied. 'One can only hope that you are thoroughly ashamed of yourself, both for your behaviour and your treatment of poor Miss Dace. She is an admirable woman, and has done much to set you on the path of righteousness, and this is how you repay her?'

'I will be given proper and just discipline in due course,' Thrift said, hanging her head meekly and praying Mrs Reynolds wasn't about to take the matter into her own hands.

'"Do nothing private in the presence of a stranger",

147

so saith the Lord,' Mrs Reynolds quoted, somewhat cryptically.

Thrift merely hung her head lower, hoping that a show of self-reproach would deflect the spanking she was sure Mrs Reynolds wanted to give her, and only surprised that it hadn't already been done. Mrs Reynolds was already moving back to the car, and Thrift made a brief and formal goodbye to James Monroe and followed. Only as she settled herself into the seat did she remember Hester Reynolds' objection to her being punished in front of Captain Langhorne, too late, as the car had barely begun to move before she had been hauled across Mr Reynolds' knee.

Both her frantic wriggling and her squealing protests were ignored as her skirts and petticoats were bundled up onto her back, her drawers unfastened and turned high, exposing her bare bottom where her cheeks stuck out from her open containment pants. The car was still gathering speed as Mrs Reynolds began to spank, admonishing Thrift for her treatment of Miss Dace as smack after smack after smack was laid across the quivering, bouncing bottom cheeks, and not stopping until she had begun to lose her breath.

'That will serve for the moment,' Mrs Reynolds stated as she fastened Thrift's drawers. 'Get up, and you may thank me.'

'Thank you, Mrs Reynolds,' Thrift managed, pouting.

As she attempted to rearrange herself Thrift saw that they were still passing between rows of cottonwoods and other native trees, with huge, open cotton fields to either side and the only sign of human habitation the sharp-pointed steeple of a small white-painted church rising above a distant wood.

'You will come to church this evening,' Mrs Reynolds said, more a statement than a question.

'I would be delighted, naturally, Mrs Reynolds,'

Thrift answered, still trying to compose herself, 'but as you see, I am not dressed appropriately.'

'You will do very well as you are,' Mrs Reynolds answered, to Thrift's surprise.

Thrift went quiet, staring out of the window as she once more began to worry about her situation. Evidently there was some turmoil in Baton Rouge, and she was very glad indeed to be safely away, which made her feel rather better about her spanking, a sore bottom being a great improvement on being lynched by vengeful Gaulistes.

They soon passed the church, a structure of no great size built of wood, set at the exact centre of a graveyard full of white crosses and surrounded by a white picket fence. There was a house beyond it, in the same style and also with a plain cross above the door, presumably the vicarage, although the bronze statue of a man in religious vestments holding aloft a snake seemed an eccentric choice for a priest.

A little way further on they began to pass houses, each set on its own in a neatly laid-out garden, only to turn in at a pair of ancient and impressively large gates before they reached anything resembling a village. Signs to either side announced the property as the Reynolds plantation, which proved to have a drive longer even than the one to her uncle's house in Scotland, ending at a white-painted mansion that was clearly the family house.

Thrift climbed from the car, waiting until Mrs Reynolds was ready before carrying on toward the house. The driver also got out, curtsying to Mrs Reynolds before she shut the door.

'I have certain matters to attend to, Miss Moncrieff, so I am leaving you in the charge of Miss Rolster until the lunch hour. Rolster, see to it that Miss Moncrieff is comfortable, but on no account are you to leave her side. If she misbehaves, spank her.'

* * *

149

Thrift stifled a yawn as she adjusted the neckline of her gown in the mirror. It had been a long, dull day, made all the more tedious by her constant apprehension about what might be happening in Baton Rouge. Nobody but Miss Rolster and herself seemed to be in the house, which had an oddly empty feeling, full of silence and dusty sunlight, with scanty furniture or adornment for people of obvious wealth.

Miss Rolster had provided very little in the way of company, responding to Thrift's attempts at conversation with curt answers at best and more usually with disapproving clucks. The lunch of baked catfish and bread had also been uninspiring, and by mid-afternoon Thrift had been so bored she'd even considered goading Miss Rolster into dishing out a spanking in order to break the monotony. In the end, the presence of a heavy wooden paddle on the wall of the room she'd been given prevented her trying, and she was very glad indeed when a gong rang somewhere in the lower house and Miss Rolster announced that dinner was about to be served.

Having made her appearance as suitable as was possible in the circumstances, she went downstairs. The meal was more appetising than lunch, a dish of chicken and spiced sausages Thrift had sampled on the *Sir Mark Twain*, but washed down exclusively with water. Both the Reynoldses were there, but their conversation revolved entirely around the estate, agriculture, local gossip and the church service that evening, which to judge by their wholehearted enthusiasm seemed to be a highlight in their lives.

'We must ready ourselves for church, Miss Moncrieff,' Mrs Reynolds announced just as Thrift was hoping there would be something for dessert.

'I am ready, thank you, Mrs Reynolds,' Thrift responded, 'if you are really quite sure I will be acceptable as I am? I thought, perhaps, a darker dress, which I would be quite prepared to borrow from one of the servants.'

'You must come as you are,' Mrs Reynolds assured her, 'as is appropriate for you.'

Thrift forced a smile, less than convinced and somewhat apprehensive about the implication of what Mrs Reynolds had said. Nevertheless, there was nothing to be done but wait patiently in the hall until the couple came back downstairs, both now so heavily clad in stiff black clothing that only their faces showed, while the only colour on either of them was the gold of the crosses on their bibles.

Dusk was gathering as they climbed into the car. Miss Rolster was driving as before, but she was also clad in unrelieved black, as were the scattering of people they passed on the way. They stopped shortly before reaching the church, parking outside the vicarage, to which Thrift was led. The door opened even as they approached, to reveal a tall, spare man with a great hook nose and large protuberant eyes beneath a bald, shiny dome. He was also in black, save for the white ecclesiastical collar. Thrift curtsied automatically, but to her surprise, instead of greeting her as she had been expecting, he reached out to place his open palm on her forehead, closing his eyes as he did so.

'I feel your sin, Thrift, my child,' he declared, 'and the Lord willing it shall be cast out!'

'Thank you, Reverend,' Thrift managed, blushing, 'but I fear you have the advantage of me.'

'I am the Reverend Leviticus Green,' he announced, 'and the man Reuben has brought your tale to me. Come then, for "an idler is like a lump of dung", so saith the Lord.'

'So saith the Lord,' both the Reynolds and Miss Rolster echoed.

'Ecclesiasticus: 22,2,' Mrs Reynolds said to Thrift in a smug whisper.

151

Thrift found herself casting a somewhat worried look at the back of the Reverend Green as he strode off down the path to the church with the others trooping behind. A good many other people had already arrived and were standing outside the little church, where a lantern held off the gathering dusk, some alone or in couples, rather more in little knots, but all of them looking at Thrift and most of them passing whispered remarks.

She hung her head, more in embarrassment than in shame, and followed the priest into the Church. The interior was as plain as the outside, with tall windows set in high, white-painted walls and a double row of pews facing a lectern on which the biggest bible she had ever seen stood open. Behind the lectern was an equally plain altar and a large font, but the north transept was unusual in being hidden by a high wooden screen, presumably to create a separate chapel.

Seating was evidently by precedence, with the Reynoldses occupying the place of honour at the very front. Thrift made to join them, knowing full well that wanton or not there was nobody present who even came close to her rank, but the Reverend Green paused at the head of the nave and took a firm grip on her elbow, steering her to the single step that rose to the chancel.

'Kneel here, my child,' he instructed. 'No, no, facing the congregation.'

Thrift did as she was told, feeling intensely self-conscious as she got to her knees. The church was quickly filling up, each and every newcomer looking at her as they arrived, faces full of curiosity and self-righteous satisfaction. Unable to meet their gaze, she hung her head and folded her hands into her lap. Evidently she was in some way the focus of the service, with which she was not at all happy, especially when the Reverend Green came to the lectern so that she seemed to be kneeling more or less at his feet. When he spoke it was in a great booming voice, full of confidence and piety,

'Praise be to the Lord, for a sinner has come among us and is willing to be cleansed!'

'Praise be to the Lord!' the congregation chorused as one.

'She is a wanton and a temptress,' Reverend Green continued. 'See how she is clad in harlot's weeds. And yet she knows her sin and is willing to repent. See how she kneels in fear of the Lord. Praise be to the Lord!'

Again his words were echoed, this time with a few loud 'Hallelujah's thrown in.

'"The fear of the Lord gladdens the heart", so saith the Lord,' Reverend Green called out, louder still, drawing an even more enthusiastic chorus from the congregation.

Thrift closed her eyes, trying very hard to think of anything except her already agonising embarrassment. As the Reverend Green continued to call out biblical quotes her sole consolation was that it could get no worse, or so she thought until he abruptly changed tack.

'Who will bear witness to the harlot's sins?' he called, now almost shouting.

'I, Reuben Reynolds. I bear witness to her sins,' Mr Reynolds called out. 'She is a wanton and a harlot, yea, the very whore of Babylon, for she tempted me with the abundance of her flesh and knows not the way of the Lord. Worthless is she, for "a woman of the streets counts as mere spittle. Ecclesiasticus: 26,22," so saith the Lord.'

He sat down abruptly, apparently out of breath, but his wife immediately rose to her feet and Thrift's face grew hotter still.

'I, Hester Reynolds, bear witness to her sins,' Mrs Reynolds intoned, her voice loud but solemn, and absolutely clear. 'She is indeed a harlot, for even under goodly chastisement she did not grow contrite of her sins but revelled in them, undergoing a great convulsion of the body as the evil spirit within her laughed at our justice.'

The moment she had finished another leapt to his feet, Seth from the store at the river landing, his words all too clear despite his drawling colonial accent.

'I bear witness too, Reverend, that I saw her go down in among the cottonwoods, and I saw her come out! With a black man, she was, a big Jamaican buck, and what she done I don't like to say, save that she needed his handkerchief to wipe it off her face after he was done, and she hadn't been eating no corn cob, but he was near as big as one . . .'

'Thank you, Seth, thank you,' Reverend Green interrupted, and gestured to Miss Rolster, who was already on her feet.

'I, Ruth Rolster, I bear witness too,' she declared, 'that she went in the trees with that big Jamaican buck and that she don't mind her sit-upon smacked all that much neither. Hallelujah!'

'Hallelujah, sister,' the Reverend Green responded, then looked down to where Thrift was cringing on the floor at his feet.

'Do you confess to these, your undoubted sins, child?' he demanded.

Thrift managed a single, miserable nod.

'Speak loud that the Lord may hear you!' he boomed.

'I confess,' Thrift managed, still weakly, but loud enough to be heard, which sent the congregation into a frenzy of 'Hallelujah's, clapping and thumping their bibles on the pews until at last the Reverend Green raised his arms for silence.

'She has confessed, brothers and sisters, and in confession there is redemption, for "if we say we have no sin, we deceive ourselves and refuse to accept the truth. But if we confess our sins to him, he is faithful and just to forgive us and to cleanse us from every wrong," so saith the Lord. The spirit of the Lilith has entered into her, the spirit of the harlot, but the Lord willing I shall cast out that spirit and in turn she shall take up the spirit of our Lord and she shall be our sister. Hallelujah!'

Another enthusiastic chorus greeted his words. Thrift hid a heavy sigh, wondering if she was going to have her head immersed in the font, as she had once seen done to a wanton girl in Scotland, or something worse.

'We will now sing hymn one hundred and fifty-seven,' the Reverend Green intoned, '"The Heathen are less than the Dust beneath his Chariot Wheels".'

As they began to sing Thrift risked a glance at the congregation. All of them seemed to be having a thoroughly good time, and taking more pleasure in the service than she had seen anyone from the middle territories do under any circumstances. The women seemed particularly happy, excited even, their faces flushed and their voices loud and high. When the hymn had finished they looked expectant, notably more so than the men, one or two of whom had even begun to look a bit fed up.

The Reverend Green stepped down from the lectern, walking around to face Thrift, looking down on her with his bible clasped in his hands and a righteous expression on his face as he spoke.

'"My daughter, if you aspire to be a servant of the Lord, prepare yourself for testing," so saith the Lord! Ecclesiasticus: 1,2.'

'I ... what sort of test did you have in mind, Reverend?' Thrift asked.

'Silence!' he thundered, then went on more mildly. 'Come, my child, we must rid you of the succubus that infests your body.'

He held out a hand and Thrift took it gingerly, allowing him to raise her to her feet. Once again he stepped up to the chancel, still holding Thrift's hand as he addressed the audience.

'"Do not let your eye linger on a woman's figure," so saith the Lord,' he stated. 'What must be done will be done in the Lady Chapel. Pray, my brothers, for this poor child's soul.'

The men stood back in the pews, allowing the women to troop out behind Thrift and the Reverend Green with Hester Reynolds at their head. The men in the congregation attempted to look pious rather than regretful as Thrift was led to the screen barring off the northern transept, clearly the Lady Chapel, which she entered with mounting nervousness, and as she saw the interior her worst fears were confirmed.

As in the main body of the church there were pews, but they faced not an altar but a great, dark whipping frame, the wood stained by what she could only suppose was the sweat of its victims around a number of heavy leather cuffs. It was bolted to the wall, where hung a knotted scourge the sight of which set her stomach churning, and her bladder too, so she knew that without her catheter she would have wet her pants. There were also a number of chests on the floor, while a recess in another wall held a peculiar box, made of old, dark wood and quite plain save for a pattern of small rounded holes, but fastened with a heavy catch.

'Rejoice!' the Reverend Green declared. 'For I shall scourge the devils from your body, and you shall be clean once more.'

'Um ...,' Thrift managed, holding back as she sought desperately for an excuse not to be whipped, only for the last person she'd have expected to come to her rescue.

'Sadly, Reverend,' Hester Reynolds stated, 'I fear the scourge will do no good in this case, as we learnt when she was punished on the river. Her possession is too strong.'

'Much too strong,' Thrift agreed earnestly, 'much, much too strong.'

Reverend Green gave a single, solemn nod, then spoke again.

'Very well, Sister Hester. Prepare her for cleansing with holy water.'

Thrift relaxed a little, the prospect of having her head dunked far easier to accept than the vicious whip, which she knew would cut her skin and quite possibly scar her. Even when the women clustering around her began to work on the fastenings of her clothes she grew only gradually more worried, and then only because the Reverend Green had stayed in the Lady Chapel, and was watching her with his gooseberry eyes as she was undressed. With her top clothes off and Miss Rolster working on her corset laces she finally found her voice.

'Er . . . Mrs Reynolds, if I am to be undressed, is it not improper for the good Reverend to watch? "Do not let your eye linger on a woman's figure," I think he said, after all.'

'Do not be foolish, child,' Mrs Reynolds replied. 'Reverend Green is a man of God and above such worldly temptation.'

The expression on the Reverend's face as Thrift's corset came loose and one fat breast lolled free of her chemise suggested otherwise. He looked as if he was about to burst. As her corset was removed her face had begun to go red and she was stammering with embarrassment, causing one of the women behind her to mutter something about her "speaking tongues", at which their activity grew more urgent.

In moments she'd been stripped down to her containment pants, and was frantically trying to cover her breasts and bottom with her hands, a hopeless task. The women peered at her with curiosity, especially at her containment pants, the Reverend Green with ill-concealed lust. There was no font, nor even a stoup, making her blushes hotter still as she imagined herself being dragged out into the chancel and having her head stuffed into the font there with her bare bottom stuck out towards the men in the pews.

Two of the women pulled out the largest of the chests into the centre of the floor, opening it to reveal a large enamelled tub, but Thrift's relief lasted only until she saw the thick leather straps at either side.

'Kneel in the tub, my dear,' Mrs Reynolds instructed, leading Thrift forward, 'and place your wrists in the straps.'

Pouting furiously, Thrift climbed into the tub and knelt down. She was doing her best not to make too rude a show of herself, but it proved to be impossible. As Mrs Reynolds and Miss Rolster fastened her wrists into the straps she found her breasts dangling in a way she'd always felt to be distinctly silly, and, far worse, her bottom stuck out to the audience with her cheeks wide and the open containment pants making it quite obvious that she had a plug in her anus.

'I perceive a difficulty,' the Reverend Green remarked, peering down at Thrift's open bottom cheeks as her blushes flared so hot she felt as if her skin was burning. 'The garment she wears to enforce her chastity plugs her fundament.'

'Why ... why should that matter?' Thrift asked, twisting her head back in sudden alarm as she pictured the Reverend Green sodomising her.

'So we may introduce the holy water, naturally,' Mrs Reynolds told her.

'Up my bottom!' Thrift demanded, all sense of decency lost in her rising panic. 'Couldn't I just drink it?'

'Certainly you must drink it,' Mrs Reynolds explained. 'Now do please be quiet, we are in the house of God!'

Thrift shut up, chewing on her lip, then gasping in shock as the gradual swelling of her cunt triggered the needles, which drove deep into her flesh. She was left gasping and shivering, but with no serum she remained fully sensitive, and very much aware of the plugs in her vagina and anus, also her rapidly stiffening nipples.

158

'Perhaps it might be pulled out?' Reverend Green was saying.

'Miss Rolster,' Mrs Reynolds ordered.

Thrift closed her eyes and hung her head, burning with shame as Miss Rolster ducked down behind her. She let her anus go loose, knowing it would only hurt otherwise, and bit her lip harder still as she felt the woman's hands dig into the back of her containment pants and start to pull. As she felt her anus spread she was wriggling her toes and sobbing with humiliation, then kicking her feet on the hard enamel of the tub and gasping for breath as the bulk of the plug emerged, only to squeeze straight back in up her gaping bottom hole the moment Miss Rolster let go. Thrift blew her breath out at the sudden buggering, and was shaking her head and panting with reaction as the plug once more pulled slowly free.

'I will have to hold it, Ma'am,' Miss Rolster stated.

'So be it,' the Reverend Green answered. 'Fetch the bags, sisters, and soon the sinner will be cleansed.'

Thrift kept her eyes closed, squatting miserably in the tub and snivelling as she pictured how her open bottom hole must look from behind and wishing she didn't want a large penis pushed up it quite so badly. For all her feelings her wantonness was coming out, as strong as ever, filling her head with dirty thoughts for all her bitter shame and the awful, creeping apprehension of what was about to be done to her.

She listened to the wet, rubbery noises as the enema bags were prepared, thinking all the while of how it felt to have her rectum fill with water until she could hold it no more and it exploded from her anus. Now there was no convenient facility to catch her waste, and no modesty gown to hide beneath, her bottom spread open in front of all the women and the lecherous, leering Reverend Green with his horrible pop-eyes and great bald dome.

A choking sob escaped her lips as she felt the nozzle touch her anus, but she relaxed by instinct, allowing her ring to open and take the rounded bulb designed to hold it in place up her bottom. It was big, stretching her out almost as much as the plug, so she knew her belly would fill right up before it blew out, and then when it did she would disgrace herself utterly and helplessly.

'Open wide, my dear,' Mrs Reynolds said from above Thrift, who looked up.

Mrs Reynolds was holding a horrible thing, composed of leather straps and brass buckles, designed like a dog's muzzle, only for a human head and with a hole where her mouth would go, through which a thick, red rubber tube protruded. For a moment she could only stare, but Mrs Reynolds spoke again.

'Do we have to make you put it on?'

Thrift quickly shook her head and opened her mouth, taking in the tube so deep it tickled her throat and made her gag before she could get comfortable. The straps were pulled tight around her head and buckled, muzzling her as effectively as any dog, and leaving her unable to speak. She looked up, pleading with her eyes as Mrs Reynolds attached the other end of the tube to a bloated enema bag of the same red rubber which another woman had attached to one of the cuffs on the whipping frame.

'Don't fret, my dear,' Mrs Reynold's assured her. 'You are to drink as best you can, but don't worry if a little comes out at the sides, or out of your nose, nor for what you will do behind. "There is no shame before the Lord our God," so saith the Lord.'

Thrift didn't believe it, biting on the tube in near-hysterical apprehension as a last few clips were fitted in place to make sure that none of the apparatus failed as she was filled with water. The two bags were close together, hanging fat and heavy from the cuffs, with perhaps a half-gallon in each. As the Reverend Green reached out to the first of the taps regulating the flow into Thrift's body she lost control, jerking in her straps and wriggling her body in a pathetic, futile effort to escape.

'Bear witness, sisters!' Reverend Green called out. 'Already the succubus writhes in fear of the Lord!'

An immediate chorus of 'Hallelujah' and 'Praise be' rang out, and the Reverend Green turned the taps. Thrift had forced herself to calm down, but her eyes popped as her mouth filled with cold water, forcing her to swallow as fast as she possibly could. A moment later she felt a touch of cold at her anus, then the slow, inexorable build-up of pressure had begun as the water flooded her rectum. In moments she was panting through her nose, so hard she was quickly blowing snot bubbles, while her gradually expanding belly had begun to pulse and her anus had gone into slow, rhythmic contractions on the intruding tube.

The audience cried out in delight as they saw the helpless reaction of her body, clapping and crying 'Hallelujah!' over and over, and ever louder as Thrift began to squirm in discomfort, her bottom wriggling and clenching, her breasts swinging back and her toes wriggling, and then her feet drumming on the floor of the tub as the sensations of her body grew unbearable once more.

Again she forced herself back from the edge of hysteria, looking up to plead with her eyes and shake her head in desperate remonstrance, staring wildly at the Reverend Green in the vain hope that he would turn the water off. He wasn't even looking at her face, but at her bottom and she gave in, hanging her head as she waited for the inevitable. Her belly felt huge and impossibly weighty, a fat, swollen ball beneath her, her stomach was gross and distended, while she could feel the water in her rectum pushing back on the plug in her anus. Again she looked up, begging with her eyes as her control began to slip away again. As she started to jerk in her straps and kick her feet once more he began to shout.

'Out! Out I say, foul succubus, leave this child that she may return to the bosom of the Lord! Out!'

With the final word Thrift's anus gave way. The plug shot out, exploding from her gaping hole on an arc of filthy water just as she pulled her back tight in a futile attempt to lessen the pain of her belly. The jet of dirty water missed the tub completely, spraying all over the floor in full, unrestricted view of her goggling audience, who had drawn close for a good look at her bottom as she gave in. At the same instant her bladder exploded, forcing her catheter out to leave piddle gushing into her containment pants and bubbling up over the rim and the hands of Miss Rolster, who let go with a squeal of disgust. Immediately the fat anal plug jammed against Thrift's open bottom hole, causing a second explosion of dirty water, all over her cheeks and thighs and the floor as well.

Thrift's entire body had gone into spasm, every muscle jerking and wrenching at once as she writhed helplessly in the tub, all the while spraying fluid out around her bottom to soil her body and everything around her, while the women watching went into a frenzied chanting and the Reverend Green screamed for the succubus to leave her body. Totally helpless and out of control, Thrift could barely think, save to gulp frantically at the water still flooding her mouth, and it was as this began to die away that she slowly regained her senses.

At last the water stopped, not because the taps had been turned off, but because their full contents had drained down Thrift's throat and up her bottom. It was still coming out too, bubbling from her anus, only to be cut off as the plug squeezed back into her protesting ring. Pee was still running from her cunt, and she was dizzy with reaction and a dozen powerful emotions, yet still blew her cheeks out in deep relief as the straining sensation in her belly gradually died down.

Behind her, the women had begun to clear up, tutting in disapproval over what she'd done, as if she'd had any choice. As the tube in her mouth was unclipped and pulled free, Thrift was praying her ordeal was over and trying to tell herself she would not be sneaking a climax over the memory as soon as she could manage it. Only when the woman who'd removed her tube failed to take the muzzle off or unstrap Thrift's wrists did she start to wonder if there was still more to come. Sure enough, the Reverend Green came round to her head, looking down at her as she lifted her gaze.

'You are cleansed, my child,' he stated. 'Rejoice in the Lord, for you are cleansed!'

'Hallelujah,' Thrift managed weakly, hoping it was the right thing to say.

'Hallelujah!' her entire audience chorused in response, even the woman who was wiping around her penetrated anus with a wet rag.

'You are cleansed indeed!' the Reverend Green sang out. 'Only the Test of Faith remains!'

'The Test of Faith!' the women shouted, more eager even than before.

'Do you have faith, my child?' the Reverend Green asked Thrift.

'I have faith, Reverend,' Thrift responded earnestly. 'I have been cleansed of the succubus and I have faith.'

'Glory be to the Lord our God!' Reverend Green yelled. 'She will take the test, and should she live she may return to the fold, a welcome sister, and more. "Verily I say unto you, there is more rejoicing in heaven over one sinner that repenteth, than over ninety and nine just persons that need no repentance," so saith the Lord!'

'So saith the Lord!' the women screamed, drowning out Thrift's voice as she raised a finger in a vain effort to attract the Reverend Green's attention.

'Er . . . how do you mean, "should she live," Reverend, if I may ask?'

He ignored her, raising his hands to the now frenzied women, who went abruptly quiet. Suddenly close to panic once more, Thrift craned around as he walked away, following him with her eyes as he went to the curious box she had noticed in the recess. First he bent to another, smaller chest, opening it to extract a curious glove, more like one of the gauntlets from the suits of armour in her uncle's castle. Pulling it on, he quickly unfastened the box and plunged his hand within, to pull out a writhing, wriggling, gap-jawed snake, brilliant green in colour and a good two yards long.

A soft, almost ecstatic sigh rose from the women at the sight of the reptile, but Thrift was writhing in her bonds and babbling entreaties, not quite sure what the Reverend Green intended to do with the snake, but certain that it was going to involve her and not be a pleasant experience.

'No . . . no, really, this is not at all necessary . . . ,' she urged, trying desperately to wriggle away as the angry snake was held out towards her. 'I have faith, I really do . . . I do! Reverend, no . . . this really is not sensible at all . . . Reverend! Mrs Reynolds, help! Somebody, please . . . no . . . no . . . you don't need to do this!'

'The Test of Faith must be made,' Mr Reynolds said solemnly, and thrust the creature's gaping maw directly at Thrift's bottom.

Thrift screamed and began to thrash in her bonds, expecting the stab of the serpent's fangs at any instant. Nothing happened, and she twisted violently around, straining her head back across her shoulder. The snake was visible, thrashing from side to side behind her like an insane tail, and attached to her bottom, sending her into panic-stricken convulsions again as she imagined the fangs sunk into her flesh and pumping venom. Scream after scream tore from her throat as she waggled her bottom in an absurd, hysterical effort to shake the reptile free, while the entire congregation stared enthralled and called out hallelujahs and prayers, clapping and stamping, ever louder.

Thrift felt she was going mad with fear, only to realise that the snake was not attached to her at all, but had sunk its fangs into the integument of her containment pants. Even then she was too full of horror to stop fighting, blinded with fright as the women suddenly stopped chanting to stare as Thrift's containment pants split wide, the plugs pulling from her anus and vagina, the thick integument wrapping itself around the snake and pulling free, dropping between Thrift's open thighs in a writhing ball of black and green.

Miss Rolster was the first woman to scream, Mrs Reynolds the first to run, both actions triggering the others, who hurled themselves from the lady chapel, falling over each other in their eagerness to get away, until Thrift found herself alone with the Reverend Green, who had stood his ground, with his gooseberry eyes fixed on the snake and Thrift's containment pants as they fought. At last the loser had been reduced to a limp black puddle, at which the snake started back for its box, satisfied in victory.

Thrift had gone limp with shock, her knees sliding slowly apart until they met the sides of the tub. Inside, she felt strangely calm as she watched the Reverend Green pick up the long green snake and tenderly return it to the box. There were still screams coming from the body of the church, also male shouts, and a moment later Reuben Reynolds and others appeared in the doorway of the lady chapel.

Far gone as she was, Thrift cringed in embarrassment as a dozen pairs of male eyes fixed on her naked, open bottom. The Reverend Green raised his hand, pointed at them and spoke.

'Out! Have you no shame? Sister Thrift is a wanton

no more, nor a harlot, but one among our number. Do not be concerned either, the creature was no devil, but merely the work of scientists. Now be gone, and take your womenfolk home that you may comfort them.'

The men retreated, mumbling apologies, although several managed sneaky looks at Thrift's naked body. As the last one left Thrift looked up at the Reverend Green, about to ask to be untied, only to find him staring at her with disturbing intensity. She recognised the symptoms and made to speak, hoping to appeal to his piety, but he was already lifting his robes, exposing a long, pale erection as the bang of the church door signalled the departure of the last of the congregation. Thrift drew a heavy sigh.

'Go on then,' she offered, 'as I suppose you're going to do it anyway. Just don't do it in me, please?'

'Would you have me commit the sin of Onan?' he demanded, taking hold of his cock as he came to squat over her.

'No ... it's just –,' Thrift began, and broke off with a gasp as the Reverend Green drove his cock into her body, only not up her vagina but her open, sloppy anus.

He was so deep that as he began to bugger her his balls were slapping on her vacant cunt, and Thrift knew she was going to come at once, whether she wanted to or not. His sinewy thighs were spread open across her bottom, smacking on her cheeks as he sodomised her with ever faster thrusts, his cock squelching in her hole and the fat, heavy sack of his scrotum smacking on her cunt to send jolt after rhythmic jolt to her already aching clitoris.

She closed her eyes, surrendering herself to her buggering, all sense of decency so completely stripped away that she was quickly gasping out her passion and deliberately pulling against her wrist straps to make them tighter. Her breasts had begun to swing and she let her body go a little lower, to make her nipples slither

166

and slide over the wet enamel of the tub. Little groans began to escape her lips, and pleas, a babble of obscene demands as his balls slapped ever faster on her cunt.

'Harder, please, Reverend, and faster . . . I love to be sodomised, Reverend, I really do, I love your cock up my naughty bottom . . . spank me too, Reverend, spank my naughty bottom while you sodomise me . . . spank me . . . spank me!'

'Harlot!' he hissed. 'You are no more clean than a dog!'

Thrift gave an anguished sob at his words, thinking he might stop. He didn't but began to spank her, slapping hard at her upturned bottom even as he drove his cock in and out of her slimy hole, now faster than ever, to make her scream as she revelled in being spanked and buggered at the same time, biting on her muzzle with her breasts slapping in the water beneath her, her bottom squirming against him, and then she was coming.

She screamed with all the force of her lungs as it hit her, her whole body going into violent contractions, fluid squirting from her pee hole to soak his balls and splash back over her swollen cunt. Again she screamed, and the Reverend Green was calling her a harlot and a wanton, a bitch and a whore, as he too came, jamming himself deep just as Thrift's orgasm began to fade and ejecting the full bulk of his come into her rectum.

Nine

As with so many of Thrift's acquaintances, once the Reverend Leviticus Green had reached his orgasm he became racked with guilt. In his case this involved going to the altar and tearing his garments in paroxysms of shame and self-deprecation, which gave Thrift time first to undo her wrist cuffs with her teeth, then to remove her muzzle and tidy herself up before getting dressed in comparative peace. Her containment pants she discarded, hiding what she couldn't help but think of as the corpse at the very bottom of the second biggest chest, which proved to contain nothing more alarming than an assortment of cleaning materials, some of which she put to good use.

It seemed impolite to disturb the Reverend Green while he was so obviously busy, so she contented herself with a polite curtsey in his general direction and left the church. Outside the Arkansas landscape had grown ghostly, the great open fields bathed in pale moonlight and the faintest of breezes shivering the cottonwoods and willows surrounding the church. The Reynoldses Austin Baron stood as it had been left, parked directly across the gate to the vicarage.

After a moment's hesitation she started towards the car, telling herself that if she was to be picked up at the plantation she had no option but to return with them. As she came close she caught the sound of sobbing, then

Mrs Reynolds' voice, calm and clear. Miss Rolster was apparently having hysterics, and Thrift paused, not wishing to intrude, only for Mrs Reynolds herself to climb from the car.

'There you are, you wicked girl,' the woman snapped at Thrift. 'I trust the good Reverend has admonished you?'

'Something of the sort,' Thrift admitted.

'So I should think,' Mrs Reynolds went on. 'Look at the state poor Miss Rolster is in, and all because you are incapable of containing your urges. I hope that you're thoroughly ashamed of yourself.'

Thrift hung her head, very sure that an objection to the outrageous accusation would lead to her being put back across Mrs Reynolds' knee in double quick time. Fortunately Miss Rolster began to wail and sob again, prompting Mrs Reynolds to climb back into the car, but only after darting an order at Thrift.

'Get into the car. I suppose I must look after you, and even if you are cleansed, which frankly I doubt, there is still your chastity to be taken into consideration.'

'Yes, Mrs Reynolds,' Thrift answered, again resisting temptation by not commenting on Mrs Reynolds' apparent lack of faith.

She climbed into the car, to find Reuben Reynolds in the driving seat and Miss Rolster looking distraught beside him. Neither paid Thrift any attention, nor Mrs Reynolds, save to make a suggestion to her husband.

'We must take poor Ruth home, Reuben, and tomorrow I shall have Jerbold drive to Nolan's in Dermott.'

Thrift sat silent, not wanting to get herself in further trouble, as they drove to the Reynolds mansion. She was sent to bed immediately, not only with her hands tied behind her back but with an elderly maid for company, but in any event she was too exhausted to do anything but collapse into a welcome sleep.

The following morning they left again immediately after breakfast, now with a man she vaguely recognised from the congregation at the wheel. For a long while they drove through the same monotonous landscape, and finally arrived at a village of no great size, evidently a local market town and centre for the agricultural industry.

As usual Thrift's now somewhat crumpled evening gown drew looks of disapprobation from every side as she climbed from the car outside what was evidently some kind of works, to judge by the noises from within and the smells of hot metal and grease. A discreet sign read 'Amos Nolan – Ironfounder', which merely left her puzzled as Mrs Reynolds rang a bell for attention and then held a whispered conversation with the bearded man who emerged, a conversation punctuated by frequent sidelong glances towards Thrift.

Noting the man's attention, Thrift gave a polite curtsey, but he returned a look of astonishment and continued to talk with Mrs Reynolds. At length an agreement was reached, Mrs Reynolds handed over a sum of money and returned to Thrift.

'This is hardly proprietous,' she stated, 'but needs must when mischief threatens and there is no proper facility for your requirements this side of Little Rock. Come.'

Thrift followed, still somewhat puzzled, but wondering if Mr Nolan held the agency for a supplier of containment pants. If so, it was not apparent from the interior of the works, which seemed to be a simple repair shop for agricultural equipment, and so primitive there was even an anvil in one corner, although the power for the furnace was supplied by a conventional Collins engine.

'Stand here,' Mrs Reynolds instructed, pointing to the exact centre of the somewhat dirty floor.

Thrift was left as she was while Mr Nolan quickly hustled his two assistants out of the building and locked the door. A nasty suspicion had begun to dawn on her as he collected various implements and pieces of metal from here and there, and when he pulled a large, battered padlock from among a box of odds and ends she could contain herself no longer.

'May I please ask your intention, Mrs Reynolds?' she enquired.

'What do you think?' she replied. 'I'm not risking you getting up to any of your nasty habits, not in my house. We're a respectable family. I'm putting you in an old-fashioned chastity belt, I am, until poor Miss Dace can come and collect you.'

Thrift opened her mouth to protest, then closed it again, knowing it was hopeless. Besides, Mr Nolan was ambling over towards them and the situation was embarrassing enough as it was.

'We are quite ready, Mr Nolan,' Mrs Reynolds stated.

'She'll have to take her clothes off,' Mr Nolan pointed out, scratching his head. 'I can't do nothing unless she takes her clothes off.'

Mrs Reynolds responded with a tut of irritation.

'Very well, I suppose there is no getting around it, but I'll not have any impropriety. Thrift, take your drawers off under your dress and lift your skirts.'

Thrift hid a sigh as she reached up under her petticoats to unfasten her drawers. It took quite a while to get them off, as the laces were trapped by her corset, and all the while Mr Nolan watched in curiosity, as if he had never seen a woman undress before. As she stepped out of the garment Thrift was getting increasingly flustered, but her moment of hesitation was met by a stern look from Mrs Reynolds.

She hauled up her skirts and petticoats as one, closing her eyes for shame as she exposed herself back and front, only to open them again, unable to quell her curiosity. Mr Nolan was looking at her, nodding, and had pulled an old and oily measure from the pocket of his overalls. Thrift bit her lip as he came close, his fingers brushing her flesh as he put the tape measure first around her waist where her hips began to swell out, then around the broadest part of her thighs and bottom.

As his fingers brushed her cheeks she began to tremble, and a gasp escaped her lips as he pushed his hand between her firmly closed thighs, catching the measure at the far side and taking a loose measurement from the swell of her belly to the small of her back, with the oily measure pulled against the slit of her quim and between her bottom cheeks.

Apparently satisfied, he returned to the forge, leaving Thrift shaking badly as she dropped her skirts. It seemed pointless to put her drawers back on and she bundled them in her hand, only to have Mrs Reynolds turn on her.

'Make yourself decent, you brazen hussy,' the woman snapped. 'Really!'

Thrift hastily put her drawers back on, once more thinking of smacked bottoms as Mrs Reynolds shook her head in disapproval. Mr Nolan had begun to work, hammering and bending metal into shape, constructing a crude iron cage to the approximate dimensions of Thrift's hips. It looked positively medieval, and very uncomfortable indeed, so much so that she was eventually forced to comment.

'I trust it will be padded in some way?' she asked.

'I suppose it must,' Mrs Reynolds snapped, 'although really, after the trouble you have put me to –'

'I am truly sorry,' Thrift cut in quickly. 'I do not mean to be a nuisance, but . . .'

'Well, you are,' said Mrs Reynolds sharply, 'a dreadful little nuisance, but I won't have it said I can't look after a charge. What might serve for padding, I wonder?'

'I've an old tractor seat I could cut up?' Mr Nolan suggested.

'That will never do,' Mrs Reynolds responded, her brow furrowed in irritation. 'I shall have Mrs Flaherty run up some drawers out of thick flannel.'

She gave an irritable tut as she finished and glanced at her watch, then spoke again.

'Are either of your daughters at home, Mr Nolan?'

'Mary's upstairs,' Mr Nolan confirmed.

'Then fetch her down, if you would. I need to call in at Munnings', and it's no place for a girl like this one. I'll drop in on Mrs Flaherty on the way.'

Mary was called, and with no further explanation Mrs Reynolds left the workshop. Thrift smiled and curtsied to the newcomer, a small, mousy woman whose eyes had gone round with astonishment at the sight of Thrift's gown. Realising that she had been mistaken for a prostitute, Thrift struggled for the right words to correct the error while her cheeks flared scarlet, only for Mr Nolan to speak first.

'You get back to your work, Mary. I can do well enough here.'

'But, father, Mrs Reynolds said –' Mary began, only to be cut off.

'I'm the master in this house,' Mr Nolan told her, 'so you just do as you're told.'

Mary curtsied, threw Thrift a last look and disappeared back upstairs. Mr Nolan gave a satisfied chuckle and turned to Thrift.

'Where'd they catch you then, my pretty?'

'I fear you are mistaken, sir,' Thrift began, realising that he too had no idea of the truth. 'I am –'

'I know what you are,' he broke in, 'and I know where you're going, so how's this for an offer? I've two keys to that padlock, and if you want the spare then you'll have to do johnson.'

'I am not acquainted with Mr Johnson,' Thrift responded cautiously, 'and what is it you wish me to do to him?'

'Mr Johnson?' Mr Nolan queried. 'Not Mr Johnson, girl, my johnson, my hodge, and I want you to suck him, that's what I want.'

'Your pego?' Thrift answered with an all too familiar sinking feeling. 'If I must, yes, but would you not give me the key purely in the spirit of generosity?'

'No,' Mr Nolan answered.

Thrift sighed and glanced down at the floor, which seemed to be soaked in oil.

'I have no wish to make my gown any worse than it is,' she said, 'nor to arouse Mrs Reynolds' suspicions.'

'No argument there,' he answered, twisting the key in the outside door, 'but I need to sit, at my age. I'll put some paper down, how's about that?'

Thrift gave a weak nod, telling herself that she would shut her eyes and pretend it was James Monroe or some equally attractive young man in her mouth and not the ageing and seedy mechanic who was now chuckling to himself as he put down newspaper in front of an old wooden stool.

'How about pulling those fine big bubbies out?' he suggested, seating himself with his legs well splayed as he began to work on the fastenings of his overall.

'If you insist on it,' Thrift responded, knowing that for the sake of the key she would go nude if he was sufficiently insistent.

'Oh, I do,' he assured her, shrugging the overalls from his shoulders. 'Now tell me, as you've had men right up and down the river, no doubt, how do I shape up?'

He had flopped his cock and balls over the lip of his open uniform and was holding them up for her inspection. Thrift looked down, trying to remember if she had ever seen an uglier penis, but more concerned to correct his impression of her.

'I am really not what you think, Mr Nolan,' she insisted, 'and although on this occasion it seems I have little alternative but to comply with your most ungen-

174

tlemanly request, I would like you to know that I am not in the habit of doing this, and that it is quite definitely not my trade. Nor, indeed, do I have any trade, which would be below my social rank, so you may consider yourself most fortunate to be receiving this service.'

As she spoke she indid her dress and tugged it down far enough to let herself push her breasts up out of her corset, and she realised that she should have waited until she'd finished her speech. Clearly he hadn't taken in a single word, as his eyes were fixed on her breasts and his mouth was a trifle open, a trickle of drool running from one side. He had begun to masturbate too, holding his crooked, scrawny cock between finger and thumb and pulling slowly up and down on it. Her tally stick was now plain plainly visible between her breasts, and he chuckled as he saw it.

'That one of them sticks to show how many beatings the Madam owes you, is it?' he drawled. 'Been a naughty girl, haven't you? What, run away did you? What was she going to give you, the paddle, a good strapping? Pay good money to see you strapped, a lot of folks would, me for one.'

Thrift made to correct him but thought better of it once more, contenting herself with a long sigh as she sank to her knees on the newspaper.

'So come on, what do you reckon?' he demanded, flourishing his cock at her face.

Thrift looked at his cock, now erect. He was long, but narrow and crooked, with thin skin pulled so tight on the shaft that his veins showed red beneath, while the swollen, purple helmet was not only grossly disproportionate but sported a fringe of tiny pimples where the meat curved down to the neck. To make matters worse, some of the oil from his hands had come off, leaving the long, ugly shaft covered in dirty black smears. Unable to compliment him without a lie, she did the best to hide her disgust as she answered.

'No doubt you are very proud of yourself, Mr Nolan.'

'I'll remember that, I will,' he chuckled, 'a regular dandy tart like yourself, and you say I should be proud of myself.'

'I am not . . . ,' Thrift began. 'Oh, never mind.'

She took a firm hold of his shaft and gulped him in, her eyes closed so that she didn't have to watch. He tasted of oil and unwashed cock, making her gag until she could swallow down enough spittle to get him clean. Even then the feel of him in her mouth was threatening to make her stomach come up, but still she sucked, masturbating him into her mouth as she made a cunt of her lips and licking on his fat helmet as if it were a lollipop.

Long, bony fingers reached down, taking her breasts in hand and pawing at them, to leave oily smears on her skin wherever he touched, but also bringing her nipples to erection. She began to pull faster on his cock, determined to bring him off quickly and swallow down what he made in her mouth, both to get it over with and because she could feel her inevitable wanton response starting to rise.

'No hurry, girl,' he grunted. 'She'll be a while, Mrs Reynolds. Now how about a fuck of those fat titties?'

'That was no part of our bargain,' Thrift managed, but his hands were already beneath her armpits, lifting her with surprising strength, and with a sigh of resignation she pushed her tally stick out of the way and folded her breasts around his cock.

Both were already dirty with oil, the smooth pink flesh streaked and blotched with black-brown smears, which began to mingle with her own spit as he pushed up and down in her cleavage. She closed her eyes again, trying to imagine giving the same lewd favour to James Monroe, but it was no good. She'd sucked cock for a common artisan, now she was having her breasts fucked by him, and soon he'd be going back in her mouth, to do his seed and make her swallow it, along with the oil she'd already taken down.

'I'll take those,' he grated suddenly, and had replaced Thrift's hands with his own, squashing her breasts to make her cleavage into a tighter cock slide. 'You rub yourself, if you've a mind. I know you tarts like to do that, and it'll be your last chance once I've put you in your cunt cage.'

Thrift shook her head, but it was a weak gesture. Just as he said, it might be her last chance to come for a very long time. He sighed and quickly adjusted himself, keeping a firm hold of her breasts but poking his cock at her mouth. Thrift took it in, eyes tight shut as she was groped, with the coarse material of his overalls rubbing on her nipples as he began to fuck her mouth.

'Go on,' he urged, 'I love to see a pretty little tart get her cunt off. Give it a good rub, why don't you? Get those fingers good and sticky ... stick one up your tushie if you want ...'

He was saying it for his own sake, pumping his cock in and out between Thrift's lips faster and faster as he did it, and yet it was still too much for her. Feeling thoroughly ashamed of herself, she quickly hauled her skirts up and set her knees well apart, baring her eager quim to her fingers. Her bottom hole still felt sore, but that didn't stop her tickling it gently and thinking of how the Reverend Green had buggered her before she got down to work her sex.

She had the rhythm immediately, her fingers rubbing in the wet, eager slit between her thighs as her head bobbed up and down on his penis. He'd realised immediately, his dirty chuckle sending a ripple of both shame and excitement through Thrift, and his voice was thick with arousal as he began to speak again.

'That's my girl ... that's my dirty little girl. I love a good whore, a really dirty whore, the sort who'll rub her cunt and get herself there while she sucks johnson.

You're that and more, ain't you? Stick your finger up, why don't you? And another up your tushie hole, right in, you dirty tart, while you suck down my spunk.'

He broke off with a grunt and came, full in Thrift's mouth, and so much of it that she couldn't swallow it all, her cheeks bulging briefly before she gave in to the inevitable and it exploded from her mouth and nose. Thick clots of sticky white filth spattered his balls and the upper slopes of her breasts. As he let go she put a hand to them, smearing his sperm over both fat globes as she masturbated, rubbing ever harder at her cunt as she revelled in her own dirty behaviour.

She'd sucked a common artisan's penis, let him fuck her breasts and, worse, much worse, let him order her to rub herself off, to touch her bottom hole, and all in front of him, to leave herself totally and utterly disgraced. At that thought her orgasm hit her, in wave after wave of ecstasy for her own wanton nature, dying only slowly to leave her gasping on the floor, her head hung low in shame but her fingers still working his oily come into one nipple.

The garment Mrs Flaherty had made for Thrift did not merely look like a nappy, to all intents and purposes it was a nappy. Composed of several layers of thick cream-coloured towelling, it hugged her hips and bottom exactly as a nappy would, even to the extent of having extra material sewn in between her thighs and immediately below her cheeks. Mrs Flaherty had erred on the generous side in any case, so that great puffs and bulges of material stuck out through the holes in her chastity belt. There was even a large safety pin to hold it up, prominently positioned at the front, although the iron lattice cage kept it firmly in place in any event.

Being put into it by Mrs Reynolds as Mr Nolan watched had been, if anything, more humiliating than going down on her knees for him, with her skirts held high to show herself off at back and front while the towelling was wrapped around her hips and pinned in place. Then had come the chastity belt, which featured twin hinges across the seat of her bottom and a catch at her waist so that with the padlock open it could either be swung open to allow her to use the convenient facility, or taken off completely. The result was that from the front both her nappy pin and padlock showed the condition she was in clearly to anyone who lifted her skirts, pushing out through the front split of her drawers, which were rather too small to hold everything in.

There were two consolations. Firstly, however ridiculous the nappy-like garment might look, the thick material prevented any chafing, although it also made her walk like a duck. Secondly, Mr Nolan had kept his bargain, and the spare key to her chastity belt was carefully secreted, tied in among the folds of her drawers, which was at least some consolation as she sat in the Reynoldses' drawing room on her hot bottom cheeks, wondering why it was that every woman she met seemed determined to get her bare and smacked.

Mrs Reynolds had done it as soon as they were home, citing the trouble Thrift had put her to, but clearly keen to make the best of her last opportunity to dish out some discipline. Thrift had therefore been taken into the drawing room, her chastity belt unfastened, her nappy removed and her bare bottom spanked across Mrs Reynolds' knee, while a maid continued to tidy the room and stifled her giggles at Thrift's normal spanking tantrum.

She had then been put back in her nappy and chastity belt, although, as Mrs Reynolds had remarked, it scarcely seemed worthwhile when Miss Dace was sure to apply yet another punishment the moment she arrived. Therefore, when Thrift heard the crunch of tyres on gravel her stomach began to flutter in apprehension, although she knew rationally that another spanking was the least of her worries.

'Come then, that will be your car,' Mrs Reynolds stated.

Thrift rose, following the older woman from the house to where what was obviously a hired cab stood on the carriage sweep. The driver opened the door and Thrift swallowed the lump in her throat, only to realise that the woman inside was not in Miss Dace's conservative black but in white set off with a rich blue in typical Louisiana style, and that it was not Miss Dace at all but Felicity Adams. She was also smiling, and greeted Thrift with a friendly if somewhat improprietous kiss before turning to Mrs Reynolds.

'Very good of you to help out, Mrs Reynolds, and please be sure that your loyalty will not go unappreciated. I'll be sure to put in a word to the Minister, and who knows, it might be worth keeping an eye on the papers after the King's birthday.'

'I have done no more than my duty, Miss Adams,' Mrs Reynolds simpered, bobbing curtsies at the same time, 'while Miss Moncrieff has been a most delightful guest and charmed everybody, including the Reverend Green when she attended church.'

'Splendid,' Miss Adams replied, 'but we must be getting on.'

'Of course,' Mrs Reynolds replied, curtsying once more. 'Oh, there was one little personal detail Miss Dace will need to take care of. Perhaps if you would be so kind as to give her this key?'

She passed across the key to Thrift's chastity belt, which Felicity Adams accepted before climbing back into the car. Thrift followed, taking her seat and letting her breath out as the car began to move off. The driver was a man, and neither woman spoke save to exchange pleasantries as they drove back to the Mississippi landing. A sleek, powerful motor cruiser was moored a little way out in the stream, evidently a Diplomatic Service craft, which Felicity Adams signalled as the car drove off.

'A personal problem?' she enquired with a trace of amusement in her voice.

'I . . . I lost my containment pants,' Thrift admitted, blushing. 'Mrs Reynolds put me in a chastity belt.'

'How very resourceful of her,' Miss Adams replied, 'but how on earth did you get rid of those over-fancy containment pants?'

'A snake killed them,' Thrift responded. 'It's all rather complicated.'

'A snake?' Miss Adams echoed. 'What . . . never mind, we'll save that story until later. For now, we need to put our thinking caps on and sort out this wretched business with the late Jean-Jacques Rougon. What did happen, by the way? Snivels says she came out to find you bending over his corpse. Old fellow couldn't handle you, I suppose?'

'Yes, he became over-excited,' Thrift admitted, 'and just died. Am I in terrible trouble?'

'Oh no,' Miss Adams assured her, 'although it's a damn shame that ass Ademar Mareschal had to walk in on you, or we might have had a chance to manage a decent cover-up. As it is we've had to tell the truth, except for you being Diplomatic, naturally.'

'Will there be charges?' Thrift queried.

'Good heavens, no. Hang on a minute.'

A boat was already putting out from the launch, and Felicity Adams walked quickly to the store, where Seth was roused from sleep and went inside with much bowing and scraping. Thrift watched, awestruck by the way Felicity Adams coped with people so easily and always seemed to get exactly what she wanted, with little thought for the conventions. More outrageous still, Miss Adams emerged from the shop carrying a squat bottle in one hand, and even displayed the label to Thrift.

'Sour mash,' she explained. 'Filthy stuff, but it helps you think, I find.'

Thrift nodded, glancing at the bottle, which had an elaborate label bearing the name 'Old Red Eye' in florid script. In Baton Rouge Thrift had regarded Miss Adams as a role-model, but as Tobias Kobo handed them into the boat her attitude had become worship.

They were no sooner on board and the boat stowed than the launch started up, a triple bank of big Collins Engines hurling the spray up behind them as she swung out into the Mississippi in a grand curve. Below deck, Miss Adams led Thrift to a wide lounge looking out over the stern of the launch, where Miss Dace was seated, as prim as ever, in pure black right down to the sling that supported one arm.

'Are you hurt, Miss Dace?' Thrift asked immediately, her genuine compassion only somewhat diluted by the fact that it was Miss Dace's spanking arm in the sling.

'A minor fracture only, thank you, Miss Moncrieff,' Miss Dace responded in an icy voice.

'The silly thing slipped on the stairs as she came to fetch me,' Miss Adams explained. 'Piece of luck, really, as all the men stopped to assist her and I managed to get to your rooms first and make the late Jean-Jacques look a bit more human.'

Thrift's mouth came open as she remembered the hideous expression on Mr Rougon's face and imagined touching the corpse, but Felicity Adams was plainly unconcerned, continuing blithely as the launch began to pick up speed in the open channel.

'Unfortunately, not everyone's willing to swallow the official line, least of all the Gaulistes, so we've a bit of a problem on our hands. Sort it out cleanly, and we'll all be mentioned on King Bertie's birthday. Foul it up and we'll be cleaning latrines in Alaska.'

She stopped to put the bottle she'd bought on the table, and from a cupboard took three small glasses which she filled with a rich red-brown liquid that made Thrift's nose wrinkle as she smelt it.

'Bottoms up, as they say in the navy, and not without good reason,' Miss Adams remarked, and swallowed the contents of her glass at a gulp.

The remark was lost on Thrift, but she saw that Miss Dace had gone slightly pink. Attempting to imitate Felicity Adams, Thrift swallowed her drink in one, only to end up in a coughing fit as the burning liquid seared her mouth and throat.

'Gets you like that at first,' Miss Adams observed, slapping Thrift on the back, 'but enough playing the fool. This is the position, Thrift, so let's see what you make of it. We knew Pierre Mareschal would drop Rougon's damn-fool idea, but what we didn't expect was for him to be such a firebrand. He's been preaching his message like a regular bible thumper, and dropping some heavy hints about British assassins along the way, for all that he knows damn well why Rougon kicked the bucket. It's working too, not that the Libertistes are impressed, but the frog-eaters in general are, and they're not too interested in the subtleties. We need to restore the equilibrium, but this time it's no good just giving the Libertistes a leg-up, because the problem is that the rest of them have begun to take notice.'

'Could we not discredit Mr Mareschal?' Thrift suggested.

'We have considered that, in detail,' Miss Dace put in.

'They'll be watching out for it, you see,' Miss Adams explained, refilling the glasses, 'and he wouldn't be so easy to deal with in any event. What we need is some way to calm the whole thing down, a distraction perhaps, or something to bring everybody together in a common cause, but as we're highly unlikely to be invaded by the Nicaraguans it's not easy to see what to do.'

'If we were to circulate a rumour that Mr Mareschal had worked hand in hand with the British to kill Mr

Rougon,' Thrift went on, 'might not the Creole population be disgusted with him?'

'Possibly,' Miss Adams admitted, 'but others might consider that it marked him as a strong leader. More to the point, though, it leaves us looking pretty damn sinister. Sorry, won't do.'

'Then might we not convert Mr Mareschal to the cause of Empire?' Thrift asked cautiously.

'Bribe the fellow?' Miss Adams responded. 'Perhaps. I'm not saying he's incorruptible, but he plays a remarkably straight bat, for a Frog. Besides, there's only so much we can offer, and even if we were to fix it so he became Governor I expect he'd still be bellyaching about French rule.'

'Blackmail? Bribery?' Miss Dace put in. 'I had not realised you had such an affinity for your work, Miss Moncrieff.'

'Then you should have read her file properly,' Miss Adams answered, 'and for goodness sake call her by her first name. There's only the three of us, damn it.'

'I would be most gratified if you would, Miss Dace,' Thrift said politely, 'and I would be honoured if I might return the compliment.'

'I hardly think, when you are under my discipline –' Miss Dace began, but Miss Adams interrupted.

'You'll be under my discipline in a minute, Snivels, bad arm or no bad arm. Now come along, you two, let's have no more nonsense. What in Hell's name are we going to do?'

'In the Chinese Empire,' Thrift remarked, 'if a noble grows too ambitious he is summoned to the Imperial Court, where his talents may be both directed and rewarded. Perhaps we might do something similar?'

For a moment there was silence, before Felicity Adams spoke again pensively.

'Now there's a thought. I bet he'd jump at the chance of being ambassador to France, but what about the chap who's in the job at the moment?'

'Lord St Paul,' Thrift supplied.

'That's the fellow. We can't just have him handed his gold watch and told to keep bees in Sussex, can we? I don't suppose even your uncle would have that kind of clout, Thrift?'

'Unfortunately not,' Thrift admitted.

'Perhaps he might be appointed as special emissary to study the Louisiana question?' Miss Dace suggested. 'In France.'

'Yes, but what if the bugger succeeded in talking the French government around?' Felicity responded, her language growing coarser with the Old Red Eye.

'We'd be cleaning latrines in Alaska,' Miss Dace admitted, for once showing a trace of humour.

'Mr Fanshaw gave us to understand that the French government is adamantly opposed to any such move,' Thrift volunteered, 'but might he not simply be awarded a suitable title and invited to take his case to London? Without his rhetoric, support here would hopefully fade.'

'Do you know, that might just work. The fellow's head is certainly swollen enough, so I bet he'd jump at a chance like that. We just need the offer to come direct from Whitehall, which can be arranged easily enough if Fanshaw backs us up, and I dare say a call to Daddy wouldn't do any harm, eh, Thrift?'

'Is your father in the Service?' Miss Dace enquired cautiously.

'My father is Sir Kincardine Moncrieff, Senior Assistant Secretary in the Foreign Office,' Thrift responded, and had the pleasure of seeing Miss Dace go ever so slightly paler than she already was.

Felicity filled their glasses, then put the bottle firmly down at the centre of the table and raised her own, swallowing the contents at a gulp.

'It would seem to be our best option,' Miss Dace said. 'We can only pray he accepts.'

'Pray be damned,' Felicity answered, causing Miss Dace to start in shock at the open blasphemy. 'I intend to make sure he accepts, but not by applying pressure to him, as more or less anything we could do is sure to make him suspicious and have the opposite effect to that intended. He's too wily and too tough for easy manipulation, but his son is a very different sort, as you know, even something of an embarrassment. Now they're pretty thoroughly debauched, these frog-eaters, and Pierre's no exception, but I bet even he would draw the line at young Ademar having an affair with the girl who he's doing his best to imply bumped off their late and revered leader.'

'You wish me to allow Ademar Mareschal to seduce me?' Thrift asked.

'You're our honey trap,' Felicity pointed out, 'and he's already as keen as mustard to bed you. Speaking of honey and mustard, order up some tucker, would you, Snivels, I'm famished.'

Miss Dace went to the telephone, leaving Felicity to reassure Thrift.

'Don't worry, old thing, you needn't go too far. In fact you mustn't, because what we need is to get him interested, and you know what men are like, one decent go at you and they bugger off with some other filly.'

'Felicity, really, I believe you are drunk,' Miss Dace objected from across the room.

'Not in the least,' Felicity answered her, 'well, no more than enough to oil the old synapses. That's the way, Thrift, give the fellow a taste, then play coy.'

'But does he not believe I murdered Mr Rougon?' Thrift objected, unwilling to defy Miss Adams but desperate for a way out.

'Oh no,' Felicity answered casually. 'He was there when the doctor pronounced the cause of death as a heart attack. If anything, I'd say it rather increased your glamour in his eyes.'

'I have ordered devilled kidneys and a dish of eggs, with toast,' Miss Dace stated as she sat down. 'How will we go about this?

'I will have Toby arrange a dinner party,' Felicity explained. 'Strictly for young bloods, nothing to do with politics, plenty of guests so that nobody will think twice about both Mareschal and Thrift being there. You'll have to go too, as Thrift's companion, naturally. Here's to success then. Bottoms up.'

She swallowed her shot of Old Red Eye, then spoke again as she dug in the pocket of her dress.

'Speaking of bottoms up, that reminds me. This is for you, Snivels. Old Mrs Reynolds has to put Thrift in an old-fashioned chastity belt, it seems.'

As she spoke she pushed the key over to Miss Dace, quite casually, and oblivious to Thrift's blushes and sulky pout.

Ten

Baton Rouge, Louisiana, March 2006

Thrift bit down her homesickness as she replaced the receiver on its cradle and tried to concentrate on her sense of satisfaction instead. The telephone conversation she had just completed with her father had been the final confirmation of the plan to render Pierre Mareschal ineffective, and would now allow her to bask in the full warmth of Felicity Adams' approval, which she found she wanted more than anything else in the world.

Pierre Mareschal was to be offered a post as advisor on Creole culture and relations in London, where he would be on a generous salary and able to indulge his personal convictions to the full. The only question that remained was whether he would accept the post. If he did, it seemed likely that, in order to prevent his influence in Louisiana being too heavily eroded, he would support the ineffectual Lucien Fargues as his successor, thus restoring the equilibrium between Gaulistes and Libertistes.

'Well?' Felicity Adams demanded as Thrift turned from the telephone. 'Did Fanshaw kick?'

'Not at all,' Thrift assured her. 'Everything is arranged. You are only required to call Mr Fanshaw when you feel the time is right and the post will be offered to Mr Mareschal immediately.'

'Excellent,' Felicity responded, smacking her hands together in satisfaction. 'Just as soon as you have young Ademar firmly on the hook we can go ahead. Speaking of which, shouldn't you be getting dressed? Come along, Snivels.'

'I shall attend to the matter directly,' Miss Dace promised, taking the last sip from her cup of tea.

'You do that,' Felicity advised, 'and remember, Thrift is to be immaculate.'

'What of my chastity belt, Miss Adams?' Thrift queried. 'It is somewhat awkward to sit in, and will spoil the line of my evening gown.'

'Not to worry,' Felicity assured her. 'You'll find a little present on your bed, from Claralinda's, which should serve very well.'

'Thank you, you are most kind,' Thrift responded, brightening at the prospect of a new Claralinda's dress.

Felicity responded with a dismissive gesture and Thrift followed Miss Dace towards the stairs. Her accommodation at the Diplomatic Service building was far less grand than that at the Governor's residence, but still very comfortable, a small suite of rooms usually reserved for the more senior visitors, but which enabled Miss Dace to stay with her.

As Felicity had promised, a new dress had been laid out on her bed, an elaborate evening gown with puffed sleeves, in pure white save for numerous ribbons, bows and silk flowers in a particularly rich crimson. It also had a built-in whalebone bustle made fuller still by a cluster of silk roses blossoming from directly below her waistline and hanging almost to the level of her knees.

'It's beautiful!' she exclaimed. 'How very generous of Miss Adams.'

'It will be on expenses,' Miss Dace pointed out. 'Now come along.'

'Yes, Miss Dace,' Thrift responded, and stood straight to allow her dress to be undone. 'I must wear

189

my Claralinda corset, naturally, as I don't suppose either my Scotian Restrictive or my Cantlemere and Lucas will go on over my chastity belt.'

'How very convenient,' Miss Dace responded, 'but don't worry, I'll have you back in a proper pair of pants just as soon as we have a spare moment.'

Thrift's dress had come undone, allowing her to step out of it, but rather than start on the corset beneath, Miss Dace lifted the tally stick from where it hung between Thrift's breasts.

'Let me see,' she remarked. 'Three for your routine, and I think another three for the inconvenience you have caused me, to be awarded when my arm is fully better.'

'Yes, Miss Dace,' Thrift answered meekly, knowing better than to argue.

She waited patiently as six more notches were cut into her tally stick, bringing the total to fourteen, but it was impossible not to grimace at the prospect of having her bottom attended to so vigorously.

'You may do without it for the evening,' Miss Dace stated, putting the tally stick down on Thrift's bedside table, 'in case Mr Mareschal becomes exceptionally amorous.'

Thrift made a face but said nothing and Miss Dace continued to undress her. Soon she was down to her nappy, and allowed to put on her rubber modesty gown before that too was removed. The bath was soon ready, and she climbed in, reaching for the soap only to have Miss Dace raise a warning finger.

'We'll have none of that,' she warned. 'I know you.'

Not wanting yet another notch on her tally stick, Thrift put the soap back in its dish. Miss Dace quickly removed her own dress and took the bar herself, leaning in over the bath as she began to work up a lather between her hands. Thrift closed her eyes, once more wishing that Miss Dace would either leave her alone or

190

make a proper job of it, perhaps washing her and then stripping off to climb in, or merely sticking her bare bottom over the edge of the bath to be licked from behind.

She knew it wouldn't happen but, as Miss Dace began to rub the soap in, it was impossible not to think about it, and to wonder why not. It was also impossible not to grow aroused, especially when Miss Dace's hand began to go up under Thrift's modesty gown, pushing it up as her thighs and belly were soaped. The gown was lifted over her breasts as Miss Dace's long supple fingers began to massage soap in over the fat, sensitive globes. Thrift was struggling to hold back her reaction and wondering if just for once Miss Dace might give in and enjoy her.

'Legs apart,' Miss Dace ordered.

Thrift obeyed eagerly, and was forced to bite her lip as the soap bar pressed against her sex, rubbing in among the folds of her slit and bumping on her clitoris. To all intents and purposes she was being masturbated, and the urge to roll her thighs higher, take her big, soapy breasts in her hands and give in to ecstasy was close to overwhelming. One word of encouragement from Miss Dace and Thrift would have done it, but the word never came, only a command.

'Roll over.'

Still hoping, Thrift obeyed, turning over onto her front with a splash. Miss Dace immediately began to soap Thrift's neck, every touch of her fingers on the sensitive skin provoking a little ecstatic shiver. Having her back and legs done was little better, but as Miss Dace's hand moved to Thrift's bottom she could simply no longer hold back, sticking it up out of the water to make her cheeks part and offer herself for a warming spanking and attention to her quim.

'Do not be lewd, Thrift,' Miss Dace remarked, but her hands had gone to Thrift's cheeks, rubbing in the soap.

191

Again Thrift bit her lip, trying desperately to tell herself that Miss Dace really was just soaping her bottom for no reason other than personal hygiene, as the bar was rubbed in gentle circles over and between her cheeks. When Miss Dace's finger touched her anus it was more than Thrift could do to hold back a whimper, and another as the slim digit probed inside, cleaning her hole to leave it stinging and a little open.

'I warned you once, Thrift,' Miss Dace said calmly as she slopped water between Thrift's cheeks to rinse the soap away. 'That will be one more on your tally stick.'

'I can't help it, Miss Dace,' Thrift said miserably, 'and . . . and I think you do it on purpose!'

'Are you saying that I am a wanton?' Miss Dace asked.

'No,' Thrift lied, 'just cruel.'

'I assure you that I am concerned purely for your welfare,' Miss Dace replied, 'and after all, cleanliness is next to godliness.'

As she spoke she tickled Thrift's anus with a finger-nail, and finished with a firm smack to each wet bottom cheek. Thrift could think of nothing to say, as bewildered as she was aroused. Miss Dace gave no further explanation either, but began to work on Thrift's hair.

Thrift was kept face down as her hair was washed, rinsed under the shower hose, shampooed, rinsed again, conditioned and rinsed yet again, which meant that her face was repeatedly pushed under the soapy water and held under until the job was done. Her bottom was also smacked occasionally, leaving her with a warm glow that made her helpless arousal worse still, which the repeated dunkings did nothing to abate.

'Last rinse,' Miss Dace announced as she pulled Thrift's head up from under the water once more. 'Sit up.'

Gasping for breath and spluttering soapy water, Thrift obeyed as best she could with her eyes tightly closed, glad it was over, only to go into a fresh bout of gasping and spluttering as she discovered that Miss Dace had turned the shower to cold. Her hair was thoroughly rinsed, also her face, back and chest, leaving her shivering and with both nipples painfully stiff, but at least able to open her eyes.

'Stand up,' Miss Dace ordered.

'Am I finished?' Thrift asked.

'Almost,' Miss Dace answered, and picked up a large, long-handled wooden scrubbing brush from a rack.

Thrift gave an involuntary wince as she saw how good a spanking implement the brush would make, but Miss Dace was at least holding it the right way around. Five minutes later, after having her entire body vigorously scrubbed, she was wishing she had been spanked with it, only to change her mind as Miss Dace applied two hard swats, one to each cheek of Thrift's now bright-pink bottom.

'What a fine brush,' Miss Dace remarked. 'Out you get then.'

As she climbed out, Thrift's lower lip was thrust out in a sulky pout, and it took all her efforts not to make a further comment about Miss Dace's behaviour. She was pink all over and her skin stung, while her quim felt puffy and ready for cock, not the condition she'd hoped to be in for dinner with Ademar Mareschal.

She was wrapped in a towel so big it enveloped her entire body and her modesty gown was pulled off over her head. Miss Dace began to dry her, again paying special attention to Thrift's breasts, bottom and sex, until by the time she was dry she was praying to be able to sneak a rub of her quim before she was put back in her chastity belt.

'Hands behind your back, Thrift,' Miss Dace spoke as if reading her thoughts. 'Don't think I don't know what's going through that dirty little mind of yours.'

'Sorry, Miss Dace,' Thrift answered, hanging her head as she crossed her hands behind her back.

The cord specially purchased for tying Thrift's wrists was quickly applied, leaving her helpless as Miss Dace went to fetch the cotton modesty gown. It was draped over Thrift's head, covering her but doing very little to reduce her sense of exposure and nothing to calm her arousal. In the bedroom a fresh nappy of the same sort made for her in Arkansas had been laid out on the bed, open, just as if a baby were about to be put into it, only on a larger scale.

'Climb on to the bed with your bottom in the nappy,' Miss Dace instructed, her voice perhaps showing the very faintest trace of amusement at the humiliation she was about to inflict.

Thrift sat down in the open nappy, enjoying the feel of the soft towelling on her bottom despite herself. Lying carefully down with her bound hands a little to one side, she waited as Miss Dace carefully cut another three notches into the tally stick, not daring to question the total.

'Come along, legs up,' Miss Dace instructed, only to walk back into the bathroom the moment Thrift had brought her knees up and let her thighs apart.

She stayed in position, acutely aware of her vulnerable quim and torn between the desire to close her legs and to be mounted for the stiff fucking she so badly needed. Miss Dace took her time, but eventually emerged with a tub of powder, which she shook over Thrift's prone body, paying special attention to under her breasts, between her bottom cheeks and in among the folds of her quim.

With Thrift's cunt and anus powdered and dry, her nappy was folded up between her thighs and around her hips, then pinned into place, adding a fresh flush of humiliation for her absurd babyish look. Nor was Miss Dace done, making Thrift hold up her modesty gown behind her back as she was put in her chastity belt and the padlock closed. Her modesty gown was pulled off

194

and she was left briefly topless in her nappy before her hands were at last untied, her hair wound into a towel and her drawers and chemise put on.

Thrift's hair was done while she was seated on the bed, dried and brushed and styled and jewelled, until at last she began to resemble less a bedraggled urchin and more a young lady of the Quality. The image grew stronger as she was put into her corset, her petticoats and underdress, and finally the beautiful Claralinda gown, which, as promised, completely concealed her chastity belt. Stockings, gloves, shoes, a fur and a bonnet completed her attire and she at last looked as she felt she should, although the Louisiana-style gown added a certain something she found both embarrassing and exciting.

Dressed and ready for dinner, she was at last able to calm down a little from the state of arousal she had been brought to in the bath, although she remained both resentful and curious as she was escorted downstairs and Miss Dace returned to complete her own preparation. Possibly, Thrift considered, it had been done in order to make her ripe for the plucking and so ensure success with Ademar Mareschal. It seemed likely, although it was clear that Miss Dace enjoyed being cruel for the sake of it, making Thrift wonder if her companion was not at that moment stretched out on her bed with her fingers busy between her thighs.

Within half an hour Miss Dace had come back downstairs, now in her modest black evening gown and suitable accessories. Tobias Kobo had also arrived, handsome in immaculate black tie, to announce that a car was waiting. The dinner proved to be in an upstairs room above a restaurant in the most fashionable part of Baton Rouge, with a fine view across the Mississippi from a broad balcony that encircled the building.

Thrift quickly found herself slipping into the familiar routine of introductions and polite conversation, although some of the customs were less precise than in London and perhaps not entirely suitable for the Quality. There was at least a seating plan, with neatly written cards at each place, although Tobias Kobo had stretched the rules of precedent somewhat, with Thrift seated to his right as was proper, but with Ademar Mareschal beside her in preference to at least two of the other men present.

No comment was made, and with grace said Thrift sat down, a little stiffly in her chastity belt but otherwise comfortable. As referring to the events surrounding the death of Jean-Jacques Rougon would have been the height of bad manners, she had little to fear in the way of awkward questions, but nevertheless found herself extremely uneasy as Ademar Mareschal lowered his bulk into the chair beside hers. He immediately turned her a somewhat oleaginous smile, his eyes flickering to the swell of her chest as he bowed his head.

'Are you enjoying your visit to Louisiana, Miss Moncrieff?' he enquired, and then made a sudden, fussy gesture with one hand. 'No, no, here we are French, and as, were I to visit England, you would no doubt expect me to follow your customs, here I must ask that you follow ours. Are you enjoying your visit to Louisiana, Miss Thrift?'

Despite colouring slightly at the grossly impertinent familiarity, Thrift managed to force what she hoped sounded like a coy titter before she replied.

'Louisiana is a most delightful territory, thank you, Mr Mareschal. Indeed, among those I have visited, I think it the most delightful.'

'Uh, uh,' he chided gently, even raising a finger as if to tick her off, 'you must follow our customs, remember? You may address me as Ademar. I am glad you enjoy Louisiana, although God knows it's no surprise after coming down river among the bible thumpers. I imagine you were bored rigid?'

'New York was ... interesting,' Thrift managed, feeling that she ought to say something to defend the other territories although not entirely sure why, 'and I understand that Boston is really quite grand, although I did not visit on this occasion. The middle territories I confess I found a trifle staid, perhaps, although Arkansas is not without its charm, and the wilderness is very pretty.'

'There is no wilderness to compare with our own bayou,' he answered. 'You must see it before you return, although it can be dangerous and you would certainly need an experienced escort, a task I would be delighted to take on myself.'

Thrift blanched somewhat at what was to all intents and purposes a proposition, and made even before the first course had been served, but managed to look away and simper at the same time, causing Ademar Mareschal to make a curious bubbling noise in his throat. Not entirely sure how to respond to the outrageous suggestion, she was glad to be able to accept a bowl of soup from the waiter.

Ademar Mareschal continued to talk, praising the local shellfish used to produce the soup and smacking his lips in a manner Thrift found especially revolting, but as they ate she managed to compose herself once more. Evidently there would be no difficulty at all in attracting Ademar Mareschal, but it still remained to find the right balance, ensuring that his father would be thoroughly embarrassed while keeping his access to her body to a minimum.

The soup was followed by baked catfish in a piquant sauce, which was followed in turn by an elaborate and spicy chicken dish. Each was served with a different wine, and the main course of Texan steak with two of contrasting vintages. To Thrift's surprise the cheese was then served rather than the pudding, causing some confusion with the cutlery and providing Ademar

Mareschal with an excuse to put his arms around her back. His touch made her stomach squirm, but she managed a convincingly stifled giggle and to balance the tone of her reproach so that it seemed otherwise.

She had done her best not to drink too much, although with his attention it was tempting to take as much as possible. He had had no such restraint, swallowing glass after glass and making comparisons with French and Australian equivalents, about which he clearly knew very little. When a dessert of bread pudding with hot rum sauce was served he even went so far as to feed her a spoonful. Thrift felt forced to accept, and found herself blushing furiously at the resulting looks of disapprobation from other women around the table.

With her acceptance he evidently believed he had seduced her, his hand finding her knee beneath the table, which caused Thrift to start so violently she choked on the sticky sweet wine served with pudding. Deciding that she had allowed things to go quite far enough, she removed his hand, gently but firmly, then spoke in an undertone.

'Mr Mareschal, please, you go far beyond the bounds of propriety.'

He nodded, as if in understanding if not apology, but replied as soon as their neighbours were distracted, his hot whisper oozing with lecherous passion.

'Come, Thrift, do not deny that your desire for me burns in your bosom just as mine does for you. I have a boat, moored just minutes away. You and I could slip away, into the bayou, where they could never find us. We could give free expression to our love, and when we return, let them do their worst!'

'Mr Mareschal, please!' Thrift repeated, genuinely flustered and wondering how to turn him down but maintain his interest. 'I cannot possibly go with you on any such enterprise. My companion . . .'

'Is deep in conversation,' he urged. 'She would never notice, and once we are away we would be safe. I have known the bayous since I was a boy, Thrift, my darling, they would never find us, never!'

'Nothing would give me greater pleasure than to run with you,' Thrift responded, 'but I cannot. Think of my position, my family –'

'Be bold,' he cut in, 'and without wishing to offend, do you think I do not know you are disgraced? Why, it was the talk of the deck when we travelled on the *Sir Mark Twain* together. Oh, how I yearned to spare you as I listened to the smack of that wicked harridan's paddle on your poor tender flesh! How I yearned to kiss it better, to . . .'

'Mr Mareschal!' Thrift exclaimed, genuinely shocked as a picture of him kissing her freshly smacked bottom rose up in her mind. 'Please, I beg you. You . . . you are making me quite distraught!'

'And you I!' he answered, then suddenly dropped his voice once more and went on in a more level tone.

'I understand, my darling. I know how it is for you British ladies, but understand that my love for you is too strong to be thwarted, and what I do is for the best. Would you pass the cream, please?'

Surprised but relieved by the sudden non sequitur, Thrift hastened to do his bidding. When he spoke again it was of the chances for the local cricket team, and addressed to the table in general. She decided that not only had he given up attempting to pester her into an erotic elopement, but she had achieved her goal. Just to make sure he was still interested, she managed a sly wink when he next turned to her, which was promptly returned even as he compared the relative skills of the local batsmen and those of the neighbouring Mississippi Territory.

As agreed beforehand, Tobias Kobo had barely spoken a word to Thrift during the dinner, but paid attention to the woman on his left and the man beyond. Thrift now gently tapped her foot against his twice to indicate that she no longer needed to be left to Ademar Mareschal. He turned to her immediately, speaking in a polite tone immensely welcome after her previous conversation.

'But I have been ignoring you, Miss Moncrieff.'

'Not at all,' she assured him, 'and may I compliment you on a delightful dinner. Creole food is delicious, and really quite distinctive.'

They began to talk, Thrift gradually allowing herself to relax and wishing it was him rather than Ademar Mareschal she was supposed to be seduced by. To judge by the quality of his attention, he might not be averse to the idea either, while with the stress of her task gone and a good deal of drink inside her the arousal she'd felt earlier had begun to return. She remembered how good it had felt to indulge herself with James Monroe, and wondered if Tobias Kobo was equally well endowed and whether it would feel as good to have him swelling in her mouth, perhaps with her chastity belt undone to allow her to sneak a hand to her quim.

It was practical as well. The doors to the balcony were open, and at the rear of the building the car was parked beneath that same balcony. He would be able to lower her onto the car roof, follow and help her down, and once within they could do as they pleased. With luck they might even manage to return to their places suspected of nothing worse than conversing together on the balcony.

She glanced down the table, to find Miss Dace in deep conversation with the companion of one of the other ladies. Ademar Mareschal was explaining the leg before wicket rule with the aid of a piece of celery and a pepper shaker. Briefly she thought of the tally stick hanging between her breasts, but there were already seventeen notches on it, and there was only so much Miss Dace could do. It was worth it. Rising to her feet, she spoke in a calm, clear voice, making very sure Kobo could hear.

'I feel a trifle faint. Please excuse me while I take a breath of air.'

He smiled and nodded politely. To her relief none of the other women offered to accompany her, and in three paces she was free, standing in the cool outdoor air, listening to the music drifting up from the city, drinking in the rich scent of the air and imagining the rich scent of cock.

Knowing he would wait a minute or two before he followed, she walked slowly towards the back of the building, to where the balcony jutted out no more than a couple of feet above the roof of the car. Smiling to herself at her own cunning, she gave her dress a squeeze to make sure the key was still safely hidden in her drawers. Sucking old Mr Nolan's cock had been well worth it.

Her smile grew broader still as she caught the sound of a footfall from around the corner, only to fade abruptly as a man appeared, not Tobias Kobo but Ademar Mareschal.

'Why, but you are a little minx, aren't you?' he said, and even as Thrift began to protest he grasped her around the waist, lifted her and swung her up and over the edge of the balcony.

Her next attempt to object turned into a squeak of alarm as he dropped her from at least a foot and she was forced to snatch at the ironwork of the balcony to prevent herself falling off. He followed, chuckling as he pulled her to the ground and ignoring her remonstrations until he was hurrying her down an alley.

'There's no cause to be coy, my darling, not any more,' he declared. 'They can't hear you.'

'I didn't mean to leave,' Thrift tried to explain. 'I had only hoped to exchange a brief word in private.'

'The time for words is past,' he said ardently. 'Come, down to my boat before they realise we are gone.'

'No, really ... ,' Thrift tried as he dragged her stumbling onwards.

'You are shy, I know,' he said, 'and afraid, but you must put your fear behind you and give in to your true feelings!'

'No, really ... ,' Thrift repeated, only to break off in a squeak once again as she was hauled up onto his shoulder. 'Put me down!'

'This is best,' he assured her, 'so that you need not have to fight your feelings. Quicker too.'

Thrift gave a hiss of frustration as he broke into a slow jog, and was still protesting when they came out onto a short jetty with the Mississippi gleaming dark silver to either side and the dim bulk of a small launch immediately ahead of them, beyond an iron gate. He put her down, fumbling in his pocket. They had come down a twisting alley between high, windowless walls, shielding them completely from view save in the direction of the water.

Quickly Thrift considered her options. Running was pointless. Turning him down flat might well ruin all her hard work, even the entire assignment. Going with him was almost as unsatisfactory, which left only one choice.

'Ademar, please,' she urged, deciding that five minutes with his penis in her mouth was infinitely preferably to a night or more among the reeking swamps he had described so vividly over dinner, 'this is madness. I understand that you cannot restrain your passion for me, but to flee into the wilderness will cause no end of trouble. If you –'

'I don't care!' he declared. 'Let them do what they will.'

'What I mean is ... ,' Thrift began, only to be struck by an inspiration. 'You said how it grieved you to hear me punished aboard the *Sir Mark Twain*, but if I go with you then I will receive ten times as much!'

'Then we will flee!' he urged. 'We will live among the swamps, as man and woman. I know people among the Cajuns, good people, true men, who will shelter us. That is our destiny, sweet Thrift, for me to live as a man should, and for you to be my wife.'

'No, really, Mr Mareschal,' Thrift responded, now thoroughly alarmed and sure than even twenty minutes with his cock in her mouth was a small price to pay. 'I have feelings for you, yes, but let us not be foolish. Now please, let me assuage your passion here and now, then we will return to the restaurant.'

'No, my darling,' he urged, but stopped.

As she spoke she put a hand to his crotch, and massaged gently, sure he would be unable to resist. To make certain he knew what was on offer, she went on, hoping he'd mistake the burning embarrassment in her voice for arousal.

'You know I am disgraced, Ademar,' she told him, squeezing at what seemed to be an alarmingly large penis within his trousers, 'but you do not know why. A man seduced me, a Frenchman by the name of Monsieur d'Arrignac, and among other things he taught me the lewdest of tricks, how to pleasure a man in my mouth.'

He had been gulping like a fish as she spoke and squeezed, and as she finished his mouth came open to speak.

'Sweet Jesus, you're dirtier than a chongo whore.'

'There is no need to be vulgar,' Thrift said gently as she sank to her knees.

He had opened the iron gate, and lent back against the frame as her hands burrowed for his fly. She closed her eyes as she delved within, telling herself that she would imagine it was Tobias Kobo she was sucking, although she knew full well the trick was unlikely to work. His cock was no doubt as big anyway, a great fat thing that squirmed in her hand as she pulled it free, but very pale, almost milky in the dim light. Tentatively, she began to masturbate him, waiting until her courage rose enough to take him in her mouth.

'Pull out my balls,' he sighed.

Thrift cast her eyes briefly heavenwards and did as she was told, extracting a big, silky scrotum from his underwear. Gently, she began to tickle under his balls, telling herself she should do her best, make it quick and swallow his yield, in which case there had to be at least a chance of returning to the restaurant without Miss Dace realising the full story.

As she thought of what Miss Dace would do to her if she was caught, his cock no longer seemed so repulsive. She gulped it in, trying to tell herself she wasn't really enjoying the manly taste and the fleshy texture as she began to suck. He was groaning and mumbling as he began to grow in her mouth, but she did her best to shut the noises out and concentrate on his cock, which was not only big but thick and extraordinarily virile, curving upwards from under his belly in as fine a display of masculine pride as she had ever had the pleasure to service. He might be a buffoon, but his cock was magnificent, and she was already groping for the key to her chastity belt when light flooded over them and angry voices rang out from behind.

Thrift jerked around, leaving Ademar Mareschal's huge, pink penis thrusting up into the light of a torch shone directly on them. Blinded, she could see nothing, but there was no mistaking the two angry voices, Miss Dace and Tobias Kobo. She immediately began to stammer apologies, only for Ademar Mareschal to grab her by the scruff of her dress and haul her through the gate, slamming it behind him. He gave a wild laugh as he bundled the squealing Thrift into the boat.

'What are you doing, you idiot?' she demanded, forgetting herself for a moment, but Ademar Mareschal wasn't listening.

The torch was still on them, Miss Dace screaming at Ademar Mareschal to stop, while Tobias Kobo shook at the gate. Ademar Mareschal paid no attention to either, or to Thrift, who was doing her best to explain to him why it was a bad idea to abduct her. Instead he quickly released the painters and twisted a key into a small Collins engine. A moment at the controls and a great fan at the rear of the boat whirled into motion, sending them skimming across the waters of the Mississippi with the shouts of Miss Dace and Mr Kobo fading into the general background noise of Creole music.

'Mr Mareschal,' Thrift began for perhaps the eighth time, but stopped.

He stood at the back of the boat, one hand on the tiller that controlled the fan, his greased hair dishevelled and blown back by the wind, his rounded face set in an expression of bliss, a dramatic posture made ridiculous by the large, flaccid penis hanging from his open fly. Thrift pulled herself up, first to her knees and then onto the bench at the side of the boat.

'Mr Mareschal,' she said once more, patiently, 'this is foolish. Take the boat somewhere quiet and I promise I will assuage your needs as best I can. Then let us return to the party. I will undoubtedly be beaten in any case, but –'

'No, no, my love,' he broke in. 'Never again will that terrible woman touch your body. You are mine now, for ever, but yes, I need you, and I need you now, as I see you need me.'

Thrift hid a sigh. They were now well out into the river and heading downstream at a speed she was sure was ill-advised, with only the lights from Baton Rouge and the channel buoys for guidance. He had begun to massage his cock too, his face set in feverish glee.

'Come,' he demanded, 'take me in your mouth as we speed through the velvet night, there is no time for more.'

'Not unless you pull in to the bank,' Thrift insisted, 'or you will wreck the boat.'

'I have known these waters since I was a boy!' Mareschal laughed, only to have to swerve violently as the bulk of a low barge loomed out of the darkness.

'No doubt that barge was not moored there at the time,' Thrift remarked once she had picked herself up from the scuppers. 'Please, Ademar?'

The boat was still wallowing somewhat from the sudden turn, and he seemed to have lost some of his nerve. With a quick glance back towards Baton Rouge he swung the tiller around, heading the boat for the west bank, which showed only as a fringe of trees, black against the wrack of clouds illuminated by the moon. Thrift let her breath out, telling herself that once he'd come he could probably be persuaded to take a more realistic and less hot-headed view of the situation.

He at least seemed to know what he was doing, slowing the boat and guiding it first in among low, moonlit sandbanks and then reeds, which closed behind them so that they came to a stop sheltered on all sides. After a moment of groping in the dark Ademar Mareschal managed to turn a light on in the tiny cabin, before lowering himself onto the seat beside the tiller, his thighs spread wide, the bulk of his genitals hanging down between.

'Come, my love, take your pleasure of me,' he urged.

Thrift forced a smile and came quickly over. With little choice in the matter, she got down on her knees in the bottom of the boat, his cock close to her face. Taking it in, she began to suck once more, and to caress his balls, her eyes closed and telling herself she might as well enjoy the moment. He'd begun to mumble again, but she wasn't really paying attention as she sucked and licked at his rapidly swelling cock, which was simply too fine a piece of manhood not to enjoy. By the time he was fully erect she was lost in the pleasure of her task, save for a touch of irritation not to be able to masturbate as she sucked, but admitting to him that she had the key to her chastity belt seemed to be asking for trouble. Instead she pushed her breasts up out of her gown, holding one heavy globe in each hand and gently pinching her nipples as she worked on both his straining erection and his bulging ball sack.

Now thoroughly enjoying herself, she took his balls in her mouth, revelling in the feel of his bulky scrotum and rolling the twin eggs within over her tongue. He was groaning and muttering, declaring his undying love and calling her a dirty whore together, but she took little notice. She needed to come and no longer cared for the consequences, her hand burrowing for the key to her chastity belt despite being aware that this was exactly why she'd been put in it and wore containment pants.

She took his cock in hand, tugging on it as she sucked his balls and rummaged beneath her petticoats with increasing urgency, only for him to suddenly grunt, snatch his cock out of her hand and start to jerk at the shaft. Before she had even released his balls from her mouth he had come, sending a fountain of sperm high into the air to splash down into her elaborately made-up hair and over her face, then a second jet, full into one wide open eye, which set her desperately trying to get the mess out and broke the spell.

'Glorious,' he sighed, 'truly glorious.'

'I am glad you appreciate me,' Thrift managed, still wiping spunk from her eye. 'Now may we please return to Baton Rouge?'

'Baton Rouge?' he queried. 'And surrender you? Never.'

Thrift gave a heavy sigh as the fan started up once more, to reverse the boat out of the reeds and head down river at gathering speed.

Eleven

The Mississippi Delta, March 2006

Thrift awoke stiff and cold in the bottom of Ademar Mareschal's boat. They were still moving, as they had been all night, but now the sky was flushed with dawn and they were no longer on the broad Mississippi, nor the wide side channel he'd turned into shortly after she'd sucked his penis. Instead they were moving between high banks of reeds with curious-looking trees beyond, down a channel no more than twice as wide as the boat. He was yawning, and produced what was presumably supposed to be a brave smile as he saw that she was awake.

'This is the bayou,' he told her, 'a maze of channels known only to a few, my mother's people, the Cajuns, who do not welcome strangers. We are free, Thrift, my love, free to live the pure life!'

Unable to find a suitable answer that would not exceed all boundaries of polite speech, Thrift contented herself with stretching her limbs and yawning. She was thirsty, hungry, cold, and wanted a convenient facility as a matter of some urgency, all needs she could see no immediate way of satisfying, although in the last case, unless they stopped soon, she was very likely to solve the problem by going in her nappy.

'Might we stop, please, Mr Mareschal?' she asked.

208

'We'll be at my uncle's cabin soon,' he told her, 'for a true Cajun welcome!'

Thrift nodded and clenched the muscles of her belly against the pressure in her bladder. Climbing cautiously to her feet with one hand on the cabin for support, she tried to get some idea of where they might be, but found that the reeds were taller than she was, limiting her horizon in every direction. It was not even clear if the trees were growing on solid ground, while there was no sign of human habitation whatsoever.

Willing herself to be patient, she focused on her predicament instead. What Ademar Mareschal had done went far beyond merely embarrassing his father, whose reaction was therefore impossible to predict save that he was hardly going to accept a post in Whitehall while his son was somewhere in the Louisiana swamps with the daughter of a prestigious family. Clearly she had to return to Baton Rouge as soon as possible and hope that Pierre Mareschal decided that the best thing to do was remove his idiot son from the territory.

She knew only that they were west of the main channel of the Mississippi, somewhere in a maze of channels, making the idea of returning alone daunting if not impossible, while it was evidently crucial to bring him with her if she was to stand any chance of eventual success. Force was out of the question, and it didn't seem likely that he would be easily persuaded. Indeed, he was evidently enjoying himself immensely, and seemed oblivious both of her real feelings and the situation he was in, steering the boat at what seemed to her dangerous speed but with considerable skill.

Another twinge from her bladder broke her train of thought and she pressed her thighs together, ignoring the urge to simply let go. It was unthinkable to wet herself, and yet a considerably better option than doing her toilet in front of him, while the tiny open boat afforded no privacy whatsoever and not even a bucket to go into. Her bladder was now starting to hurt, and she grimaced as another long, slow wave of pressure came, dying only gradually. Knowing she would be unable to resist many more, she spoke up despite her embarrassment.

'Mr Mareschal, please could we stop?' she asked. 'I am in need of a moment of privacy.'

'So am I, my love,' he answered with a dirty grin, 'but just you keep that thought warm for a little more.'

'No, no, I mean, on my own,' she explained, blushing hotter still, 'for the sake of my convenience. How soon will we be at your uncle's?'

'Not long at all,' he assured her, 'two hours at the most.'

Thrift let go, hot piddle squirting out into her nappy and quickly soaking in over her cunt, between her thighs and up around her bottom cheeks, a sensation so good she had to fight down a sigh of relief for all the hideous embarrassment of wetting herself.

Having started, there seemed little point in stopping, and she stayed as she was, her face turned away from him as she let the full contents of her bladder run out into her nappy. When it began to trickle down her legs she pressed them together, allowing it to soak into her drawers and petticoats, although most of it was in her nappy, which now felt heavy and wet around the lower part of her bottom and up to her belly.

Not daring to sit down for fear of squeezing the pee out of her nappy, she continued to look out over the reeds, full of chagrin but still grateful that the pressure was gone. Again she considered trying to reason with him, but decided to postpone her efforts until she had quenched her thirst, eaten and changed her nappy. That meant waiting until they arrived at his uncle's house, and she forced herself to be patient, trying to ignore the now cold piddle soaking slowly into her lower clothes.

The sun was approaching the zenith when they finally reached a cluster of islands somewhere deep in the swamp. Ademar Mareschal had now begun to sing, to Thrift's added annoyance, a selection of loud and rather vulgar anthems dealing either with the virtues of France and the French or the supposed oppression of the inhabitants of Louisiana. He had even attempted to get her to join in, apparently oblivious to her rank.

Finally he turned in at a tiny channel, invisible from just a few yards away, to where a wooden cabin stood among a grove of some sort of cypress, with an elderly mule tethered at the front, chewing carrots. Ademar Mareschal pulled in at a rotting jetty where a similar boat was moored. The planking of the jetty was warped and split with long exposure to the sun, and wobbled alarmingly as Thrift climbed out of the boat. Ademar Mareschal offered a helping hand, then called out in a loud, joyful voice.

'Uncle Onez! There's somebody I'd like you to meet.'

At first there was no response, and after the steady drone of the fan the island seemed oddly quiet, with no noise other than the buzz of insects, the munching of the mule and a single bird calling from some way off in the swamp. Only as Ademar Mareschal began to start up the path did the door open, creaking wide to reveal a man in nothing more than tattered blue overalls and a decaying straw hat, barefoot, with a pipe sticking out at one side of his mouth and a bottle of some clear liquid in one hand. He appeared to be drunk.

'Uncle Onez!' Ademar Mareschal declared cheerfully, striding forward to put his arms around the man. 'Thrift, I'd like you to meet my uncle Oneziphore. Uncle Onez, this is Thrift Moncrieff, who is to be my bride!'

'You brought home a bride?' Onez queried, his eyebrows lifting in open surprise. 'I never thought to see the day you'd bring home a bride.'

'Well, it is today,' Ademar Mareschal answered, 'and we'll be staying here a while, if that's all right with you? We had a bit of trouble in Baton Rouge.'

211

'Always trouble in Baton Rouge,' Onez replied as Thrift gave an awkward curtsey. 'Full of damn Limeys, Baton Rouge. Sure you're welcome, be good to have a woman around the place for one thing. I'm starving, girl, how about you knock up some gumbo?'

Ademar Mareschal gave her an encouraging nod as he steered her towards the cabin. Within, there was a single large room, partially screened off at one end by a somewhat ragged bead curtain, and with kitchen facilities at the other. There was no sign of a convenient facility, and with her wet nappy now extremely uncomfortable, Thrift was forced to speak up.

I would be delighted in assist in the preparation of lunch,' she offered, swallowing her pride for the sake of her hunger, 'but first, perhaps you could direct me to the convenient facility.'

Her cheeks flared red as she said it, and the puzzled glance Onez threw her in return didn't help. Ademar Mareschal merely laughed, then spoke.

'This is the bayou, my love. Go out the back and you'll see a branch, just right for a seat, very convenient.'

'Oh, she wants to shit,' Uncle Onez confirmed to himself. 'You a Limey, girl?'

'I am British, certainly,' Thrift confirmed, her voice somewhat icy, which he appeared not to notice.

'Damn pretty for a Limey,' he said, 'good big tits too. Well, Miss Limey, here, you shit out the back, like Ade says, same as every other body.'

Thrift made a face, but with no choice in the matter she was forced to leave the cabin by the back door. To her dismay the ground sloped directly down to the water. It was obvious which branch Ademar Mareschal meant and it was in full view of the cabin. With her lips pursed in vexation she went behind the largest of the cedar trees.

She was shaking with embarrassment as she began to undress, and constantly glancing around the trunk in

212

case either of the men was watching. They were talking, but the window was so dirty she couldn't be sure if they were looking out or not, so she took great care to remain in the shadow of the tree. She took off her gown and hung it between two bushes, and her underdress between two more, making an effective screen.

With her petticoats and drawers off, she found the key to her chastity belt, quickly fumbling it into the padlock and praying that Mr Nolan hadn't tricked her after all. He hadn't. It worked, and a moment later she was climbing out of it to leave her soggy nappy hanging heavy around her hips. She unpinned it and pulled it off, allowing the air to her bottom and quim, a sensation so welcome she spent a moment just standing as she was, bare front and back with the dripping nappy discarded on the ground. Her stockings were wet and she peeled them off, then padded down to the water's edge barefoot and squatted down with her bottom stuck out over the water to evacuate herself, squeezing as hard as she could and praying the men didn't decide to come out, or had the decency not to try and look.

When she'd finished, she sacrificed her already damp flannel petticoat to wipe herself and generally clean up, then began to dress again. For a moment she hesitated, wondering if she should risk abandoning her chastity belt, but the joint prospect of a fucking from Ademar Mareschal and Miss Dace's paddle made her change her mind. Using her cotton petticoat as a nappy, she climbed back into the cage and fastened the padlock, replacing the key in her drawers before putting them on.

Once dressed again, with her soiled nappy and petticoat discreetly buried, she felt a great deal better, although she still had no idea what she should do beyond getting some food into her stomach. Back in the cabin, Ademar Mareschal and his uncle were seated in the only two comfortable chairs, glasses in their hands and an open bottle of whatever foul-smelling spirit they were drinking between them. Uncle Onez gave her a wink, making her wonder if he had watched her outside, then spoke, his voice perfectly friendly but also commanding.

'Come along, girl, my stomach's starting to growl. Where's that gumbo?'

'I'm afraid I don't know the recipe,' Thrift explained, 'but I shall do my best.'

She finished with a polite curtsey and made her way to the kitchen end of the cabin. There was plenty of food, and even a refrigerator, although it was mostly full of beer, but with no experience of cooking she found herself nonplussed. There was at least bread, and what appeared to be ghee, also a long string of dark red sausages which gave off a spicy waft. Lost for an alternative, she made three large sausage sandwiches, passing one to each of the men.

'What in Hell is this?' Uncle Onez demanded as Thrift sat down on a stool to eat her own lunch.

'I apologise if it is not to your liking,' Thrift explained, 'but I am of the Quality and have no familiarity with cooking.'

'I am of the Quality,' he echoed, imitating her accent. 'Hell, Ade, I hope you're going to whoop this one's ass, 'cause she sure needs it, and if you don't I will.'

Ademar Mareschal merely laughed and began to eat his sandwich, leaving Thrift hot with blushes and indignation. Despite his complaints, Uncle Onez had no difficulty in finishing the meal, washed down with the clear spirit drunk straight from the bottle. Ademar Mareschal was drinking too, if less heavily, and as he swallowed the last bite of his sandwich he adjusted the prominent bulge in his trousers. Uncle Onez noticed and gave a low, dirty chuckle, sending the blood to Thrift's face once more. Mareschal got up, stretched and spoke to Thrift, his voice betraying the amount of drink he'd swallowed.

214

'Come then, my darling, this is the moment you've been waiting for.'

Thrift gave an uneasy glance towards the bead curtain, which failed to completely conceal an unmade wooden bed beyond.

'Please allow me a moment to finish my lunch,' she said, not wanting to anger him but eager to buy some time, 'and then, perhaps, we might take a walk, a private walk, during which –'

'No need to be coy, girl,' Uncle Onez broke in, laughing. 'Hell, don't you think I know what you two want to do?'

'No doubt,' Thrift answered, 'and yet –'

'She's shy,' Ademar Mareschal broke in, 'and she's had a strict upbringing, but underneath ... You're among Cajuns now, Thrift, and that's how you'll be living. There are no secrets among families here.'

He'd reached down as he spoke, to take her hand and haul her to her feet. She still had a mouthful of sandwich, and was spluttering breadcrumbs as he led her into the bed area, pressing her mouth to his before they were even through the bead curtain. His breath smelt of spirits and his hands had gone straight to the front of her dress, pulling it wide and pushing hard to pop her breasts out of her bodice. Thrift gave a muffled squeal of alarm as he began to grope her, his thumbs greasy from the sausages as he rubbed them over her nipples. To her intense chagrin both little buds came erect almost immediately, and he was chuckling as he pulled her down onto the bed beside him, where he began to suck on her nipples, finally allowing her to speak.

'Mr Mareschal ... Ademar, please, not in front of your uncle!'

'By God I mean to have you if I swing for it!' he growled, ignoring her completely. 'Let's have those skirts up, and now.'

'Mr Mareschal, please,' Thrift urged, hastily pulling back, but his hands were already locked in her gown.

Up it came, underdress, petticoat and all, as she was tipped backwards onto the bed with her legs up and open. Taking no notice of either her squeals of protest or her efforts to bat his hands away, he quickly pulled her drawers wide, only to stop with a curse.

'Hell! You're wearing some infernal device to guard your chastity, aren't you? What's it made of, solid iron?'

'I fear so,' Thrift admitted. 'Now please, Ademar, take me outside and you may use my mouth, but this is not decent, not in front of your uncle!'

'Nonsense,' he answered her. 'Things go differently around here, Thrift. In a cabin like this, why, nobody thinks twice about sharing a little love. He'd be offended if we didn't let him watch, and really, a young girl like you, it's your duty to keep the men happy.'

'Keep the men happy? Including –' Thrift began in outrage, only to break off. 'What are you doing?'

'Looking for the key,' he said, groping among her underwear.

'I don't have it!' Thrift protested. 'My companion does, always, precisely so that I may not be molested! Mr Mareschal!'

He'd turned her skirts up as far as they would go, covering Thrift's face as he continued to search among the folds of her corset and drawers. She could still hear him, though, and there was very little of the gallantry of the night before in his voice.

'It's here somewhere, I know it is. How else did you evacuate yourself if you can't get it undone? Never mind, Uncle Onez has a hacksaw somewhere, I expect.'

'Oh, very well!' Thrift snapped. 'I have the key, tied in at the side of my drawers, but really, must you be so importunate, and so rude?'

'It's for your own good,' he replied. 'I mean to teach

216

you the way of true pleasure, Thrift, living as a woman should, for her man.'

'And for his relatives?' Thrift queried. 'Ademar, really, could you not at least put up a proper screen?'

'I explained all that,' he told her. 'Ah, here it is.'

He extracted the key and made quick work of opening the padlock. Thrift lay back as her chastity belt was removed, now half-resigned to a fucking in front of Uncle Onez, but still wanting to put up a fight. The old man had turned his chair to get a better view, so that as the petticoat Thrift had used as a nappy was unpinned she was left with her quim spread open to him. To her shock she saw that he had his cock out and made to speak, only for her voice to break into a gasp as Ademar Mareschal buried his face between her thighs.

His tongue went straight to her clitoris, lapping vigorously to fill her with such ecstasy that all she could manage was to give a weak groan of protest before she gave in. As he took her thighs to spread them wider still she was still wriggling in her embarrassment at being done in front of his uncle, but her arousal was simply too high to let her push him away. With a final, broken sob, she let her hands go to her breasts and she played with herself as she was licked, still wriggling, only no longer in protest but in ecstasy.

Ademar Mareschal gave a wry chuckle as he finally pulled away, and in a moment he had climbed onto the bed, straddling Thrift's body to flop his half-stiff cock onto her face. She took him in, sucking and trying not to think about her naked lower body being on show to the ageing uncle, or the prospect of him rolling her legs high again and pushing his cock in up her cunt while his nephew held her down.

By the time Ademar had changed his position and begun to fuck her breasts Onez had pulled his chair closer, now sitting to one side and watching openly through a gap in the ragged bead curtain as he masturbated a large dirt-coloured penis. A whimper of shame escaped her throat as she saw, but then her hands went to her breasts, pushing them together to make a slide for Ademar's erection.

'I want to suck it again,' she sighed, abandoning herself completely as he began to climb off. 'Then you can have me.'

Ademar obliged, cocking his leg over her head to drive his cock down into her open mouth. Thrift pursed her lips, allowing him to fuck her head, but after a few thrusts he pulled out, to dangle his balls into her gaping mouth. As she sucked on his scrotum his hand went back, burrowing between her thighs to manipulate her cunt. One finger slipped up her, easily entering her juicy hole, and a second, before his thumb found her clitoris.

Thrift's back arched in pleasure as he began to masturbate her, and as he lifted his balls from her mouth she spread her thighs in an open invitation to being mounted. Instead he moved a little forward, presenting his anus to her mouth as he rubbed harder still on her cunt. Another whimper broke from Thrift's lips but her tongue was already poking out, to lick at his anal star and the underside of his balls.

'That's my little English whore,' he sighed, lowering himself to rub his scrotum in Thrift's face and allow her tongue deeper in up his anus. 'Now I aim to have you, and when I'm done, I want you to go over to Uncle Onez, naked and pretty, and show him how friendly you are by taking him in that sweet mouth.'

Thrift gave a muted whimper, then was left gasping and pushing her cunt out for attention as he once more climbed off her. She'd been on the edge of orgasm, and there was no resistance left in her as he lifted her fully onto the bed to climb between her thighs and sink his cock deep in, up her ready hole. Her hands were on her breasts as he began to fuck her, squeezing and groping at the fat globes, lost to all sense of decency as his big cock moved in her cunt. Before she could stop herself her mouth had fallen open, a clear invitation to Uncle Onez, who obliged, shuffling over to jam his big, greasy cock deep into her throat.

Ademar made no comment, merely pumping a little harder into Thrift's cunt, but for no more than a dozen strokes before he pulled free. A grunted comment from nephew to uncle, and Thrift had been flipped over onto her knees with her disordered petticoats turned up on her back and her breasts swinging free of her corset as Ademar once more drove himself to the hilt in her body. Her mouth was agape and quickly filled by Onez's cock, the two men rocking her back and forth on their erections.

Both were beginning to grunt, and she quickly pushed her hand back between her thighs, willing and debauched as they used her at each end, clutching at her cunt in her eagerness to come while they were in her. They were calling her a trollop and a whore as they used her, but she no longer cared, masturbating to the ecstasy of having two big cocks in her body with no thought for anything but the orgasm already bubbling up in her head.

She never made it. Ademar came, heedless of the risk of pregnancy, perhaps even on purpose, spunking deep in her hole, and Thrift was too far gone to stop him. As the thick, sticky mess squashed out of her cunt with the next pump, she was immediately masturbating in it, her orgasm broken right at the edge but rising again, only to break once more as he withdrew.

'I've got to have that arse,' Onez panted, pulling back from Thrift's mouth, 'that fat white arse.'

'Do it ... take me,' she gasped, 'but keep in it me until I've had my pleasure, I beg you!'

He merely laughed, but moved round behind her and eased his cock in deep up her cunt, now so open and so sloppy she barely felt it. Ademar had moved too, feeding his gradually deflating cock into her mouth to make her suck up her own juices as his uncle took a firm grip on Thrift's hips and began to fuck her, only to stop just as she had once more started to stroke her cunt.

'Hell, you always did stretch 'em,' Onez complained, and he pulled out.

'No, please ... do me ... ,' Thrift begged, spitting Ademar's cock away to gasp out her words.

'I aim to,' Onez told her, and he wiped his slippery cock between her bottom cheeks, smearing her anus with a mixture of her own juices and his nephew's come.

'Oh, God, no ... ,' Thrift sobbed, but made no effort to stop him as he pressed the head of his cock to her bottom hole.

She cried out as she felt her ring spread, and again as he gave another push, but she was taking him, the tight muscle gradually giving way as he forced it, easing inch after inch of thick brown cock into her rectum until she felt swollen and bloated inside, and had once more began to masturbate.

'Dirty, dirty, bitch!' he said happily as he jammed the last of his shaft inside her, pressing his balls to her busy fingers. 'You've got yourself a live one here, Ade!'

Thrift was whimpering with pleasure as she was buggered, and wishing there was another man there, or two, to fill all her eager holes at once as she came. It was going to happen anyway, the sensation of having her anal ring pull in and out on Uncle Onez' big cock too good to let her hold back. She screamed as it hit her, and again, her whole body tight as the orgasm tore through her, and at the very height of her ecstasy she felt him jerk, heard him grunt and knew that he had spunked up her bottom.

With that she cried out once more, the first of a series of glorious peaks, fading only slowly as he pumped her rectum full of seed, and she was still in ecstasy as he withdrew. Even as he came around to push his filthy cock at her face she was too high to resist, taking it in and sucking down her own juices until he was clean. His sperm was still bubbling from her anus as she sank slowly down on the bed, her hand still on her now aching cunt, completely spent.

Uncle Onez staggered back to his chair, poured most of what remained in the bottle down his throat and almost immediately collapsed into a stupor, his cock still hanging out of his trousers and dribbling sperm down one thigh. Ademar Mareschal had at least put his away, and stood and stretched before taking the bottle from his uncle's limp fingers. Sitting down with his back to the bed, he swallowed the last gulp of drink, then addressed Thrift.

'Wasn't that just fine!'

'Yes,' Thrift admitted, already sulky about the way they had used her.

'Yes, there's nothing like giving a girl a good fucking to get a thirst,' he went on. 'Fetch me a beer.'

'Yes, of course, Ademar,' Thrift promised, rising from the bed.

'Good girl,' Ademar Mareschal responded, his final words before Thrift brought the heavy iron chastity belt down on the back of his skull.

Twelve

Felicity Adams pushed a bottle of Old Red Eye into the centre of the table as she spoke to Thrift.

'How did you get the fellow into the boat? Damn it, he must weigh fifteen stone.'

'I tied his feet to his uncle's mule,' Thrift explained, 'and once he was on the jetty I used a piece of plank as a lever.'

'Most ingenious,' Miss Dace remarked.

Thrift managed a nervous smile, not sure how to read Miss Dace, who seemed as impressed with her as anybody else, outwardly, and yet there always seemed to be a sting of sarcasm hidden just below the surface of her words.

'A fine show in any case,' Felicity went on, 'and as Pierre has taken the bait, I think we may be allowed to celebrate.'

She poured out three shots of Old Red Eye and raised her own.

'Bottoms up.'

'Bottoms up,' Thrift managed, getting the rude word out with a little difficulty.

Miss Dace merely raised an eyebrow in Thrift's direction and swallowed her own drink. Outside the window of the Diplomatic building an airship could be seen attached to the summit of the Baton Rouge tower. She was the *Sir James Scarlett*, scheduled to leave for London the following day with Thrift aboard. Pierre Mareschal was booked to follow a week later, in company with his son.

'I'd give fifty guineas to have been a fly on the wall when Pierre interviewed Ademar,' Felicity said with a chuckle, then puffed her cheeks out and sat up rigidly straight in imitation of Pierre Mareschal. 'It is bad enough that you abducted a British girl, Ademar, but to allow her to overcome you and return you here tied in the bottom of a boat! You are a disgrace to the Gauliste movement, and to France!'

Thrift laughed and smiled, basking in the warmth of Felicity's admiration.

'Just as well you had the key though, naughty girl,' Felicity went on, chuckling to herself as she poured out a second round of Old Red Eye.

'No doubt Miss Moncrieff would have found something else suitable to the purpose,' Miss Dace put in quietly.

'You have no sense of style, Snivels,' Felicity answered. 'To brain a man who is attempting to ravish you with your own chastity belt, that is sheer poetry.'

Thrift smiled again, blushing with pride and at the memory of what had happened in the swamps, the truth being somewhat different from the official version, in which Uncle Onez had already been insensible with drink and she had deliberately allowed Ademar Mareschal to find the key and open her chastity belt so that she could hit him with it.

'I only wish I'd been there,' Felicity said. She drained her drink and refilled all three glasses before addressing Thrift again. 'Let's see this remarkable piece of iron-mongery then.'

'I ... but ... ,' Thrift stammered in sudden shock, although the thought of being exposed in front of Miss Adams had sent a powerful jolt of desire through her.

'No call to be shy,' Felicity insisted, 'not when we're all ladies together. Come on, skirts up, drawers down.'

Thrift's face was burning as she stood up, but she found herself unable to disobey. Both women were watching as she hauled her skirts and petticoats high, her embarrassment growing stronger still as she fumbled with her drawers, and reaching a peak as they fell down, exposing the iron cage and the new nappy Miss Dace had put her in just hours before. Miss Adams raised both eyebrows. Miss Dace allowed herself the faintest of smiles.

'Good God!' Miss Adams swore. 'I'm damn glad I never had to wear anything like that. A pair of Dr Mountjoy's was good enough for us, eh Snivels? Not that a chastity belt is exactly normal nowadays.'

'You . . . you wore containment pants, Miss Adams?' Thrift managed to say, made bold by surprise and the drink, which had gone straight to her head.

'Of course,' Miss Adams confirmed as Thrift quickly rearranged herself. 'They keep you in them until you're thirty, generally, although Dr Mountjoy's Patent were more designed to keep the boys out than anything much in, eh, Snivels?'

Miss Dace, who had been growing rapidly redder during the conversation, finally found her voice.

'I really think, Felicity, that we should mind what we say in front of Miss Moncrieff . . . Thrift, who is after all, very much our junior and should be properly respectful of her elders.'

'Don't be so damn stiff,' Miss Adams responded, taking another swallow of Old Red Eye. 'You enjoy smacking her behind well enough, eh? Don't you suppose she knows how much you enjoy it? After all, you were at Weathercote, weren't you, Thrift? From what I hear, once you've been there you know damn well how the land lies.'

Miss Dace had lapsed into a sulky silence, staring out of the window at the airship mast and sipping from her

224

glass, while Thrift was red-faced with embarrassment but trying not to giggle at the thought of Miss Dace in a pair of containment pants. Miss Adams filled their glasses once more, insisting Miss Dace take her share, and after a moment to savour the heady liquid she spoke again.

'How about a round of Tears at Bedtime? What do you say, Snivels, for old time's sake?'

'Is that the question game?' Thrift asked as Miss Dace's blushes started again, richer and darker than ever.

'That's the one,' Felicity went on, 'only with just the three of us we'd better take it in turns. What do you say? I bet you'd be glad to get out of that damn chastity belt, for one thing.'

'It is somewhat uncomfortable,' Thrift admitted, hesitant, although the thought of a playful spanking from Miss Adams was sending shiver after shiver of pleasure through her.

'I really think –' Miss Dace began, only to be cut off.

'Nonsense, whatever you were going to say,' Felicity Adams stated. 'You're playing. Besides, I bet you'd love a go at me after all these years, eh?'

Miss Dace tried to retain her haughty look, but failed, allowing an expression of deep longing to cross her face. Felicity laughed and got to her feet as she spoke again.

'Just let me lock the door and we'll begin. Girls' secret, obviously, in which case, Susannah, I suppose we'd better make Thrift an honorary Omega Pi, don't you think?'

'Without doubt,' Miss Dace agreed.

Thrift wasn't sure what Felicity meant. Miss Dace had brightened considerably, which was worrying, and more so as Felicity continued.

'Maybe we'll even haze her after the game. It's years since I hazed a girl.'

Felicity locked the door and pulled the curtains. When she sat down again the lounge had been plunged into a warm gloom, the single set of bulbs she'd left on casting glittering light on the whisky. Already somewhat drunk and more than half in love with Felicity Adams, Thrift found it impossible to resent what was about to happen. She could already feel her quim swelling and juicing at the prospect of exposure and more.

'These are the rules,' Felicity was saying. 'We go around the table, question by question. One wrong answer and you go bare, two and it's over the knee with you, three and . . . Do you have your paddle to hand, Snivels?'

'Yes,' Miss Dace admitted. 'I shall fetch it.'

'And something for Thrift's hazing,' Felicity instructed as Miss Dace rose. 'You know the form. So where was I? Yes, three questions wrong and you get the paddle. Keep the questions fair, because if they're challenged the third person gets to adjudicate. If an adjudication goes against you, you get the forfeit instead. First girl to get the paddle is the loser. All clear?'

Thrift made a face, in no doubt whatsoever whose bottom the paddle was likely to be applied to, while Miss Dace's arm seemed entirely better. Now she herself had a chance to apply it, but she was not sure she was physically capable of doing it, and definitely not to Felicity.

'I suspect you're keen to give Snivels a good whacking?' Felicity remarked. 'And I confess I've wanted to give you a go ever since we met, so we'll go clockwise if you don't mind?'

'Not at all,' Thrift answered, glowing with pleasure at Felicity's words, which also meant that she would be spared Miss Dace's attention.

Miss Dace was soon back, hurriedly locking the door behind her and pulling the big wooden sorority paddle out from where she had concealed it beneath her skirts.

'They know we're not to be disturbed,' she said,

laying down the paddle on the table. 'I suppose you had better go first, Felicity, as you are senior.'

'I'd say so,' Felicity agreed, 'and we've decided to go clockwise. Thrift, here's an easy one to kick off with. In which year was Louisiana ceded to the British Crown?'

'Nineteen twenty-six,' Thrift answered promptly, the knot of apprehension that had been building in her stomach growing a fraction looser, only to tighten again at the prospect of questioning Miss Dace and the inevitable consequences once Felicity Adams was no longer there.

'Miss Dace,' she began, intent on asking an easy question to spare her own bottom.

'Uh, uh,' Felicity interrupted. 'No formal names among girls. The rules say nicknames, as it happens, so we really ought to give you one.'

'Nappies,' Miss Dace said promptly, 'which she is not only wearing, but suits her for the fuss she makes over punishment.'

'You two make a fine pair then,' Felicity laughed. 'Nappies it is.'

Thrift had gone scarlet, but couldn't find it in herself to protest.

'Miss . . . Susannah . . . Snivels,' she managed, almost choking on the word as she pictured the state her bottom would be in once due revenge had been taken. 'Which is the largest county in England?'

Miss Dace looked completely blank, then cross.

'I protest,' she said, turning to Felicity. 'I don't know anything about English geography.'

'You did it at school,' Felicity pointed out. 'Fair question.'

Miss Dace looked far from happy as she turned back to Thrift.

'Norfolk.'

'No, Yorkshire. I'm sorry . . .'

'Don't be,' Felicity said cheerfully. 'Come on, Snivels, let's see that bare bottie!'

Miss Dace stood up, lips pursed in consternation as she bunched up her severe black dress and the petticoats beneath, exposing her drawers. It took her a moment to pluck up courage, and then she turned to pull the rear split wide, exposing her neatly turned pink bottom for just a moment, but keeping herself bare as she sat back down.

'Freckles,' she said. 'Name all fifty-six traitors who signed that document known as the Declaration of Independence.'

'All fifty-six?' Felicity demanded. 'That's far too obscure.'

'It also seems to me to be fifty-six questions,' Thrift put in cautiously.

'Absolutely,' Felicity agreed. 'So you rule for me, Nappies?'

'Oh, I didn't know I was adjudicating,' Thrift answered, 'I just . . .'

'Adjudicated,' Felicity finished for her. 'Unfair question. Come along, Snivels, over you go.'

Miss Dace opened her mouth, closed it, opened it again, closed it and very slowly got up, holding her raised skirts and petticoats to leave her bottom bare behind her. Felicity pushed her chair back to make a lap, smiling broadly as Miss Dace very slowly laid herself down into spanking position, little pink bottom raised naked and ready. Thrift could only stare in mingled fear and delight, her eyes flicking between her tormentor's bare bottom and the angry pout of her face.

'Watch this,' Felicity said, giving Thrift a wink as she twisted Miss Dace's arm high.

'She . . . she always ties my wrists,' Thrift said, unable to hold the words back.

'Good point,' Felicity admitted.

Thrift watched in both awe and rapidly mounting arousal as Felicity pulled out Miss Dace's drawer strings and quickly lashed both wrists together, finishing with a neat bow. Now helpless, with her wrists crossed and bound behind her back and her bottom quivering as she awaited her spanking, Miss Dace closed her eyes, mumbling what might have been a prayer and broke to a yelp as Felicity's hand delivered the first smack.

The spanking was hard, delivered full across Miss Dace's bouncing, squirming bottom cheeks, fast and furious. At first Miss Dace bit her lip to stop herself crying out, but she lost control almost immediately, and Thrift's hand went to her mouth in giggling delight as the woman who had punished her so often and so hard began to wriggle her bottom, to kick her feet, to gasp and pant, and finally to go into a full-blown, howling, blubbering spanking tantrum. The tears were streaming down her face, and before long snot as well, two long streamers hanging from her nose, and, as she sniffed them back up with a noise for all the world like a pig snorting, Thrift burst into helpless laughter.

'Now you know why she's called Snivels,' Felicity said with a chuckle, and stopped. 'There, that should do you. Back to your chair, and keep that bottie bare for the paddle.'

Miss Dace's face was as red as her bottom, also streaked with tears and snot, but as soon as she'd been untied she wiped both away and sat down, bare on the seat, contenting herself with a single venomous glance at Thrift before speaking.

'Your question, Freckles, and please stop ganging up, it's not fair.'

Thrift immediately felt guilty for the sorry tone in Miss Dace's voice, only to remember how she'd been treated herself.

'Fair enough,' Felicity answered. 'Nappies, name one American territory where you would expect to find cowboys.'

Thrift said nothing, completely lost and wondering what a cowboy even was. It sounded like the result of some particularly horrible genetic experiment, and after her visit to Smith and Smith that didn't seem all that unlikely.

'Tennessee?' she ventured.

Felicity clapped her hands in delight as she answered. 'No. We'll have you bare please, then, Miss Nappies.'

Thrift stood, genuinely reluctant and yet thrilled at the prospect of being laid bare in front of Felicity. Both women were watching her as she lifted her skirts and petticoats, showing the heavy padlock of her chastity belt hanging through the open front of her drawers. Miss Dace looked pleased with herself as she inserted the key, allowing Thrift to open the padlock, tug open her drawer strings and unpin her own nappy, but as she began to push it all down Felicity raised a finger.

'Uh, uh, we show bottoms.'

A bubble of shame and desire had risen in Thrift's throat as she turned around, pushing out her bottom a little as she continued her exposure. Her drawers and the chastity belt came loose easily, but she had to step out of them and pull her nappy down separately, adding a last, strong flush of arousal as her bottom came fully bare to Miss Adams for the first time.

'Very pretty,' Felicity said admiringly, 'full, and yet so firm and smooth. You have wonderful skin, Thrift.'

'Thank you,' Thrift managed, and shivered as Felicity reached out a finger to stroke one rounded cheek, just gently, but enough to leave Thrift's heart pounding.

'Now you can sit bare,' Felicity went on, 'and it's your turn.'

'Um ... Snivels,' Thrift said, lowering her naked bottom onto the chair. 'Where are the Caledonian mountains?'

'Scotland,' Miss Dace answered, although she looked worried.

'Correct,' Thrift told her.

'Freckles,' Miss Dace said immediately, 'which book of the bible comes after Kings?'

'Chronicles,' Felicity answered without hesitation, leaving Miss Dace looking crestfallen. 'Nappies, in which country was the inventor of the Collins Engine born?'

Thrift knew the answer, but hesitated, shame and arousal warring in her head as she thought of how it would feel to be put across Miss Adams' knee and spanked. At last she answered.

'Wales.'

'No,' Felicity replied, sounding immensely smug. 'He was Russian. Over you go.'

Thrift stood, trembling hard as Felicity once more pushed her chair back to make a lap. Even as she laid herself into spanking position she felt as if a few touches to her quim would make her come, and she was unable to resist pushing her bottom high to make herself as available as possible.

'Tie her wrists,' Susannah Dace said pointedly.

'I know,' Felicity answered, tugging the back of Thrift's dress up to get at her corset laces.

Eyes closed, melting in submissive ecstasy, Thrift let her wrists be taken up behind her back and tied firmly off, leaving her deliciously helpless. Felicity's hand settled on her bottom, gave a gentle, warning pat, and then it began, a hard, stinging, no-nonsense spanking, much too painful for her to hold herself in, and yet bliss from the very start. She let her body go, wriggling in her pain and quickly streaming tears, a natural reaction to a punishment she wanted more than anything, save perhaps to be put on her knees and made to lick by the woman who was doing it.

'I've wanted to do that since the moment I met you,' Felicity said happily, planting a final slap to Thrift's now hot bottom.

'You . . . you should have done,' Thrift panted.

'You're a disgrace,' Susannah remarked, but there was no malice in her tone.

Thrift was shaking badly as she got up, now dizzy with both arousal and drink. One more question wrong and she was going to be paddled, a prospect that filled her with both longing and fear. Yet it was her go, and unless her question was ruled unfair she still had a chance of escape.

'Snivels,' she said, 'in Edinburgh, between which two streets does the western boundary of the Quality Enclave run?'

To Thrift's amazement, there was no challenge.

'Haggis Street and Bagpipe Street,' Susannah answered.

'Like that, is it!' Felicity laughed. 'That's the knack with Snivels, Thrift, spank her well and she'll get it bare for anybody. Over you go then, you little trollop.'

Susannah made a face but got up, moving the bottle and glasses to bend across the table and take a firm grip on the far side. Thrift also stood, still unsure she could actually beat the woman who had punished her so often and so hard, but nevertheless picking up the big sorority paddle. Felicity had got up too, grinning as walked around the table to admire the view of Susannah's neatly rounded bottom, on full show between the open flaps of her drawers. A pert, brownish cunt showed between elegantly turned thighs, somewhat puffy with arousal and also distinctly wet, while the tiny, dark brown anal star had begun to wink lewdly in fear of the paddle.

'A dozen dozen, I think,' Thrift said, unable to hold down her glee as she rubbed the paddle against her tormentor's bottom.

She was going to do it, hard enough to hurt, hard enough to make Miss Dace cry, and if that felt cruel, she knew she'd be getting the same soon enough. The paddle came up and down, landing across the pert little bottom with a satisfyingly meaty smack. Susannah cried out in pain but with the same wanton breathlessness

Thrift knew only too well from her own beatings, and with that the last of her doubts fled. She laid in, landing smack after smack after smack across Miss Dace's naked bottom, to set her kicking and dancing on her toes, squealing and snivelling, so like a pig that both Felicity and Thrift were soon laughing.

After just a dozen Susannah was crying again, and by two dozen she was blubbering her heart out, beaten into full, wanton submission, and before the halfway mark she had broken completely. Her belly came up, her hand went back, and she was rubbing her cunt as she was spanked, masturbating openly in front of them even as the tears and snot streamed down her face, her fingers working furiously in the wet pink mush of her slit as smack after smack landed across her dancing cheeks, and finally coming with an ear-splitting scream.

Thrift gave the final half-dozen gently and Susannah got up, running straight to Felicity's arms to sob her heart out. Fully aware that she was witnessing a very private moment, Thrift waited, speaking only when Susannah had had her nose wiped and been kissed better.

'I would like a cuddle too, after you punish me, please?' she said.

Susannah nodded, still too emotional to speak, and held out an arm to include Thrift in the embrace. Fighting back tears, Thrift allowed herself to be held and kissed, and her bottom patted, until Felicity at last broke away.

'There, nothing like a good game of Tears before Bedtime, is there? So now, Ladies, we need to make Nappies an honorary Omega Pi.'

'I suppose you're going to paddle me too?' Thrift asked.

'No,' Felicity told her. 'A pledge – that's what we call a probationary member – has to choose between a dozen of the paddle and being spanked across the

President's knee, and as I've just spanked you that will do. The other half is what we call hazing, to make sure you never tell anyone else, and by God I've yet to meet the girl who'd break her promise. We're going to make you a glove puppet.'

'A glove puppet?'

'You'll see. Over the table with you.'

Thrift obeyed, laying herself into the same vulnerable position Susannah had adopted to be paddled. Her petticoats had fallen down, but she quickly adjusted them, knowing she should be bare bottom, and wanting to be.

'What did you get, Susannah?' asked Felicity, and to Thrift's amazement Miss Dace giggled as she replied.

'I found some kumquats in the kitchen, and a pat of butter.'

'Perfect!' Felicity said happily. 'I haven't done this for years! Bottie up, Miss Pledge, and let's have those legs well apart.'

Thrift did as she was told, unable to resist the laughing Felicity, lifting her bottom and parting her feet in a way that she knew left both quim and anus fully exposed. Susannah had picked up the sorority paddle, but instead of applying it to Thrift's bottom she laid it down on the table. Felicity planted a single, firm swat across Thrift's cheeks instead, making her gasp once more.

'She makes a damn sight less fuss about it than you did, that's certain,' Felicity remarked with a chuckle, addressing Susannah, who answered in a curious, coy, slightly sulky tone Thrift had never heard her use before.

'I was younger, and you used great big plums.'

Felicity merely laughed, and Thrift felt her quim twitch in anticipation for what was about to be put inside her, only for her eyes and mouth to go round when a warm, buttery finger touched not her vagina, but her anus. Still she was unable to hold back her whimpers of pleasure as Felicity began to finger her bottom hole, rubbing butter around the ring and probing deep long after Thrift had been adequately lubricated.

'You always were rude with us,' Susannah said, as sulky as before, but not without a trace of arousal.

Felicity gave a wicked chuckle in response and eased her finger free of Thrift's anal passage. A moment later it was replaced by the firm, rounded tip of a kumquat, which slid in easily, to lodge in Thrift's rectum. A second followed, and a third, leaving her in a state of wanton bliss and eager for more rude treatment. The fourth kumquat was pushed in past her ring, the fifth, and Miss Dace spoke to her.

'Do you, Miss Thrift Moncrieff, pledge yourself . . .'

There was more, but as Felicity worked the sixth kumquat in up Thrift's bottom hole she kept her finger up, using it to stir the kumquats about, which was too distracting for Thrift to concentrate on anything else. By the time Susannah finished Thrift was dizzy with reaction and wanted to rub her quim, but she managed what seemed the most appropriate response.

'I do.'

Miss Dace gave a solemn nod and went to the cupboard once more, returning with more of the small glasses from which they'd been drinking. Carefully, she laid them out in a line on the sorority paddle and filled each one. Stepping back, she began to speak again.

'Miss Thrift Moncrieff. As proof of allegiance to the Omega Pi sorority, and to ensure that you never reveal the secrets of your initiation, you are to obey myself and Miss Felicity Adams until such time as we deem you worthy to join us.'

'About five minutes in this case,' Felicity chuckled, and eased a second finger in up Thrift's bottom.

'Do you so swear?' Miss Dace demanded.

'I swear,' Thrift gasped, her fingers now clawing at the table in reaction as her anus was forced wider still by a third finger.

'She's nearly ready,' Felicity said. 'Yes, I think she's ready.'

Thrift's mouth came wide as her bottom hole spread to the full circumference of Felicity's fist, right up to the knuckles, then deeper still, engulfing the entire hand and more. She began to whimper and kick her feet as she felt her rectum bulge, with Felicity's arm now half in, creating a swollen sensation beyond anything she had known before.

'Now you're my glove puppet,' Felicity chuckled, wriggling her hand inside Thrift's body.

Miss Dace giggled, her hand to her mouth, a girlish gesture quite at odds with her normal behaviour, but lost on Thrift, who was dizzy with drink and ecstasy.

'Feed her,' Miss Dace urged. 'I want to see.'

'Now who's the naughty one,' Felicity laughed, and she had begun to withdraw her arm from Thrift's bottom.

Having it taken out had almost as powerful an effect on Thrift as having it put in, and she was left mewling and shaking her head, with her anus agape behind her and in urgent need of being filled once more.

'Open wide,' Felicity ordered.

Thrift had barely been aware of what the others were saying, so she had a shock when Felicity's hand uncurled in front of her mouth. She was being offered one of the kumquats that had so recently been up her bottom, but her mouth came open before her shame and disgust could get the better of her and she took the little slimy fruit between her lips.

'She's doing it, the dirty pig!' Miss Dace laughed in delight as Thrift took the fruit properly in her mouth. 'Go on, Thrift, eat it, eat it all up!'

Her voice was full of cruelty and arousal, ending in a squeal of delight as Thrift bit on the kumquat, which burst to fill her mouth with bitter-sweet juice. She swallowed and Susannah gave a squeal of delight, her knuckles pressed to her mouth in sheer joy at watching Thrift's humiliation.

'Now a glass of Old Red Eye,' Felicity ordered, her voice calmer, but also full of cruel pleasure.

Thrift put one trembling hand to the first of the shot glasses and tipped the contents down her throat. Immediately a second kumquat was offered to her mouth, which she took between her lips, wanting to please the two women who were enjoying her subjugation more than anything else in the world. Again she swallowed down a shot of drink, and with the third kumquat she deliberately lifted her head to let them see it between her lips before she ate it.

Susannah burst into delighted giggles, clapping her hands and jumping on her toes, her eyes alight with sadistic joy. Felicity's hand found Thrift's bottom, stroking then smacking. Thrift stuck it up, eager for more as she swallowed another shot of Old Red Eye. The spanking grew firmer, and Susannah joined in, the two women holding Thrift at either side and smacking a cheek each as she was offered the next kumquat. Again she took it between her lips, showing off as she ate it and revelling in the taste of her own bottom as she was spanked.

Another shot of drink and Thrift was given the fifth kumquat, her bottom now warm and glowing as it bounced and wobbled to the hard smacks, while both women were cuddled close to her, calling her a naughty girl and kissing her face and neck. Thrift ate the kumquat, opening her mouth to show the sticky orange pulp inside before swallowing it down. A pause to swallow the last of her drinks and she took the sixth kumquat, nuzzling it out of Felicity's palm and bursting it in her mouth, just as Susannah's lips met hers. She gave in to the kiss, sharing the sticky, bitter-sweet pulp as their tongues moved together, first with Susannah, then Felicity, with both still spanking her.

Now completely lost to her needs and the others no better, Thrift gave in. Her gown was tugged down at the front and her breasts spilt out. Her nipples were sucked and licked, her breasts squeezed and slapped. She was upended on the table and the paddle applied to her bottom, each woman giving her several dozen hard smacks that only served to make her more eager still. Her gown and petticoats were pulled off, to leave her in just her corset, her breasts and bottom and cunt bare and available. She was rolled onto her back and mounted, Felicity dropping a neat curtsey into her face, spreading her soft, womanly bottom cheeks over Thrift's mouth so that she could push her tongue in up the tight, musky hole between.

Thrift licked, willing and eager, burrowing her tongue as deep as she could up Felicity's bottom hole, wanting nothing more than her own utter subjugation as she gave pleasure. Her legs were rolled up as she licked and Felicity took hold of her ankles as Susannah began to spank once again, to her usual firm, relentless rhythm, first across the chubby tuck of Thrift's bottom, then higher, right on her swollen, eager cunt.

'That's the way, Snivels,' Felicity sighed, 'spank her cunt. Make her come while she licks my bottom, Snivels, make her come.'

The smacks at once grew harder as Thrift's legs were rolled higher still, to leave the lips of her quim pouting from between her thighs as they were spanked, every impact sending an ecstatic jolt to her clitoris as she probed deep up Felicity's bottom hole with her tongue. Felicity began to wriggle, rubbing her bottom in Thrift's face and the spanking grew harder still. At that, the orgasm hit, Thrift's entire body going into violent contractions as she came, every smack of her cunt driving her higher, and earnestly wishing Felicity would just give in completely and fill her mouth.

Only as she came down did she withdraw her tongue from Felicity's anus, and as soon as she'd been helped up the three of them cuddled together, kissing and stroking each other's bodies, until, without a word being said, Thrift got to her knees. Felicity went first, skirts high and drawers pulled wide to expose herself as Thrift crawled between her legs. She was in a state of adoring bliss as she licked, paying plenty of attention to Felicity's bottom hole as well as cunt before finally applying herself higher to trigger orgasm. Susannah followed, sitting in the same lewd pose and playing with her open cunt as Thrift crawled over, only to lift the heavily notched tally stick in her fingers.

'Don't think I've forgotten this,' she said.

Thrift merely nodded and buried her face in her lover's cunt.

nexus

The leading publisher of fetish and adult fiction

TELL US WHAT YOU THINK!

Readers' ideas and opinions matter to us. Take a few minutes to fill in the questionnaire below and you'll be entered into a prize draw to win a year's worth of Nexus books (36 titles)

Terms and conditions apply – see end of questionnaire.

1. Sex: Are you male ☐   female ☐   a couple ☐?

2. Age: Under 21 ☐   21–30 ☐   31–40 ☐   41–50 ☐   51–60 ☐   over 60 ☐

3. Where do you buy your Nexus books from?

☐ A chain book shop. If so, which one(s)?

_____

☐ An independent book shop. If so, which one(s)?

_____

☐ A used book shop/charity shop
☐ Online book store. If so, which one(s)?

_____

4. How did you find out about Nexus books?

☐ Browsing in a book shop
☐ A review in a magazine
☐ Online
☐ Recommendation
☐ Other _____

5. In terms of settings, which do you prefer? (Tick as many as you like)

☐ Down to earth and as realistic as possible
☐ Historical settings. If so, which period do you prefer?

_____

☐ Fantasy settings – barbarian worlds
☐ Completely escapist/surreal fantasy

- ☐ Institutional or secret academy
- ☐ Futuristic/sci fi
- ☐ Escapist but still believable
- ☐ Any settings you dislike?

_____

- ☐ Where would you like to see an adult novel set?

_____

6. In terms of storylines, would you prefer:

- ☐ Simple stories that concentrate on adult interests?
- ☐ More plot and character-driven stories with less explicit adult activity?
- ☐ We value your ideas, so give us your opinion of this book:

_____

_____

_____

7. In terms of your adult interests, what do you like to read about? (Tick as many as you like)

- ☐ Traditional corporal punishment (CP)
- ☐ Modern corporal punishment
- ☐ Spanking
- ☐ Restraint/bondage
- ☐ Rope bondage
- ☐ Latex/rubber
- ☐ Leather
- ☐ Female domination and male submission
- ☐ Female domination and female submission
- ☐ Male domination and female submission
- ☐ Willing captivity
- ☐ Uniforms
- ☐ Lingerie/underwear/hosiery/footwear (boots and high heels)
- ☐ Sex rituals
- ☐ Vanilla sex
- ☐ Swinging
- ☐ Cross-dressing/TV

☐ Enforced feminisation
☐ Others – tell us what you don't see enough of in adult fiction:

_____
_____
_____

8. Would you prefer books with a more specialised approach to your interests, i.e. a novel specifically about uniforms? If so, which subject(s) would you like to read a Nexus novel about?

_____
_____
_____

9. Would you like to read true stories in Nexus books? For instance, the true story of a submissive woman, or a male slave? Tell us which true revelations you would most like to read about:

_____
_____
_____

10. What do you like best about Nexus books?

_____
_____

11. What do you like least about Nexus books?

_____
_____

12. Which are your favourite titles?

_____
_____

13. Who are your favourite authors?

_____
_____

14. Which covers do you prefer? Those featuring:
   (tick as many as you like)

☐ Fetish outfits
☐ More nudity
☐ Two models
☐ Unusual models or settings
☐ Classic erotic photography
☐ More contemporary images and poses
☐ A blank/non-erotic cover
☐ What would your ideal cover look like?

_____

15. Describe your ideal Nexus novel in the space provided:

_____

_____

_____

_____

16. Which celebrity would feature in one of your Nexus-style fantasies?
   We'll post the best suggestions on our website – anonymously!

_____

THANKS FOR YOUR TIME

Now simply write the title of this book in the space below and cut out the
questionnaire pages. Post to: Nexus, Marketing Dept., Thames Wharf Studios,
Rainville Rd, London W6 9HA

Book title: _____

nexus

NEXUS NEW BOOKS

To be published in January 2007

WHIPPING TRIANGLE
G. C. Scott

Rhonda, Paul and Muriel form a love triangle with a difference. They are drawn together by their love of sex with bondage, and live a curiously intertwined life – in and out of one another's beds, now dominant and now submissive as the urge strikes them.

Rhonda is the true dominant, relishing her control over the men and women she meets and takes into her circle. Paul finds himself attracted to her as a mistress, and at the same time he is drawn to Muriel, the submissive bank manager who loves to be restrained and ravished.

They all meet at Rhonda's country house in order to fulfil their mutual desires for domination, submission, pain and pleasure.

£6.99   ISBN 978 0 352 34086 3

INSTRUMENTS OF PLEASURE
Nicole Dere

Two musically gifted young cousins, Max (the girl with the boy's name) and Toni (vice versa) have been brought up under the tyrannous rule of Aunt Charlotte. Their lives are dramatically transformed when Charlotte gifts them to the charismatic Professor Labat, known as The Maestro.

His talents extend far beyond his musical genius, and he prepares his protégés for a novel kind of serfdom, in which their skill is combined with erotic artistry to refresh the jaded palates of the wealthy clientele in The Pleasure Dome, mansion of the notorious Lady Letitia (Tiny) Laycorn.

£6.99   ISBN 978 0 352 34098 6

WIFE SWAP
Amber Leigh

The *Nexus Enthusiast* series brings us a definitive adult novel about a couple's adventures as Swingers. Mark and Anne have been tempted by the idea of wife swapping since their first shared sexual fantasies. They have the desire, the determination and a watertight relationship. Only thing missing is the right couple to swing with.

But that small hurdle is overcome when they move next door to the sexy and exciting Johnny and Lisa. Their new neighbours are avid swappers and engaged in organising the season's largest swinging party.

As Mark and Anne take their first tentative steps into the waters of swapping they are soon immersed in a tidal wave of new experiences. The only thing left for them to discover is whether or not their relationship is truly watertight.

£6.99   ISBN 978 0 352 34097 9

If you would like more information about Nexus titles, please visit our website at www.nexus-books.co.uk, or send a large stamped addressed envelope to:

Nexus, Thames Wharf Studios,
Rainville Road, London W6 9HA

This information is correct at time of printing. For up-to-date information, please visit our website at www.nexus-books.co.uk

All books are priced at £6.99 unless another price is given.

- - - - - - ✂ -

Please send me the books I have ticked above.

Name   ....

Address   ....

                    ....

                    ....

                    .... Post code ....

Send to: **Virgin Books Cash Sales, Thames Wharf Studios, Rainville Road, London W6 9HA**

US customers: for prices and details of how to order books for delivery by mail, call 888-330-8477.

Please enclose a cheque or postal order, made payable to **Nexus Books Ltd**, to the value of the books you have ordered plus postage and packing costs as follows:

UK and BFPO – £1.00 for the first book, 50p for each subsequent book.

Overseas (including Republic of Ireland) – £2.00 for the first book, £1.00 for each subsequent book.

If you would prefer to pay by VISA, ACCESS/MASTERCARD, AMEX, DINERS CLUB or SWITCH, please write your card number and expiry date here:

....

Please allow up to 28 days for delivery.

Signature ....

Our privacy policy

We will not disclose information you supply us to any other parties. We will not disclose any information which identifies you personally to any person without your express consent.

From time to time we may send out information about Nexus books and special offers. Please tick here if you do *not* wish to receive Nexus information.   □

- - - - - - ✂ -